INCONVENIENT EVENTS

Ian Ellis

ISBN: 978-1-3999-4231-7

This is a work of fiction. Names, characters, places and incidents are either the product of the author's imagination or are used fictitiously, and any resemblance to actual persons, living or dead, business establishments, organizations, companies, events or places is entirely coincidental.

My gratitude and love, as ever, to Vicki and Rebecca. Without their support and encouragement this book would not have happened

Thanks to Jane for my use of her pseudonym

PREFACE

The pond was set just inside the edge of the woodland. It had been undisturbed for a long time. Over years, many years, it had become overgrown and almost hidden. Dead and broken trees together with undergrowth and other plants had covered the black, lifeless water when they first saw it. They'd been hired by the farmer to clear away this accumulation of rotten debris and open up the pond to make it visible and accessible. They said it would take a week.

Danny was operating his grimy, yellow, elderly JCB digger, which had seen better days. Karl had been using a chainsaw to cut the dead and decaying trees that were in and around the pond into manageable sections or pieces. These he attached to straps hanging from the bucket loader for the JCB to drag away. Karl had needed to clamber precariously onto the trees that had fallen across the pond to cut them up. On several occasions his legs had slipped into the foul water, much to Danny's amusement. Sections of trees removed had been piled by the JCB into a huge stack, which would later be burned by the farmer once it had dried out.

Now Danny was using the digger's bucket to remove stuff left in the water.

The JCB's large mud-covered rubber tires rolled down the pond's bank into the water's edge. Danny operated the large hydraulic-powered bucket to scoop up mud and debris from below the water's surface and lift it out. With each bucketload the stench increased as the pond's putrid bottom was disturbed and brought up. The JCB's tires fought for grip and slipped and skidded as it scrabbled to reverse up the bank with another bucket-load to add to a growing pile of black, wet, oozing, stinking mud and rubbish. Churned mud seemed to be everywhere as the JCB's tires created a quagmire of the ground already saturated by recent heavy rain.

Karl's dog, a spaniel called Boris, played nearby and was covered in the slime and mess.

"What's he got now?"

Danny had opened the cab window and shouted to Karl as he pointed at Boris.

Karl looked at his dog which was pawing with what appeared to be a football. He plodded through the mud to look and bent down to pick it up but suddenly stepped back.

"It looks like a head," Karl shouted back as he stared at the thing.

Danny climbed down from the cab to have a look. Karl pulled the dog away. There was little doubt they were staring at a human skull—a rather dirty and slimy one, but still a skull.

"Bloody hell. That's going to mess us up," Danny muttered.

"Why not just ignore it? Chuck it back into the pond and forget about it?"

"Shouldn't really, but it's not a bad idea."

Boris let out a yelp. He'd gone over to the pile of oozing wet mud just emptied from the JCB's bucket. They both turned and watched as he pulled at something and ran to them carrying it in his jaws. Boris placed it at Karl's feet.

"That settles it then. I wish you'd not brought your bloody dog."

They both stared at a bone—a large bone, like a human bone.

"Better let the old bugger know. He's not going to like it," Danny muttered as he took out his phone and keyed in the number.

"Danny here, Arthur. You'd better get over here quick."

"Why, what's the problem now?" came the reply.

"You come and see for yourself. It's serious."

It took nearly ten minutes before a red tractor stopped beside them. Arthur, the farmer, climbed out of the cab. He was a big, scruffy, grim-looking man in his midfifties.

"What is it then?"

Danny pointed at the skull and the bone. "Looks like human remains to me. Came from the pond."

Arthur peered at the skull and then the bone.

"This all there is?"

"We've not looked for anything else."

"Then don't look. Chuck this back into the pond and forget it. Get things tidied up and then leave it alone."

"That's not right, Arthur. It should be reported. You just can't ignore human remains."

"Who says they're human? What do you know?"

Danny sighed and pointed at the skull. "Look at it. That's human. It's bloody obvious."

"It's not obvious to me. Anyway, it's old, years old, ancient. Probably a hundred years old or more. It's not important. Get rid of it."

"I'm not moving it, Arthur. You've got to report it, or else I will."

Arthur turned and glared at Danny. "You'd bloody better not. You'll bring the police all over us, and they'll close all this area off and start searching about and asking questions. You'll not get paid, and you'll get no more work from me, nor any other farmers around here."

Danny glared back at Arthur, and then turned to Karl, who looked unhappy but just shrugged his shoulders. Danny didn't like Arthur; few people did. He had a justifiable reputation as a bully. He was unpopular among other farmers and suppliers; few had a good word to say about him.

Danny squared his shoulders and faced Arthur. "You're always slow to pay us anyway. Pay us now for the whole job, and we'll go.

But we're not touching anything more. What you do next is up to you."

Arthur stared and then smirked. "You must be joking. You've only half done the job. Tidy up and remove this as I said, and I'll pay you up to today. Otherwise, you'll get nothing."

Danny stood quietly. Then he took out his phone.

"Don't you dare," Arthur said with a snarl.

"Don't worry, you old bugger. I'm not going to phone the police. Not yet anyway." Danny turned away from Arthur and with his phone took a photo of the skull and bone and then turned back and took a few photos of the scene around the pond, including the pile of black, stinking mud that had been dredged up for the pond.

Danny grinned at Arthur, "Just a bit of insurance. You pay us for the whole job by tomorrow. OK? Otherwise, you may regret it."

Arthur moved forward and raised his arm as if to hit Danny but then held back. Danny was more than a match, and Arthur knew it.

"You're a fool, Danny. You haven't got the guts. You'll get nothing from me. Now clear off my land."

Danny walked to his old JCB and as he climbed into the cab shouted, "Don't forget, Arthur. Full payment into my account by tomorrow."

CHAPTER 1

It was two days later when a detective police constable called at the farmhouse. She rang the bell, and a dog barked from inside. The door was opened by a pleasant-mannered woman aged perhaps around sixty, who asked if she could help.

"I'm Detective Constable Imogen Duggan, ma'am. I'd like to speak to Mr. Arthur Symonds please."

Duggan presented her warrant card.

"He's not here. I'm his wife. Can I help?"

"I really need to speak to him. Do you know where he is?"

"They're working in the long field today."

"Can you show me where or perhaps call him to come here?"

The woman looked at Duggan's shoes and said, "I think it's best I call him. The field is very muddy. Come inside. Don't mind the dog."

The dog was a scruffy collie, which stood inside the back door wagging its tail. Duggan followed the woman into a large kitchen area and watched her pick up a phone and press a number.

"Hello, Arthur; it's Aggie here. There's a police lady here to talk to you."

Aggie went quiet, but Duggan could hear something being said in reply. Aggie looked worried and said, "But what shall I tell her?"

Duggan could hear the noise of a reply and held out her hand and took the telephone receiver from Aggie.

"Detective Constable Duggan here. Are you Arthur Symonds?"

There was a short hesitation before a man's voice answered. "Yes, what do you want?"

"I need to see you and talk to you, sir. It is important."

"What do you want to talk about?"

"We've received a report of some human remains found on your farm."

"I know nothing about that."

"I still need to see you and talk to you."

"Well, it's not convenient. Come back tomorrow morning."

Duggan turned to Aggie. "How long will it take to get to that field?"

"A good twenty minutes to walk or five minutes in a tractor."

Duggan spoke into the phone. "Sir, this is urgent. Please come to the farmhouse; otherwise, I shall have to come and find you."

The phone went quiet for a moment before he replied, "Have it your way then. I'll come, but it's a waste of time."

It was ten minutes later when a red tractor arrived outside the farmhouse. Symonds stepped inside the back door and removed his muddy boots before walking into the kitchen. His expression was unfriendly.

"Thank you for coming back, sir. It'll make things much easier. Tell me about the human remains found on your farm two days ago, please."

"Don't know anything about it."

Duggan saw that Aggie was looking distinctly anxious. She took some photographs from a folder and laid them on the kitchen table. One showed muddy ground alongside a pond with a heap of black mud and a JCB digger near the bank. Also in the photo was a red tractor and an angry-looking Arthur Symonds. One of the photos clearly showed a human skull lying on the ground.

"I want you to take me to this place and show me that skull, sir."

Symonds looked uneasy before replying, "Look, there's nothing to see. Just a muddy mess."

Duggan stared at him before gathering up the photographs. "You'd better show me. I'll get my wellies from the car."

Duggan sat in a small jump seat alongside Symonds in the grimy tractor cab. To her surprise he drove away from the farmyard, through the gate, and onto the narrow country lane outside. They followed the lane for nearly a mile, and then Symonds turned the tractor off the lane and onto a muddy track, then through an open gate into a field. The pond was on the right at the edge of a wood. As they approached, Duggan could see a blue tractor fitted with a digger bucket.

"What's that tractor doing?" she asked.

"That's Gertie just tidying things up."

Symonds's tractor stopped by the pond; Duggan climbed down from the cab and plodded toward the red tractor and waved her arms at the driver. It stopped, and the cab window opened. Gertie peered out, and Duggan shouted, "Switch off the engine and leave the cab please."

Gertie looked at Symonds before switching off the engine and climbing down to join them. Duggan estimated that Gertie was around thirty years old. She was slightly plump with a serious expression on her face and brown hair showing beneath her woolen hat, and, like her father, she was dressed in grubby overalls with muddy boots.

Duggan showed her warrant card before asking, "Who are you and what are you doing?"

"He's my dad," she nodded toward Symonds. "We're clearing up the mess left by some men who worked here."

Duggan looked around. She could recognize the area shown in the photos, but the piles of rubbish and debris had largely disappeared. Nor was there any sign of the skull.

Duggan took out the photos and displayed them to Gertie.

"Where has all this stuff gone, Gertie? Where is this skull?"

Gertie was quiet and looked nervously at Symonds, who put his finger to his lips. Duggan saw the gesture.

Symonds answered instead, "Don't know anything about any skull. We're just clearing up the mess left behind by two useless idiots who didn't finish the job. I didn't pay them, so they're just trying to cause me trouble."

Duggan looked at them both and said, "Please, do not touch anything and wait here."

Duggan walked out of earshot and made a phone call.

Five minutes later, Duggan finished the call and walked back to them. While on the phone, she'd watched Symonds and Gertie talking. Rather it was Symonds who did most of the talking while Gertie looked at the ground. They both turned to look at Duggan as she approached.

"My instructions are that you must remain here until my sergeant arrives with a team of officers. We have reason to believe that a crime has been committed. You'll be questioned and probably be taken to—"

Duggan was interrupted by Symonds, who said angrily, "That's rubbish. You can't tell us what to do. We've done nothing wrong. We're not hanging around here. Come on, Gertie; let's get back to the house."

"Don't do that, sir; otherwise, I shall have to arrest you—"

"Don't make me laugh. How do think you'll do that. Look at you: a little thing like you against us two."

Duggan stared at them both. Symonds didn't move, and Gertie looked anxiously at her father and said, "Dad, let's not make trouble. Please, let's do as she says, please."

It went quiet until Symonds spoke. "Look, this is stupid. We've done nothing wrong, and there's work to do. We can't hang around here."

"If that's the case, sir, then it'll all be over quickly. My sergeant and some officers will be here within thirty minutes. To save time and for your sakes, I'm going to give you a formal caution. Can I have your full name please?"

Symonds made as if to protest but then replied, "Arthur Richard Symonds."

Duggan entered it in her notebook and then said, "And you, Gertie; your full name please?"

"Rosemary Ann Symonds."

Duggan looked surprised. "That's a pretty name. Why are you called Gertie?"

"Dunno really. Everyone calls me Gertie."

Symonds laughed. "It's because she was a dirty little girl. You know, 'Dirty Gertie.'" He laughed. "She still is. The name's stuck."

Duggan stared at Symonds with unconcealed contempt before writing the name in her notebook and then spoke to them both.

"OK. As I was saying, you'll be questioned when my sergeant arrives. You may be taken to Kidlington police station for that; it'll depend on the sergeant. Before that I'm going to give you the usual caution or warning; it's for your benefit, both of you. Here goes.

"You do not have to say anything, but it may harm your defense if you do not mention when questioned something which you later rely on in court. Anything you do say may be given in evidence. Do you understand?"

They both stood quietly, looking at Duggan before they each nodded agreement.

"OK. I suggest that you say nothing and wait quietly until they arrive. It shouldn't be too long."

It was less than thirty minutes later when three police 4x4 vehicles drove through the gateway, although it had seemed longer to the father and daughter.

A slim woman in her late twenties with dark hair and wearing plain black clothes climbed out of the first vehicle. She changed from her shoes into waterproof boots, commonly known as wellies. A total of six uniformed police officers also climbed from the three vehicles, and Duggan walked over to join them.

"OK, Duggan, bring us up to date with what's happened."

"Yes, sergeant. You can see what's happened by looking at the photos."

As the scene was compared with the photos taken by Danny two days previously, Duggan explained what had happened since she'd arrived at the farm. After a brief discussion, they went over to the farmer and his daughter.

"I'm Detective Sergeant Teagle, sir. DC Duggan confirms that she has issued a formal caution about anything you say. So can you please tell me where the skull in this photo has gone?"

Symonds looked at the photo in Teagle's hand.

"No idea. Must have been taken by a fox or something."

Teagle gave him a smile. "I suggest you do better than that, sir. Remember that you are under caution. Why didn't you call us when human remains were discovered on your land?"

Symonds shrugged. "Didn't seem worth it. They were just old, probably been around for centuries. Didn't want the fuss with your lot poking about and disturbing us. We've got work to do running the farm."

"So you decided to get rid of the evidence then?"

Symonds said nothing. Teagle waited a moment watching him. She could sense his uncertainty about what to say. She turned to Gertie, who stood nervously alongside her father. "What can you tell us about it, miss?"

Symonds spoke up before Gertie could reply.

"She knows nothing, can't tell you anything."

"I suspect she knows quite a lot. Now I suggest you stop this nonsense and tell us what you've done with the skull and the bone and everything else."

Symonds was briefly silent before shrugging his shoulders. "All right. I didn't want the bother and disturbance. Anyway, it was just two old bones from the pond—prehistoric rubbish, that's all. Didn't mean anything. Now your lot'll bugger us up with all your procedures. It won't lead anywhere, so why all the fuss? Total waste of time. It's not as if there's any harm done."

"Thank you, sir. It's a pity you didn't contact us straightaway and leave things undisturbed. Now you've caused us and yourself even more bother and disturbance, as you put it. What did you do with the skull and bone?"

"Chucked 'em back in the pond where they belong."

"What about all the other stuff dredged from the pond?"

"Just spread it around in the woods."

Teagle sighed. "That was very stupid, sir. You'd better show us everything you've done."

CHAPTER 2

"OK, Teagle, what's happening at Wootton?"

Detective Chief Superintendent Graham Barnes gestured for Teagle to take a seat. They were in his office at Thames Valley Police HQ in Kidlington, just north of Oxford.

Alice Teagle was assistant to Barnes. In police jargon she was known as his "bagman." Barnes never used that term; to him she was his associate.

It was just two days since Teagle had first visited the farm at Wootton about eight miles north of Kidlington and stood by the pond.

"Not good news, sir. As you know, the scene was disturbed, almost destroyed, by the farmer; it's made life more difficult for us. The pond has now been drained, and human remains have been found. Incomplete skeletons of what looks like four people have been discovered in it. The debris taken from the pond and scattered around in the woods is being searched, and a few human bones have been unearthed so far. The police pathologist has brought in a forensic anthropologist to assist. Between them they still trying to piece things together. Nowhere near getting any identification of the remains. At this stage they are reluctant to say much. We don't know how or when the bodies got there, nor how they died."

"What does the farmer say?"

"His initial bullying bravado has disappeared. I've explained the seriousness of what he's done. But he's starting to complain again about how we're upsetting his farm. I've impounded the two tractors he used until forensics have finished with them, and that's annoyed him."

"Have you interviewed the man who reported it and took the photos?"

"I have, sir. It confirmed what Duggan reported. He and his mate noticed a skull when they were clearing the pond. Told the farmer, who wanted them to get rid of it and say nothing. They both refused, and the farmer said he therefore wouldn't pay them. He took the photos as insurance and gave the farmer twenty-four hours to pay for the work. Farmer didn't pay up, and so he reported it. That was two days after the discovery, by which time the farmer had tried to get rid of everything."

Barnes sat quietly thinking. Teagle sat quietly waiting. She was used to it; it was one of the superintendent's traits. He liked to get his thoughts together before making any decision. She admired him for it.

When the report of the photos of a skull came in, he'd instructed Teagle to look into it. He'd read her reports and now listened to her. He thought through the implications of the investigation. It was, almost certainly, going to be a slow process with a good deal of forensics and technical input and routine legwork required. He could, and possibly should, assign it to one of his inspectors, but they were all already more than busy with other cases. Anyway, he rather liked the sound of it and decided he and Teagle would handle it and fit it in with their other work.

He smiled at Teagle, but before he could speak, she said, "You're going to handle it yourself, aren't you, sir?"

"Not quite, Teagle. We are going to handle it together. Let's go and look at this crime scene."

When Barnes and Teagle drove into the field, they saw that a large area of the farm and the adjoining wood had been cordoned off as a crime scene. This area had become more extensive because of the farmer's attempt to clear away all traces of the debris produced from clearing the pond.

A forensics team in white protective clothing was painstakingly working across the area when they arrived. A large white tent had been erected. The police pathologist noticed them and waved. They walked over to him.

"Good to see you, Superintendent. I rather thought you'd turn up; this type of case always interests you."

"Good to see you too, Doctor. What can you tell me about the bodies?"

"Well, I'll give you an opinion, but don't hold me to it. There's a huge amount of work to do yet. The remains we've found so far indicate four human bodies. All are male. We estimate they've been in the pond for maybe ten years. They've decomposed to skeletons. Unfortunately, the scene has been badly disturbed, as I'm sure you know. It's making things more difficult. We've also found some clothing, or the remains of some. I expect there'll be more to come. Ideally we'd like to find credit cards, driving licenses—something readily identifiable—but we've not found anything like that yet. We're still in the process of finding and tagging things, trying to piece them together. It'll be a while before I can give you much of a report."

The superintendent looked around at the scene then asked, "Any idea about cause of death?"

The pathologist grinned. "Knew you'd ask, and the answer is no. There's no initial evidence of blunt trauma—blows to the head, broken bones, that sort of thing. It's quite likely we'll not be able to identify the cause of death because we've only got the skeletal remains, and they've been disturbed. We're trying to sort out which bones belong to which skull; it'll take time, and we'll need to get everything to a laboratory."

"What about finding their identity?"

The pathologist grimaced. "From what we have so far as

remains, that's not going to be easy, either for me or you. We'll get some sort of DNA, and the teeth might help. We might have more luck with any personal effects we can find. Still, we've not yet retrieved everything; a lot still to do. Sorry, but it's the best I can give you for the time being. Must get on if you'll excuse me."

With that he walked away and into the tent. Doctor Jacob Watson, the police pathologist, was generally known to be gruff and curt in his manner. He was short and overweight and not given to wasting time.

The superintendent stood looking at the pond and its surrounding area. He wondered how it could be possible to dump four bodies into the pond without them being noticed for ten years. The human corpse usually sinks into the water initially, but the decomposition process releases gas inside the body and brings it to the surface. Only as the decomposition process advances will the body, or its remains, sink back under the surface.

"What do you think, Teagle? How could it happen?"

"Does seem difficult to believe, sir. Although it is an isolated spot, and the pond had been neglected for a long time. The gate into the field is kept locked, and it's the only access to this part of the farm, so there'd be no passersby."

"Let's go and look at the gate."

The police officer by the gate recognized the superintendent. "Hello, Chief Superintendent. PC Warren; can I help?"

"Thank you, Warren. Can you please tell me how this gate is locked?"

"Very basic, just this chain and a padlock. Let me show you."

The gate itself looked old but very sturdy, galvanized steel with cross bars and uprights, hinged at one end to one gate post and wide enough for any farm machinery to pass. There was barbed wire fixed across its top. The two gate posts were large, made of oak, and set in concrete. A barbed-wire fence ran through the thick hedge and undergrowth on either side of each post. The heavy chain was passed through the gate's bars and around the post and fastened together with a big padlock. Very simple and effective, and secure.

The superintendent studied it. "Very difficult to get past it, especially with a vehicle."

"Not without the key, sir." The officer held up the padlock's key. "Or unless you have a strong chain cutter. Nor can the gate be lifted from its hinges because this rider is inverted."

"Not easy to climb over it either or get over the barbed wire fence on either side."

They walked together the thirty yards along the muddy track between trees to the road beyond. It was in fact a narrow country lane.

The superintendent looked both ways along the lane. There were no houses or buildings in view. He asked the officer, "Warren, does much traffic pass by?"

"Very little, sir. The farmhouse and yard are nearly a mile that direction, and beyond it along the lane only three more properties before the tarmac peters out into a rough track. You came in from the other direction, which joins the road back to Kidlington after a mile or so, and you probably saw only a few houses on the way. Only four vehicles have gone by in the last three hours or so whilst I've been on duty here."

They turned back toward the gateway, and on the side of the track was a sign. The words were crudely painted, but the message was clear enough.

Private Property
Keep Out

"Not much of a welcome. I reckon the farmer doesn't want any visitors in his field."

"I suspect you're right about that, Warren. Thank you for your help."

The superintendent walked back toward his car with Teagle.

"I suppose it's possible. Isolated and off the beaten track. Accessible only to the farmer and anyone who was let in or had a key. Even so, four bodies dumped in the pond unnoticed is still difficult to accept."

"The farmer has made it very difficult for anyone to trespass in this field. Not easy to lift a body over that gate and then carry it to the pond either. Doubt it could be done by one person alone, sir."

"Certainly looks that way. Let's see what we can find out. We'll start with the two men who first found the skull, and then we'll talk to the farmer and his daughter. Get them in as soon as you can."

The following morning at Kidlington HQ, Danny and Karl sat in an interview room opposite the superintendent and Teagle. Danny gave his explanation about what had happened, and Karl confirmed it.

The superintendent studied them before asking, "Would you have kept quiet about finding human remains if you'd been paid by farmer Symonds as you asked?"

Danny hesitated before nodding. "I suppose we would have. But it is his land, and it should really be him who reported it, shouldn't it?"

"You all had a legal duty to make sure it was promptly reported. As it is we've lost two days, during which time the area was cleared to erase the evidence."

"We didn't erase anything. We refused to get rid of the bones as Symonds demanded. We left it as it was. I brought you the photos; that's how we left it. We did our bit. We only wanted to get paid for our work."

Danny and Karl looked uncomfortable as the superintendent stared at them.

"How do you suppose a body could be dumped there and not be noticed for all that time?"

"Ah, that's easily explained. Before we started clearing the pond, you could hardly see it. Totally overgrown, surrounded by old trees, brambles, and other stuff. The surface of the water was almost covered by old trees and plants as well. It hasn't been touched for years, decades even. Anything thrown in wouldn't be seen. Not like it is now since we opened it up."

"It's a pity we can now only try to imagine what it was like."

"I can show you how it was. I took some photos; always do that before we start a job."

Danny reached into his pocket and produced a cell phone. He pressed a few buttons and turned the screen toward the superintendent, who took it from him.

There was a series of photos, each showing an overgrown area of trees, bushes, and undergrowth. One photo was a close-up looking through the bushes, and it was just possible to make out the surface of the pond.

"That's very useful, sir. I'm going to borrow your phone for a short while to get these printed." He passed the phone to Teagle.

"There'll be other photos, anyway," Danny remarked. "You'll get them from the application."

"What do you mean?"

"Well, you don't think Symonds would use his own money to clear a pond, do you? He's as tight-fisted as they come. No, it's all part of a government initiative to encourage wildlife. Grants to clear ponds or plant areas for wildlife and so on. He got a government grant for this. All the farmers are applying for the grants, and we've had a lot of work because of it. By not paying us, he's pocketed the grant money at our expense."

"So you think there'll be more photos in the application for the grant?"

"Certain of it; there has to be. Gertie will have taken 'em and done the application. She's got the brains, although you wouldn't know it hear Symonds talk about her, poor girl. She used to be an attractive young woman, but Symonds made sure she never had any boyfriends. He's a stupid bully and a nasty piece of work. He wouldn't know where to begin to do a grant application. He's a useless farmer as well; not a patch on the old man when he ran things."

"So Symonds took over the farm from his father then?"

"No, no. The farm belonged to Aggie's dad. Ben Gladwell was his name. He was a good chap and a good farmer. Been dead for a few years now."

"That's very interesting. Thank you, sir. I'm sorry it's not worked out for you, and I guess you'll not be doing any more work for farmer Symonds?"

"Not likely, been bitten once too often by him. Don't imagine anyone else will either."

The superintendent gave a faint smile. "Mind you, if he'd not refused to pay you, we'd probably never have known about this."

Danny smiled back. "And you wouldn't be all over his farm, making life difficult for him."

After Danny and Karl had left, the superintendent studied the photos printed out from Danny's phone. He passed them back to Teagle.

"These photos put a different light on things, Teagle. It could be the ideal place to get rid of a body without it being noticed. Whoever did it would need prior knowledge of the pond and its isolation, so they'd have been on the farm beforehand. There'd be little chance of being seen dumping a body. But they'd still need to get past that gate with it. There's no way round it, only over it."

"Ideally, they'd want to drive a vehicle with the bodies up to the pond, sir. They'd need a key for that padlock or else have to cut through the chain, assuming the gate is always padlocked. Even then it'd still be difficult for one person to drag a body from a vehicle and through that undergrowth into the pond. My money would be on two people involved. To lift a body over the gate and carry it across the field to the pondside would need at least two, I think."

"Cutting the chain would be noticed fairly quickly by the farmer. Interesting. It's time we had a serious talk with farmer Symonds."

The interview with Symonds was delayed because of having a solicitor present. Symonds also demanded to be present with Gertie
when she was questioned.

"She can't tell you anything, so no point in asking her questions
anyway. She doesn't want to be alone; you lot make her nervous.
She needs me, her father, with her."

The superintendent overruled him. Gertie was an adult, and
the solicitor would be alongside her.

Symonds was first. He and Teagle sat opposite Symonds, and
the solicitor and went through the formalities before the superintendent began the questions.

"Mr. Symonds, can you tell me about the farm please? How
long have you worked on it?"

"About thirty years."

"Who owns it?"

"It's mine. Previous owner died, and I took it over."

"Did he leave it to you in his will when he died?"

"That's right."

"Why didn't he leave the farm to his daughter?"

"It's all the same. She's my wife, so it's my farm."

"He left it to her then?"

"OK. But it's the same thing. What's hers is mine, isn't it?"

The superintendent sat quietly looking at him. He could sense
Teagle wanting to disagree, so he said, "I wouldn't like to say, sir.
Now when did your wife's father die? Ben Gladwell was his name,
I think."

"Gladwell, that's right. Been dead well over five years now.
Stupid old bugger, always interfering. We never liked each other."

"How long have you been married to Aggie?"

"Don't see that's any of your business. About thirty years. Look,
where's all this leading?"

"Just trying to get some background. What does Gertie do on
the farm?"

"She helps me. Does as I tell her."

"So presumably she's not a partner in the farm?"

"You must be joking; she's useless. I told you, she helps me."

"How much do you pay her?"

"I give her all she needs."

"Is she your only child?"

"Yes, more's the pity. I wanted a lad. One who'd be useful, but we only have Gertie."

"Presumably Gertie will own the farm one day?"

Symonds hesitated before laughing and then saying, "She doesn't know the first thing about running the farm. No, I'll sell it first, should get a good price, and then I'll pack up, stop work, retire."

"What will happen to Gertie?"

"Hadn't really thought about it. Look she doesn't know any of this, nor does Aggie, and I don't want them to find out. Not yet anyhow, do you understand me?"

The superintendent gave him a smile and said, "Oh, I understand you all too well, sir."

It went quiet for a minute or two. The superintendent reflected upon what had been said.

"Now, sir, the only access to the field with the pond is from the lane and through a padlocked gate. Is that correct?"

"Yes. I have the padlock key. There are some spares in the farmhouse, just in case."

"So nobody can get into that field without you knowing?"

Symonds hesitated before shaking his head. "Not through the gate. I suppose it's possible someone could climb over it."

"Someone could cut the chain perhaps?"

"I'd soon know if they did. Nobody's ever done that while I've been on the farm."

"Have any keys ever gone missing?"

"I suppose over the years we've lost the odd key, but nothing as I remember."

"How many people work on the farm?"

"Got two farm hands who look after the cattle. Otherwise, it's me and Gertie. We used to have more when the old man was alive, but it was a waste of money. I got rid of them when he packed up."

"Presumably Mr. Gladwell would have carried keys. Did he live on the farm until he died?"

"Not quite. We put him in a care home for a while before he died. For his own sake really. By then he wasn't up to doing anything useful. Not that he ever was much use; he just got in the way. Look, are all these questions necessary? Can't I go? There are urgent things I've got to do."

The superintendent looked carefully at Symonds and glanced at the solicitor.

"That's probably enough for today, sir. We're still trying to find out what's happened, and it'll be a while before we get a forensics report. I shall definitely want to talk to you again. Remember that you deliberately interfered with a crime scene, which is a serious matter, but we'll deal with that another time."

"What crime scene? Just a few old bones, could be anything. I don't suppose you've found much else; otherwise, you'd be asking different questions."

Symonds was unaware of what had since been discovered in the pond. The superintendent wanted to keep it that way for the time being.

"We'll talk to your daughter next, Mr. Symonds, but someone will bring her back home to the farm afterwards. So, there's no need for you to wait around; you can get straight back to your urgent business."

"There's no point in talking to her. She knows nothing more than I've told you. Don't want you frightening her into saying things that aren't true. She might as well come back with me."

The superintendent looked directly into Symonds's eyes for several seconds and then leaned toward him. "I shall neither frighten nor intimidate her, sir. However, if I find that you have already tried, or try in the future, to prevent her from answering my questions, then I shall charge you with perverting the course of justice. That is a very serious offence, as your solicitor will confirm. Is that clear?"

Symonds averted his gaze and looked downward. "I suppose so, but I just want to protect her."

"We shall protect her. Thank you for coming in, sir. We'll not delay you any further. Sergeant Teagle will see you out."

Symonds stood up hesitantly, and Teagle went and opened the door and beckoned, "This way, sir. I'll escort you from the station." Symonds followed her with the solicitor.

Teagle returned to the interview room a few minutes later.

"He wasn't keen to leave without Gertie, sir. But I took him to his car, and he's driven away. She's waiting outside. I didn't let Symonds talk to her."

"Well done, Teagle. There's a lot more I want to ask Symonds, but that was useful background information. It's given me plenty to think about. We'll talk it all through after we've interviewed Gertie. Bring her in, please."

"Thank you for waiting, Miss Symonds. Your father's gone back to the farm, and Sergeant Teagle will drive you home when we've finished. There's no need for you to be concerned. I just need to get some background information. Is that all right?"

Gertie nodded.

"Can you please tell me your age?"

"I'm thirty."

"And you've lived on the farm all your life?"

"Yes, except when I went to agricultural college, but Dad didn't like that, thought it was a waste of time and money, and I didn't finish the course."

"Were you disappointed?"

She shrugged her shoulders. "I was. It was good, and I was learning a lot about farming. Grandad set it up for me and paid for it, and he was upset when I left the college. Had an argument with Dad."

"Did you like your grandad?"

"Yes, he was nice. We had fun. The farm was busy then, and things were always happening. He'd take me to the county farm shows and introduce me to other farmers. He bought me a pony. When I got older, he took me to visit his friends and their families. He took me to the tennis club, where I learned to play. Dad didn't like it though.

"Everybody called me Rosemary or Rosie then; only dad called me Gertie. Now everyone calls me Gertie, except Mum.

"Grandad also arranged driving lessons for me and then bought me a car for my birthday. Dad didn't like that either."

"Do you still have the car?"

"Not anymore. Can't afford to run one. Dad sold it."

"What was your grandmother like?"

"Didn't really know her. She died when I was small."

"Was your mother disappointed when you stopped college?"

"She was, but in the end, she does what Dad says."

"Do you have any boyfriends?"

Her faced colored with embarrassment, and she looked at Teagle, who smiled at Gertie and said, "Don't worry Miss Symonds; the superintendent is just trying to gather some background information. He's trying to understand who might have visited the farm."

"Sorry, no I don't. I did have some when Grandad was alive. One was the grandson of one of Grandad's friends and then a boy I met I met at the tennis club, and a boy from college. When Grandad was here, I got invited by his friends to dances and barbeques, sometimes a family wedding. Grandad had a lot of friends. But Dad didn't like me going out. He said boys were only interested in me because they wanted to get their hands on the farm."

"Why did your dad say that?"

"Grandad always said that one day the farm would be mine."

"Will it?"

"I don't know. Dad doesn't talk about it, nor does Mum."

"Do you regularly go to the field with the pond?"

"Not often. It's used for grazing sometimes, but it's so far from the main farm, so it's a chore getting the cattle up there and tending to them. It's nearly a mile along the lane; there's no other way. I think Dad is planning to sell it. He's sold some other fields."

"Were you surprised at the bones found in the pond?"

"There weren't any bones when Dad took me there. He'd already done some clearing up and told me to help him with the rest of it. He was keen to get it finished."

The superintendent sat quietly, thinking about what had been said during the interview before saying, "That's been helpful, miss. I think it's a good time to stop. Please wait here a few minutes. I need a quick chat with Sergeant Teagle before she takes you home. Thanks for your help."

Teagle and Gertie chatted together during the drive from Kidlington to the farm.

"Do you still keep in touch with any of your boyfriends? They sound nice."

"Not really. Dad frightened them off. One sends me a birthday card each year. If Dad knew he'd go berserk, but Mum takes in the post, and she gives it to me without him knowing. He's called Freddy. I really liked him, still do."

"Do you write back or phone him?"

"I'd like to, but I'm scared Dad would find out. Freddy sent me a card on my birthday last month, always puts his address and phone number in it. I've got a mobile phone, need one on the farm, but Dad seems to know everything I do with it. The postman picks up our outgoing post, and Dad would notice if I tried to send a letter. There's no post box nearby that I could get to. Dad refuses to let me see anybody. He's frightened away all my friends. There was a student who worked on the farm one summer years ago. She was a good friend. We had fun and spent a lot of time together. She came along with me a few times on grandad's outings, but then she went back to university, and I've not seen her since. She left suddenly without saying goodbye; it upset me. Dad told me to forget her."

"I could post a letter for you if you'd like."

She looked at Teagle and smiled. "Thanks, maybe. Will I see you again?"

"Certainly. While we're working at the pond, I'll be visiting, and I'll come by to see how things are. Here's a card with my contact details in case you ever need it."

Gertie took the card and studied it before slipping it into her pocket.

"Have you thought about leaving the farm and getting a job elsewhere?"

"Used to do that a lot. But how could I? I've no money and nowhere else to go. Anyway, I couldn't leave Mum alone."

The car stopped by the farmhouse, and they both went inside. Symonds and his wife, Aggie, were in the large kitchen.

Symonds directed his words to Teagle. "You took your time. I suppose you've been asking her stupid questions. A total waste of time when we could be doing something useful."

Teagle smiled at him. Aggie was looked nervous as she pretended to busy herself by the kitchen sink. Gertie was quiet.

"I didn't think we'd been very long, sir. Anyway, Chief Superintendent Barnes has asked me to thank you and Miss Symonds for your time. It has helped with some background information. When we know more about what's happened at the pond, he'll probably want to see you again."

"I thought so. It's all been a waste of time, but you can't bring yourself to say so. Waste of public money as well."

He glowered at Teagle, who simply smiled back.

"We'll have to wait and see what happens. Just in case you think of something which might be useful or would like to contact us, I'll leave you a card with my number."

Teagle put her business card on the kitchen worktop. Symonds picked it up and looked at it before screwing it up and throwing it into the wastebin.

He smirked and said, "That's what I think of your card and you lot. We won't be needing it."

Teagle stood looking at him and gave a gentle smile. "That was very foolish, Mr. Symonds. The chief superintendent will not be pleased. I'm going to give my card to each of you; consider them police property. There'll be no excuse for not reporting to us in future—promptly reporting, instead of destroying evidence."

She took out three cards and handed them out.

Symonds snorted at her. "Don't try to be smart with me, girlie. You people think you're so high and mighty, you—"

Teagle interrupted. "Better you don't do or say anything you might later regret, sir. I'll be seeing you again soon. Cheerio."

She nodded and smiled at Aggie and Gertie as she left the farmhouse.

CHAPTER 3

The superintendent listened as Teagle gave a report on what had happened.

"I feel sorry for Gertie, sir. It's a waste of her life. Symonds is a nasty piece of work, and I wouldn't be surprised if he's violent. Aggie and Gertie are frightened of him."

"I agree. But it may be that this domestic situation is not relevant, although I imagine that what we've discovered and heard so far will contain some important clues when we know more about what's in that pond. Meanwhile make sure you get everything written up, and then put it on one side until the pathologist comes back with his report. That could take a while. There's plenty of other crime to keep us busy meanwhile."

"Very good, sir. But I'll call in to the farm again just to check how things are. I've got an uneasy feeling."

The superintendent looked thoughtfully at her.

"OK, do that. I've also got a few pieces of information I want you to gather for me."

He passed over a piece of paper containing a handwritten list. She studied it before replying.

"I can understand why you want the grant application for clearing the pond, but the other things are a surprise. Although I can see what you might be thinking."

"I expect you can. It isn't a marriage made in heaven, as they say!"

It was in fact nearly four weeks before the pathologist sent in his report. During that time Teagle visited the farmhouse on three occasions.

The first time was two days after she'd taken Gertie home. Aggie was alone in the farmhouse and obviously nervous that Teagle had visited.

"Is everything all right, Mrs. Symonds?"

"Yes, but you ought not to be here. Arthur won't like it."

Teagle studied her. Aggie was a frightened woman.

"There's nothing to be afraid of, Mrs. Symonds. I just wanted to check that everything was OK. Where is Mr. Symonds?"

"In the barn down at the bottom of the yard. They're dealing with some cattle to go to market."

Teagle walked along the farmyard toward the barns. Everything looked uncared for and untidy. She could hear animals bellowing. She followed the noise and found Symonds with Gertie and two men trying to get some cattle into a large trailer that had been reversed into one of the pens. The ground inside the pen was covered in manure, and the air was full of its pungent aroma.

The cattle were quite obviously reluctant to go up the slippery ramp into the trailer, and Symonds was shouting as they all heaved and pushed the cattle along a makeshift gangway that led to the ramp. Everybody inside the pen was smeared with manure and filth. Teagle stood watching until eventually, after a great deal of noise, four animals were coerced and pushed to struggle up the ramp into the trailer, and the doors were quickly closed behind them. Symonds noticed her and shouted, "What do you want? You can see we're busy."

"Just called by to check that everything is OK, Mr. Symonds. I told you I would."

"You're wasting your time. There's nothing to tell you. We've got things to do. Let's get these to market, Jim. You clean up, Gertie."

Teagle smiled at Gertie. "Hello, Miss Symonds. How are you?"

Gertie gave a brief nervous smile in return before saying, "OK, thanks."

They all looked at Teagle, who smiled again and gave a wave. "I can see you're rather busy now, so I'll let you get on. I'll call by again in a few days; perhaps you'll have more time then."

As she walked back to her car, she heard Symonds shout. "We're always busy, so don't bother coming back."

She arrived on that next visit in the early evening. She presumed they'd have finished farm work for the day. Gertie answered the farmhouse door and invited her inside. Symonds was in the kitchen with Aggie sitting at a table. They were just finishing a meal.

"Hello. I hope I'm not interrupting your supper."

"You're always interrupting something. What do you want now?"

Symonds was as unwelcoming as ever, but Teagle smiled and said, "Just a couple of questions. When was the area by the pond last cleared?"

Symonds looked puzzled. "Not ever been cleared before as far as I remember. Can you remember, Aggie?"

"Must be well over twenty years ago. Dad used to keep it tidy in the old days."

"He would. A waste of money. The pond isn't any use."

"Well, Arthur, when the farm was bigger, we used to keep more animals up there, and they drank from the pond."

Symonds looked displeased with Aggie and turned to Teagle. "What's it matter anyhow?"

"Well, sir, we wondered why you'd decided to spend your money clearing it recently, if it isn't any use."

Symonds laughed loudly and leaned back in his chair and said, "Didn't cost me a thing. Those two didn't finish the job, so I didn't have to pay them."

Teagle studied him. It was difficult not to show her distaste for him.

"But you would have expected to pay, so why do it?"

"Thought it needed tidying up. None of your business what I do on the farm."

Teagle looked at Aggie and then Gertie; each face had a blank expression.

"Well, thanks for that. I'll leave you to it. I'll call again if anything else occurs to us. Goodbye to you all; pleasant evening."

As she turned to go, Gertie said, "I'll see you out, Sergeant."

Gertie held open the outside door, and Teagle brushed past. The door was closed behind her. It was dark as she reached her car and drove from the yard onto the lane. She pulled up when she was out of sight of the farmhouse and looked at the envelope that Gertie had pressed into her hand. She studied the address; it would need a postage stamp.

It was two days later when she was called by the Kidlington HQ reception desk.

"There's a visitor at the front desk asking to see a sergeant called Alice. Thought it could be you, Sergeant. Says it's personal."

"What's the name?"

"Freddy Hawthorn."

The man waiting near the front desk looked about thirty years old, fair haired, slim and pleasant looking—quite handsome, in fact, thought Teagle.

"Detective Sergeant Alice Teagle, sir. Can I help?"

"I hope so. Do you know Rosie Symonds?"

"I do, Mr. Hawthorn. Let's go somewhere to talk."

Hawthorn explained that he'd received Rosie's letter. It explained how she'd try to smuggle it from the farm by giving it to a nice police sergeant from Kidlington called Alice to post. She said he must not reply because her father had a habit of intercepting the post deliveries. So he'd driven to HQ to ask for a sergeant Alice.

"What's going on, Sergeant?"

"What did she tell you in the letter?"

"It's a lovely letter, quite long and personal. I always dreamed she'd contact me, but she's never done so for eight years. I send her a card each birthday, hoping it'll get to her. I know her father tries to stop her getting any post, but I'd thought a birthday card might reach her. I can tell she's unhappy and frightened. Having gotten this letter, I desperately want to see her, but I thought it might cause more trouble if I went to the farm. Her father forced me off the farm last time, and Rosie was in tears. He told me never to go back there. So I came to find you, to try and find out what's happening to her."

Teagle sat quietly thinking. She felt sorry for him, sorry for them both, in fact. Gertie—or more properly, Rosie—had trusted her to keep a secret from her father. If Hawthorn visited the farm, it would almost certainly create uproar from Symonds, especially if he found out what had happened. Teagle was conscious that she should not get involved in taking sides over what was a domestic issue. But she was already doing that by offering to secretly post Rosie's letter for her. On the other hand, there were clear indications of bullying and intimidation from Symonds; otherwise, Rosie could have posted it herself.

"I don't think it would be wise to go to the farm. It would make things very difficult. You already know what farmer Symonds is like. Perhaps you should write a reply to Rosie, and I'll try to deliver it to her without her father knowing?"

After Hawthorn had gone, Teagle sat thinking about what she had let herself in for. She was certain that the superintendent would strongly disapprove. Better not to mention it, she decided.

The following day Hawthorn left a large envelope marked for her attention at Kidlington HQ reception. Inside was a smaller sealed envelope addressed to Rosie Symonds.

Teagle puzzled about how to get it to Rosie without her father finding out. She made a phone call, and Aggie answered.

"Hello, Mrs. Symonds, DS Teagle here. We've got a copy of an application from the farm for a grant to do work on the pond, the pond we're investigating. Can you tell me who prepared it?"

It went quiet, and Teagle could imagine Aggie struggling what best to say.

"Mrs. Symonds, was it your daughter, Rosemary, who prepared it?"

"Yes. Rosie does some of the paperwork for Arthur."

"That's what I thought. I need to see her to ask some questions. Can you ask her to call me please?"

Again, it went quiet before Aggie replied, "I'll have to tell Arthur first. He may not agree."

"Mrs. Symonds, this is a serious police matter. Please give me Rosemary's phone number, and I'll call her."

Teagle already knew Rosie's number but decided it was best to pretend otherwise. Aggie repeated it to her.

"DS Alice Teagle here, Miss Symonds. Your mother gave me your number. I need to see you to ask some questions about the application for the grant to clear the pond. Nothing to worry about, but can you get to Kidlington HQ today?"

"Not sure that I can. I've no transport unless Mum or Dad can give me a lift."

"No problem. I'll send a police car to pick you up. It'll be there in an hour; please be ready. Don't worry; it's just some questions about the grant application."

She cut the call and waited. It was less than ten minutes before she was informed that Arthur Symonds was on the line.

"What do you want to talk to Gertie about?"

"You didn't tell us about the grant you received to clear that pond, Mr. Symonds."

"It's none of your business."

"Well, it is because the grant application describes the pond as it was before you interfered with it."

"So what? Anyway, Gertie's too busy to come to Kidlington."

"Mr. Symonds, you have already interfered with a crime scene. Don't make it even worse for yourself by obstructing us further in our investigation. A police car will be on its way for Miss Symonds. Please make sure she is ready; otherwise, I shall come and arrest you. Do you understand?"

There was a short silence before he cut the call.

Rosie arrived as planned. She'd had time to get changed from her work clothes and looked smart and fresh. Teagle sensed her excitement.

"Did you post my letter?"

"I did, and I've met Freddy Hawthorn. He came here to find me."

"Oh! What did he say?"

"He told me a lot. He's given me this letter for you."

Rosie studied the envelope before carefully opening it.

Teagle said, "I'll leave you alone for a few minutes." Rosie just nodded as she stared at the letter.

When Teagle returned, Rosie was sitting sobbing with the letter in her hands.

"It's surely not bad news?"

"No," she sobbed in reply. "it's a lovely letter, I just don't know what to do."

Teagle stood quietly, watching Rosie.

"Why not call him, speak to him? Use the phone here. Let me know when you've finished."

It was nearly half an hour later when Teagle returned to the room. Rosie smiled and looked happy. "Thank you, Sergeant. I feel better now. Freddy's coming here to pick me up. He lives near Bicester, so he'll be here soon. It's hard to believe that I'll see him again after all this time. He's going to drive me home, but he'll drop me off at the farm gate. Dad won't know what's happened today. Thank you so much."

Teagle smiled. "We'd better look at your grant application. I do need some details from you, and it's also your cover story."

Symonds was an angry man. When Rosie arrived home, he demanded to know what had happened, and what Rosie had said, and why the police were interested in the grant application, and how they'd found out about it. Rosie had her answers prepared; Teagle had told her what to say.

Rosie went to bed happy that night. She and Freddy had a plan.

The pathologist's report was long and detailed, full of written and photographic information. It emphasized that the poor condition of the remains made accurate analysis difficult.

In summary there were four skeletons found in the pond. Tests indicated they had been in the pond for between six and eight years. They were all male, estimated to be between twenty and twenty-five years old at the time of death. Examination of the skulls indicated they were probably Caucasian, although one might have African ancestry.

There was a large section of technical data for each skeleton with estimates of body size and height, diet, state of health. And another section about the site included a chemical analysis of the pond's water and the subsoil, pace of decomposition, and more.

There was no evidence as to the actual cause of death for any of the skeletons.

Clothing remains and other objects found were detailed and where possible were attributed to individual skeletons. Nothing to provide easy identification had been found; no driving licenses, no credit cards, no mobile phones, no wallets, nor anything with a name.

There were some items that might provide a line of inquiry, but it was not going to be easy to discover the identity of any of the skeletons.

After studying the report, the superintendent and Teagle went to the School of Anthropology at Oxford University to meet

Professor Lionel Cornelius, a visiting American academic spending a year teaching at Oxford. Doctor Jacob Watson, the police pathologist, was also there.

Cornelius was a famous forensic anthropologist. He was also a friend of Watson's and had eagerly accepted the invitation to assist with the investigation. The skeletons and other remains were in his laboratory.

Introductions were made, and Watson gave a wry smile. "Well, Superintendent, this little puzzle is likely to keep you busy for a while."

"Your report doesn't give us much to go on, Doctor. I was hoping for rather more."

"I thought that we'd done quite well considering the mess made at the pond. What do think, Lionel?"

Cornelius was a tall, stooping, bespectacled figure in his sixties with frizzled gray hair. He spoke with only a slight American accent.

"It's certainly not been easy, but we've finally pieced the bits together. Let me show you."

Each skeleton was exhibited on a separate large trestle table with the remains of clothing alongside it.

"As you know, Superintendent, the crime scene was very disturbed, and much of what we have here was scattered around a wide area. Some remains were discovered in the pond, and others were found amongst the slurry and mud dumped around the wood. There are still a few parts of the skeletons missing, but I don't believe they are material.

"Each table has the skeleton of a body together with other remains, clothing etc., which we believe belong to it."

The superintendent walked around the tables and studied the exhibits.

"Quite an achievement bearing in mind the mess made by the farmer. But there's very little for us to work on. No indication of identity, not even a suggestion of cause of death. In fact, are we sure there's even been a crime?"

Watson gave a guffaw. "You disappoint me, Superintendent. The remains of four men in a pond with all forms of identity missing. Are you suggesting they all may have died accidentally and not been noticed? Perhaps they slipped whilst paddling, having forgotten to take their shoes off? Or maybe drowned having a swim fully clothed?"

The superintendent gave Watson a broad smile. "That's more like it, Doctor. Thought I might provoke a response. That's not what you put in your report. Let's get down to business. Tell me what you think has happened."

Watson shook his head at the superintendent and gave him a rueful smile. "I presumed you could read between the lines!"

"We are but simple policemen, Doctor. Why not spell it out for us?"

"OK, but this is just a possibility, only our interpretation at this stage. Lionel and I have spent a lot of time trying to work it out, and this is our best guess, if you like."

Cornelius nodded and took over. "That's right. We think, from our tests, that we have the remains of four adult males, each very nearly the same age, born within a year of each other. The dead bodies were put into the pond separately over a period of less than two years. So we can presume they were killed individually within the space of two years or less before being dumped into the pond. OK so far?"

"Yes, excellent. That's much more specific than the report, Professor. But can you give me more? What year were they born, for instance?"

Cornelius nodded to Watson, who took over. "In our opinion, and to put it simply, they would each be thirty years old today, if still alive."

"Now that is very interesting, Doctor."

"I thought it would be, and we've more. The earliest or first death was eight years ago, and the latest or last was six years ago or maybe slightly less."

"Also very interesting. You said when we first talked that you thought the bodies had been in the pond for about ten years, but now it's only six in the last case?"

"I do remember. That was my initial thought, and that's normally how long it would take to get that level of decomposition in such an environment. However, Lionel has analyzed the pond water, and we now know it was full of rotting debris and bacteria, which has hastened decomposition. Not nice water, more like a deadly germ-laden soup, not wise to go swimming or even paddling in, if you value your health. Now that the area has been opened up and cleared, and sunlight can reach it, I imagine the water quality will improve dramatically."

The superintendent stood thinking until he heard Cornelius speak. "I've put them in order, Superintendent. Exhibit Body 1, 2, 3, and 4. So this was the first man to die."

Cornelius led them to the table marked Exhibit Body 1.

"The clothing remains, and the few personal effects might be interesting for you, Superintendent."

The superintendent looked closely at the various items on the table. The remains of a jacket displayed a tailor's label, and he could make out some writing inside a shoe.

Watson spoke. "We're photographing and classifying everything for you, Superintendent. It should give some clues for you to follow up."

"Another thing that's noticeable"—it was Cornelius who spoke—"each of the men was above average height, and I'd imagine from the bone structures that they would be strong men. Hope that's helpful."

"Thank you, Doctor, and you too, Professor. You've both given me a great deal to think about. I appreciate all you've done, and I'm grateful for your helpful assessment."

"Please remember, Superintendent, that what we've told you is just our assessment, our best guess, so don't jump to too many conclusions yet."

The superintendent smiled. "I wouldn't dream of it, Doctor, but good of you to be so helpful."

Watson grimaced. He was about to say something but decided against it.

As they sat together in the car on the way to Kidlington, Teagle remarked, "You seem in a hurry to get away, sir."

"There's nothing there that won't wait a bit. A line of inquiry has occurred to me."

"You've not jumped to a conclusion, have you, sir? Remember what Doctor Watson said!" Teagle grinned at the superintendent.

"Not a conclusion exactly, Teagle, but a possibility which we'll have to follow up at some point, so we may as well do it first. Who's our most likely suspect for these murders?"

Teagle thought for a moment. "There aren't yet many to choose from, so I suppose it's farmer Symonds."

"Exactly. You've told me he's capable of violence, and we know he's the only person we know who has ready access to that field with the pond."

"That's true, but who would he want to kill?"

"Those men in the pond would each be thirty years old today. That's a clue. If I'm wrong, then we'll soon know. Come and see me in my office in two hours, and I'll tell you what to do."

The car arrived at HQ, and the superintendent quickly got out and ran up the entrance steps. He was in a hurry.

CHAPTER 4

Two hours later Teagle was listening to the superintendent.

"OK, Teagle, I know this is perhaps a long shot, but here's how it looks to me. The pond was overgrown in a field hardly visited. Access is made deliberately very difficult by farmer Symonds. To gain entry it needs the padlock key, and farmer Symonds holds the key."

"Symonds said there were spare keys, sir, and don't forget all this happened years ago when the farm was apparently busier."

"Good point, and I've thought about that. I said it was a long shot, but hear me out. Each victim would be about thirty years old today and were killed over a period of two years. The first victim would have been twenty-two, and the last twenty-four years old.

"Rosie is aged thirty, and she says that all her friends were frightened off by her father, Symonds, when she was in her early twenties when her grandfather, her protector, was ailing. Symonds wanted Rosie isolated at the farm with no friends for some reason."

"I follow your thinking, sir. Rosie said her grandfather led her to understand she would inherit the farm one day. She also said that Symonds had told her that any boyfriend was only interested in getting his hands on the farm. But you asked me to get a copy of Ben Gladwell's will, and it turns out he hadn't made one, so surely that rules out that motive?"

"Good reasoning, Teagle. I thought about that. Gladwell would have still been alive when these murders took place, and farmer Symonds would have still imagined there would be a will in favor of his Rosie at that time."

"So you think Symonds frightened off her friends to keep her isolated and under his control; and those that didn't go quietly he bumped off and dumped in the pond? Seems rather far-fetched, sir, don't you think? They'd have been reported missing."

The superintendent gave a shrug. "You're probably right. Although it is a possible motive especially when you bear in mind the birth and marriage certificates you obtained for me."

"What exactly do you mean?"

"Gladwell's daughter, Aggie, was pregnant with Rosie when she married Arthur Symonds. Gladwell didn't like Symonds—that's very clear from everything we've heard, but Aggie was in her thirties and unmarried and pregnant. Aggie maybe felt she had no alternative but to marry Symonds; perhaps she even loved him then. So Gladwell had no choice but to accept it. I'm guessing that Symonds had done what he was frightened one of Rosie's suitors would do. By finding a way to marry the farmer's daughter, Aggie, he intended to get his hands on the farm, and he didn't want anyone marrying Rosie and getting in the way."

It went quiet. They looked at each other. Teagle's mind was racing. She remained uneasy that the superintendent was on the wrong track. Unfortunately, he made it sound so compelling.

"You did say that it wasn't a marriage made in heaven, sir. But aren't you letting your imagination run riot?"

"Don't worry, Teagle; it is only a possibility, just speculation, and we've no evidence, but it justifies being investigated. If I'm wrong, then we'll quickly rule it out and get on with other lines of inquiry. However, I am certain that these murders are connected to someone who knows that farm.

"Something is rotten about that farm, or more precisely about farmer Symonds. He needs checking out. Another thing that's bugging me is why old Ben Gladwell didn't make a will. He was intelligent, owned a valuable farm, and had indicated to his grand-daughter, Rosie, that she'd inherit it all one day. Without a will that was never going to happen."

"So, what shall we do, sir?"

"Without sounding alarm bells, I want a list of all Rosie's past friends and anyone else who regularly visited the farm socially or worked on it between, let's say, five and twelve years ago.

"So far, we've been lucky with the media; the possibility of a few very old human bones found in a pond has not attracted any real interest. When it's known we've found the remains of four relatively recent bodies, then it'll hit the national news, and that publicity could be very unhelpful at the moment. So let's try and keep things quiet for a while longer.

"You talk to Rosie again—she seems to have confidence in you—and I'll interview Aggie. Let's see who we come up with, and then you can check if any of them went missing. That'll soon tell us if I'm wasting our time."

"Symonds won't like you talking to Aggie alone, sir."

"I imagine he won't, especially if he is involved in the murders. Nevertheless, you get Aggie here and arrange for a solicitor to be present just to be safe."

Teagle wondered if she should mention Rosie's boyfriend, Freddy Hawthorn. Maybe not yet, she decided.

The superintendent took the call.

"Listen, that sergeant of yours says you want to talk to Aggie. Well, you can't. I won't allow it. If you've anything to ask, then you can ask me. Same goes for Gertie; you've already spoken to her, and she's too busy to waste any more time."

The superintendent let Symonds finish and paused for a few seconds before replying.

"Tell me, Mr. Symonds, why are frightened of me talking to Mrs. Symonds?"

"I'm not frightened, not of you or anyone. Aggie can't tell you anything more than I can. But she's nervous of you, and you'll get her to say things she doesn't mean."

"A solicitor will be alongside Mrs. Symonds. I simply want to ask her some questions which might help my investigation. Your turn will come when I next interview you."

"You don't get it, do you, chum? I've already told you: Aggie is not coming to Kidlington. Nor is Gertie. You'll have to make do with me, when I'm good and ready to see you. Is that clear?"

"Perfectly clear, sir. I expect to see you very soon."

"When I'm good and ready, I said. That won't be this week or next. You'll just have to wait. You people nosing about have messed me up, and you've found nothing. All a waste of time."

When work on the farm had stopped for that day, Teagle walked into the farm kitchen. As she expected, they were eating supper together.

"Who invited you in? What the hell do you want now? I told your guv'nor to piss off."

"That was the gist of what he told me, Mr. Symonds. So I'm here to arrest you and take you to Kidlington."

"Don't make me laugh, girl. Look at you. How do you expect to do that?"

Two large police officers walked into the kitchen.

"I'm going to do it with the help of these officers, sir. You are under arrest for obstructing the police and interfering with a crime scene."

Teagle nodded, and they quickly handcuffed Symonds before he'd managed to get up from his chair. His face was red with anger. He tried to struggle, but it was in vain. The officers held him as Teagle issued the caution.

"Mr. Arthur Symonds, you do not have to say anything, but it may harm…"

Rosie could barely suppress a smile. Aggie looked shocked. Symonds cursed repeatedly.

"The officers will take you to Kidlington, Mr. Symonds. You may be kept overnight, so I'll ask Mrs. Symonds to pack you a few things to bring along later just in case."

Symonds had gone quiet, but his anger was obvious. He was hauled to his feet and escorted from the kitchen. As he passed by, Teagle could feel his rage as he glowered at her.

They heard the police car drive away, and Teagle sat down with Rosie and Aggie.

"Mrs. Symonds, the superintendent simply wants to ask you some questions. There's no need to worry, and you'll have a solicitor with you. In fact, Rosie can sit with you as well if that would help. I also need to ask Rosie some questions."

Aggie nodded. "I'd like Rosie with me please."

Rosie and Aggie smiled at each other.

"It'll be all right, Mum. They're nice at Kidlington, not at all like Dad says."

"OK, please can you both get ready, and also pack a few overnight things for Mr. Symonds. I'll clear the table and tidy up here for you."

The superintendent sat watching Rosie and Aggie sitting alongside a solicitor as Teagle went through the formalities. When they had been completed, he smiled at them both and began.

"As Sergeant Teagle has told you, my name is Graham Barnes. As you know we are investigating the discovery of some human remains at a pond on your farm. We believe that these remains may be connected to something which happened on the farm in the past, possibly between five and twelve years ago. Can you remember anything out of the ordinary happening during that time?"

Rosie and Aggie looked at each other, and it was Aggie who spoke first.

"I can't think of anything. Of course, my dad was still in charge most of that time, and there was much more happening then. He never mentioned anything to me."

41

"Did you have any unusual visitors during that time, Mrs. Symonds?"

Aggie shook her head. "There were quite a few visitors in those days and more people working on the farm. We used to be a busy farm, but things are much quieter now."

"Why is it quieter now?"

"Well, my dad really enjoyed farming, liked a lot happening, enjoyed exhibiting at the farm shows. When Dad became poorly and had to give up working, Arthur took over. He thought that we were trying to do too much. Said there was no need, and it all slowed down. Dad's friends stopped coming; we didn't go to the shows. When Dad died, Arthur sold a lot of the herd and some of the land and properties. He said they weren't profitable."

Aggie went quiet and looked at Rosie. The superintendent sensed a sadness about them both.

"It might help us if you could remember the people who regularly visited during that time, both friends and workers. Your friends, for example, Miss Symonds, who might have noticed something. People who may have spent time around the farm. Mr. Gladwell's friends perhaps."

Rosie was about to answer, but Aggie spoke. "Rosie had quite a few friends in those days, didn't you? Sometimes we had a barbeque and a party. Dad liked to do that. He had a lot of friends, and their families came as well. Dad was proud of the farm and liked showing it to people."

The superintendent smiled at Aggie. She seemed relaxed and keen to help.

"Thank you, Mrs. Symonds; that's helpful. I'd like you and Rosie to spend some time with Sergeant Teagle compiling a list of names for us. I'll come back when you've finished."

He left them to it. It was nearly two hours later before Teagle knocked on his door.

"Quite a long list, sir. I think it was a trip down memory lane for both of them. What do you want to do? I'd like to speak to Rosie separately about the grant report again before she leaves; it'll only take a few minutes."

"I've a few more questions for Mrs. Symonds. I'm unsure whether to do it with Rosie present."

Teagle looked surprised.

"They seem relaxed together."

"Mother and daughter usually are, sir. But it's helped by not having Symonds present."

The superintendent looked thoughtful. "Let's keep them together, and you can see Rosie alone afterwards."

He sat opposite them and smiled. "Mrs. Symonds, Miss Symonds, thank you for your help. Before you go home, I have a few more questions for you, Mrs. Symonds, and then Sergeant Teagle wants a few minutes with Miss Symonds."

They both sat looking at him expectantly.

"Mrs. Symonds, I think that you are the only child of your parents?"

"That's right. My own mum was an only child as well. Dad started the farm soon after they married. It was small then, but he built it up to be one of the biggest in the area."

"Quite an achievement. Your mother died soon after you married, I understand?"

"Yes. Rosie was only six when she died. Dad was terribly upset. But he loved Rosie, and that helped him through his grief. It was a sad time."

Aggie looked at Rosie and smiled, although there were tears in her eyes.

"I'm sorry, I don't mean to upset you Mrs. Symonds. I'm just trying to understand the background. Were you surprised when your father died without leaving a will?"

Aggie almost jerked in her seat, and her face went pale. Her head went down.

Rosie looked alarmed. "What's wrong, Mum? Don't be upset."

The solicitor started to say something, but Aggie blurted out, "I'm sorry, Rosie, so sorry."

Rosie gently held Aggie's hand and spoke softly. "Don't worry, Mum; it doesn't matter."

The solicitor finally managed to speak. "Chief Superintendent, are these questions relevant? I can't see that they've any bearing upon your investigation. They are clearly very upsetting to Mrs. Symonds."

Teagle looked puzzled, and Rosie continued to console her mother.

The superintendent sat watching them before deciding.

"I think that will be all for now. I'm truly sorry that my question upset you, Mrs. Symonds. I'll leave you with Sergeant Teagle, and after she has spoken to Rosie, she'll take you both home."

Aggie looked calmer, and Rosie said, "Thank you, Superintendent. I'll look after Mum. She'll be fine."

The superintendent looked at Teagle. "Come and see me for a few minutes before you set off."

Teagle took Rosie to a separate room, leaving Aggie with the solicitor.

"Sorry that your mum is so upset."

"Don't worry, she'll be OK. I'll look after her."

"That's good. I told the superintendent that I had a few questions to ask about the grant application, but that was just an excuse to see you alone."

Rosie looked excited. "Has Freddie been in touch?"

"He left this for me to give to you."

Teagle took a small package from her pocket.

"I can guess what this is."

Rosie took it eagerly. Her eyes were shining, and she smiled. "It's a mobile phone. Now I can contact Freddie without Dad knowing."

"You'd better hide it in your pocket then. I'll take you back to your mum, and I'll be along very soon to take you both home."

The superintendent was leaning back in his chair thinking about events when Teagle entered his office.

"What do you make of all that, Teagle?"

"Seems to me that they both expected Ben Gladwell to leave a will which would in some way favor Rosie, but he didn't. Aggie is upset about it and feels sorry on behalf of Rosie, so she said sorry to her. Rosie seems to accept it."

"Maybe; it's a plausible interpretation. Of course, the lack of a will would mean Aggie would inherit, and she could put any disappointment right by passing the farm to Rosie, if she wanted to."

"I don't imagine Symonds would like that. He calls the shots, from what Aggie was saying about the way he runs things."

"I agree with you there. There could be another explanation."

"What do you mean, sir?"

"I'll tell you tomorrow. We'll soon know if I'm wrong. Meanwhile, I'm going to keep Symonds here overnight. We'll charge him in the morning. It'll give Aggie time to calm down. On your way back to the farm with them, play down the importance of my question about the will and suggest they don't mention it to Symonds."

"Good idea, sir. I expect they'll be happy to keep it to themselves. I don't think Symonds will like being kept here overnight."

She smiled at that thought as she left the office.

The following morning, Symonds was formally charged with deliberately interfering with a crime scene and attempting to obstruct police inquiries. He was released on police bail pending a court hearing to be arranged. Although unhappy, he remained subdued as he was escorted from the building to make his own way back to the farm.

Teagle sat waiting in front of the superintendent's desk. His face was expressionless. She knew from experience that he was gathering his thoughts.

"It's quite likely that your interpretation of what happened yesterday is correct, Teagle. Gladwell talked about leaving the farm to

Rosie but failed to make a will for some reason. Maybe Gladwell talked about Rosie inheriting to bait Symonds, to wind him up; he certainly didn't like him. Gladwell wasn't a fool and would know that without a will, Aggie would inherit but simply presumed she'd pass it to Rosie in due course. In doing so he misjudged the greed and determination of Symonds."

"Sounds about right to me, sir. Certainly explains the reaction of Aggie and Rosie."

The superintendent went quiet again before saying, "The problem I have is that from what we know about Ben Gladwell, it doesn't ring true. At least not to me."

"Sir, I know you don't like Symonds—neither do I—but aren't you letting that interfere with your judgement, if you don't mind me saying so? It's unlikely there's anything sinister about it."

He smiled. "I never mind you giving me the benefit of your opinion, Teagle. Not sure I agree, though. It feels very sinister to me. Anyway let's find out. Find the name of the solicitor who acted for Aggie to get probate of Ben Gladwell's estate. I presume a solicitor was involved?"

"There was. He's named on the probate documents."

Barry Dalby was that solicitor. He had an office in Milton Keynes, thirty-five miles away from the farm. They met him the following day. He was a thin, bald man in his middle forties with a small practice in an anonymous, unattractive office block.

He sat looking at their warrant cards before asking, "How can I be of service, Chief Superintendent?"

"Thank you for your time, Mr. Dalby. Did you, around six years ago, assist Mrs. Agnes Symonds to obtain probate on the estate of her late father, Mr. Ben Gladwell?"

Dalby smiled. "You know very well, Superintendent, that the code of client confidentiality precludes me from answering the question."

The superintendent smiled back. "Yes, that is often a problem, sir. Fortunately for the police, your code of confidentiality does not apply if you are being used by a client to perpetrate a fraud, or any crime."

Dalby stopped smiling. "Surely you not suggesting that Mrs. Symonds did that?"

"I wouldn't be here if I didn't have strong reasons for believing a crime may have been committed. But let's talk generally to begin. I'll try to avoid putting you on the spot. We already know from the Probate Office that you acted for Mrs. Symonds. Please tell me what brought her to you."

"I seem to remember that she simply turned up and said that she was looking for a solicitor who could help her. Her father had died without leaving a will, and she wasn't sure what to do."

"Didn't it seem odd that she'd come to all the way to Milton Keynes when Oxford is much closer and has many solicitors?"

"I recall that her husband considered Oxford lawyers too expensive and slow. Said he'd heard we were what he wanted. Conveyancing and some probate work is mainly what we do."

"So Mr. Symonds came as well?"

"Yes, in fact he did most of the talking. Mrs. Symonds was quiet, seemed a bit out of her depth."

"Did you check that there was no will?"

"As it happens I did make inquiries of the registers—always do—but there was nothing. That's not unusual. So we filed for her to be the administrator for probate. You'll know, Superintendent, that when someone dies intestate—without a will—that the inheritance rules can be complicated. In this case it was simple because Ben Gladwell was a widower, and Mrs. Symonds was his only child. Consequently, his entire estate passed to her. The paperwork and formalities were completed, the debts on the estate were settled, but there weren't many of those, and probate in her favor was granted. All done quickly. The affairs of the estate had been kept in good order, which was a huge help."

The superintendent sat thinking for a minute.

"A large estate and its paperwork and affairs in good order but no will. Didn't that strike you as peculiar?"

Dalby was quiet and frowned before answering, "I was surprised at the large size and value of the estate, but it was a large farm with extensive property. Not the sort of estate I normally deal with I admit. As for no will? Well, it's not unusual for there to be no will despite it not being recommended. Many people are superstitious about wills, don't want to think about death, don't want to tempt fate, I suppose. However, there was nothing to arouse any suspicion."

Again it went quiet as the superintendent considered what he'd heard. Something was niggling away at him. He hoped it wasn't just a perverse tendency to not accept the obvious.

"So that was it, presumably the last you saw of Mr. and Mrs. Symonds?"

"It was the last I saw Mrs. Symonds, but there was still a lot of work to do after probate to get things in order, and Mr. Symonds was involved in that. Transfer of titles on all the land and properties. Also investments and bank accounts needed to pass into Mrs. Symonds's hands. It was a considerable estate, and there were tax implications. You may know that farm property has beneficial, or special, rules for inheritance tax purposes. That was outside my knowledge, and I took specialist advice. It all took time, and Mr. Symonds did get impatient."

"Presumably there was also a substantial fee for all that work?"

Dalby shrugged and smiled. "I suppose so, but it was a significant project for us, and I'd enlisted tax accountants to help. I'd expected Mr. Symonds to complain about our fees, bearing in mind what he'd said about expensive Oxford solicitors. Consequently, I billed monthly to try and avoid later problems. He never raised a query on the fees, and all the bills were promptly paid."

The superintendent sat digesting what he'd heard and then said, "Is that everything you did? The last you saw of them?"

Dalby hesitated and seemed uneasy.

"Well, no, as it happens. I shouldn't really tell you, but subsequently I've done an occasional transaction for Mr. Symonds. He's needed to sell bits of land or property surplus to requirements, and I've done the conveyancing."

"Surely you mean Mrs. Symonds?"

Dalby hesitated and sighed. "Well, technically yes. She signed the documents and had them witnessed; Mr. Symonds gave me instruction on her behalf. Everything was above board, done correctly."

The superintendent leaned forward and stared at him. "Did Mrs. Symonds sign those documents and have them witnessed in your presence, sir?"

Dalby appeared distinctly uncomfortable. "No she didn't. Mr. Symonds explained that she found traveling difficult; I understand she has difficulty walking. He took the documents away for her to sign and have witnessed. Surely you're not suggesting there is anything improper in that?"

The superintendent stared at him before replying, "What I can tell you, sir, is that Mrs. Symonds was very sprightly and happy to travel when I saw her yesterday. Was there any indication of a previous solicitor acting for the farm on any documents you saw?"

Dalby looked unhappy and uneasy. "There was an Oxford-based firm of solicitors named with all the documents provided. I'll get the address details for you."

He left the room and quickly returned. "Here you are, Superintendent. Mr. Symonds said they were a rip-off and wouldn't use them again. That happens."

The superintendent pocketed the details and stood to leave. "Thank you. That could be helpful, sir. I may want to speak to you again."

On the journey back to Kidlington, Teagle looked at the Oxford address provided by Dalby. The name on it was Curlew & Williams.

"Curlew was one of the names Rosie and Aggie provided, sir. One of Ben Gladwell's friends I think."

"Hmm, not a surprise, I suppose."

"You don't seem happy, sir. I thought what we heard seemed to make sense."

"You're right, Teagle. Ben Gladwell simply didn't make a will despite being particular about keeping his affairs in good order. Farmer Symonds didn't want Aggie to be dealing with Gladwell's old friends and so persuades her to find a new solicitor away from Oxford. Without Gladwell around Aggie does as Symonds tells her. Symonds effectively takes over the farm."

"Doesn't sound suspicious to me, sir. Ben Gladwell might have mentioned to Rosie that she'd inherit one day, and he just presumed that Aggie would pass it on. I suppose he hadn't bargained on Symonds taking over."

"Agreed that's most likely. Seems to blow away my theory that Symonds committed murder to get his hands on the farm. But Gladwell was no fool. He didn't like or trust Symonds, and he'd surely have anticipated what Symonds might do. Why not simply write a will to avoid that possibility?"

"I don't like Symonds and what he's doing any more than you, sir, but I think we should look elsewhere for our murderer."

It went quiet, and the superintendent was lost in his thoughts until he said, "OK, Teagle, we'll just tie up the loose ends. Fix up for us to see the Oxford solicitor tomorrow. I'd just like to understand why there's no will. Then we'll move on."

Curlew & Williams had premises in an old building near the center of Oxford. They met Mrs. Ravenna Curlew, the senior partner. She was a handsome, friendly woman in her late forties who seemed keen to help answer the superintendent's questions.

"That's correct, Superintendent. My father looked after Ben Gladwell's affairs. Father's been retired for over ten years now. He and Ben were good friends. In fact, we were family friends. I know Aggie and Rosie; we all used to meet socially in the old days."

"You haven't met recently then?"

"Not since before Ben died. There's been no social contact for, I guess about seven years. Ben visited me a few times on farm business in the year or so before he died, but otherwise nothing. It's a shame really because I liked seeing Aggie and Rosie, but it seems that Arthur Symonds wasn't keen on socializing."

"So we understand. Anyway, we're puzzled and hoping that you can shed some light upon why Ben Gladwell didn't make a will. He kept his affairs in good order, and surely your father would have advised him to make a will."

She gasped in surprise. "Oh but he did make a will. He was very careful about it in fact. What makes you think he didn't?"

It went quiet. The superintendent's mind was racing.

"Probate was granted on the basis that he died intestate, Mrs. Curlew."

"That can't be true, Superintendent. Aggie, and also Rosie, know there was a will."

"Can you remember what it said?"

"I believe we still have a copy, but I can remember its intention. It was a little unusual but not unduly complicated. Ben left the bulk of his estate to be held in trust by Aggie until Rosie reached the age of thirty-one, when title passed to her, if that makes sense?"

The superintendent nodded, and Ravenna Curlew continued. "Until then Aggie would manage the estate and be entitled to its income. Aggie would by then be in her sixties, and Ben thought she would be ready to retire and so left her some property and income to keep her comfortably off. He and my father spent a lot of time discussing it. According to father, Ben didn't like Arthur Symonds and wanted to preserve the farm until he felt that Rosie would be able to own and manage it."

"It seems that Mr. Symonds was generally unpopular. Do you agree?"

She hesitated before saying, "He isn't very likeable. I don't think it is a happy marriage, but that's just my personal view."

"Arthur Symonds is seven years younger than Aggie. That would be quite a difference when they married."

She sat quietly, looking at the superintendent before speaking. "I imagine you know a great deal about what happened, Superintendent. It would be true to say that it was an unexpected marriage, some might even say unwelcome."

He rather liked Ravenna Curlew. She'd been helpful without breaking any professional discretion. Just a few hints to confirm what he'd thought.

"Thank you, Mrs. Curlew. It fits with the circumstances as we know them very well. You said that Aggie and Rosie knew of the will?"

"I can't be sure they knew before Ben died, although he would have held a copy in his private papers at the farm, and he may also have told them. But when he died, as is usual, I sent them each a copy because they were beneficiaries. We had expected to act on it and obtain probate, but Aggie wanted to change solicitors. Let me get the file, and I'll see what we have there."

She made a phone call, and while they waited, the superintendent asked, "You didn't speak to Aggie about it then?"

"I tried to phone on several occasions, but either there was no answer or I was told she was unavailable. I wrote a letter of condolence, of course, but received no reply. I'd expected to see her and Rosie at the funeral, but they decided to hold a private family funeral at the Oxford Crematorium. Everyone—Ben's friends, that is—had expected a large church memorial service, but it didn't happen. It was all very sad, Superintendent."

"You mentioned that Aggie decided to change solicitors. Were you surprised?"

"More disappointed than surprised. I'd thought she would want me to help. It's not unusual for executors to change the solicitor, especially if they live far away from the deceased's solicitors. Aggie lived nearby, and I thought we were friends.

"However, Aggie was the sole executor and trustee and was

perfectly entitled to use someone else. I suspected the influence of Arthur Symonds. Aggie also requested to take away all the deeds and files we held in respect of the farm—quite a bundle, and Symonds came to collect. That was a surprise as we'd normally expect to deliver them to a nominated new solicitor in such a situation."

There was a knock on the door, and a clerk came in with some files. Ravenna Curlew opened them and extracted some papers.

"We kept a copy of the will, Superintendent. There are copies of my letters to both Aggie and Rosie enclosing each a copy of the will. Also their letters acknowledging receipt. We always ask the recipient to confirm their receipt. Also the letter from Aggie explaining that she wished to use another solicitor; she doesn't say who. She also asks for all the documents, deeds, etc., relating to the estate. Do you want to see them?"

The superintendent held up his hand to stop her passing anything to him.

"I certainly do, Mrs. Curlew, but they are evidence, and so I don't want any more fingerprints on them. Teagle, please get it all into evidence bags."

He watched Teagle don gloves and start to carefully place documents into plastic bags. Ravenna Curlew sat back and watched before turning to the superintendent.

"This is extraordinary, Superintendent. Are you saying that Aggie and Rosie pretended that Ben did not make a will? It's unbelievable. It doesn't make any sense. What would be the point?"

"We don't know exactly what has happened, Mrs. Curlew, and you must treat this discussion as confidential. We are still investigating; I'm sure you'll understand."

She nodded, and he continued. "We're told that a search of registers was made but no will for Mr. Gladstone showed up."

"That's quite possible. This will was written over ten years ago; my father advised Ben about it. At that time the registers were only starting up, and most wills went unregistered. It's more usual to register a will these days, but it's still not a legal requirement."

"Did you ever wonder what had happened afterwards?"

"I did and I felt a bit of 'sour grapes,' I suppose. We'd lost an important long-term client. However, I knew that the farm continued on with Aggie and Rosie, so everything seemed OK. I'd heard that some land and property had been sold, which surprised me, but then again it could be part of running the farm. Ben wouldn't have liked that; he'd spent his life building it up."

Teagle finished the bagging up and had written a detailed receipt for Mrs. Curlew. The superintendent stood and offered his thanks, said he expected they would talk again, and left the office with Teagle carrying the evidence behind him.

They sat in the car to Kidlington.

"You were right all along, sir."

"Not sure that's quite true, Teagle, but we've discovered something that is rotten about that farm. We need to try and work out exactly what happened and who is guilty."

"Symonds is guilty surely?"

"I'm certain he is, but we have to prove it. So far it looks like Aggie and Rosie are in the frame. It's a powerful motive for murder, though, don't you think?"

"I still don't understand that, sir. The bodies were all young men, murdered before all this happened with the will. Nor do I understand what motive Aggie and Rosie would have for pretending there was no will. It's a good job you insisted we went to Oxford to tie up the loose ends, as you put it."

The superintendent chuckled. "Funny how things happen. It certainly came as a surprise to me. It's cheered me up. When we get back to Kidlington, we'll decide what to do."

Teagle was uneasy. She had yet to confess that she was acting as a go-between for Rosie and her boyfriend, Freddy Hawthorn. It was not going to look good if Rosie was involved in a criminal conspiracy, and that was putting it mildly.

CHAPTER 5

I t was the following morning when Teagle sat with the superintendent. The previous evening he'd spent time examining the
various items of evidence, documents, and reports. He'd written
notes about the meetings with Dalby at Milton Keynes and Ravenna
Curlew in Oxford, and refreshed himself about the interviews with
Symonds and Aggie and Rosie. He'd carefully studied the copy of
Ben Gladwell's last will and testament to understand the thinking behind it. Overnight he'd gotten his thoughts together and
decided what to do.

"We'll start with Aggie and Rosie. Don't alarm them, but get
them here on the pretext of wanting some clarification on the list
of names they prepared. Have solicitors present."

Later that day, Aggie was seated with a solicitor in an interview
room. DC Duggan was with Rosie in an adjoining room, waiting.
Symonds had been at the farm when Teagle arrived there to collect Aggie and Rosie. He'd wanted to know what was going on.
Teagle said it was just a follow-up to clarify some previous information. To her surprise, that seemed to satisfy him.

"Thank you for being here, Mrs. Symonds. Can I first confirm
that you have been properly cautioned?" The superintendent was
looking at the solicitor, who nodded. "I confirm it, Superintendent,

and I've explained it to Mrs. Symonds. Can you please tell us the purpose of this interview?"

"Last time, Mrs. Symonds was upset when I asked questions about her late father's death and his estate, and consequently I curtailed the interview. I need to ask some further questions about it."

It went quiet. Aggie looked anxious, frightened even. She stared at the superintendent but said nothing.

"To begin, Mrs. Symonds, do you remember visiting the solicitor called Barry Dalby in Milton Keynes shortly after you father's death?"

"Yes."

"Can you please tell me the reason for that visit?"

"Well, Dad had died without making a will, and we needed to obtain what is called probate."

"I understand that probate was granted, and you duly inherited your late father's estate."

She nodded. "Yes, I was his only child, and that was the law."

"Quite so, Mrs. Symonds. How did you know that your father hadn't made a will?"

"Dad's solicitor in Oxford told us, and we couldn't find one in the house."

"Was the Oxford solicitor Curlew & Williams? I believe you know Mrs. Ravenna Curlew?"

"That's right. Yes, I know Ravenna."

He paused and gestured to Teagle, who placed a document in front of Aggie. It was enclosed in a plastic wallet.

"Please don't touch it, Mrs. Symonds. You should be able to see it under the cellophane cover."

Aggie leaned forward to study the document and so did the solicitor. The solicitor looked up at the superintendent. Aggie continued staring at the document.

It was quiet. Teagle felt the tension growing. She felt sadness. She was sure that Symonds had coerced Aggie to do it. Eventually Aggie looked up at the superintendent.

"I don't understand."

"It's your confirmation of receipt of your late father's last will and testament sent to you by Mrs. Ravenna Curlew. It's dated shortly after his death and signed by you."

She was agitated but emphatic. "But that can't be. There was no will. She told us there wasn't one."

He watched her and waited. She looked defiant.

"How do you explain this receipt with your signature?"

"I can't. Ravenna told Arthur there was no will."

The solicitor intervened. "Superintendent, I'm advising my client to say nothing more until I've talked with her. Can we please take a break?"

Aggie started to speak, but the solicitor put his hand on her arm. "Say nothing, Mrs. Symonds. We need to talk."

The superintendent looked at them both and nodded. "Very well. We'll leave you together and recontinue later." He nodded at Teagle, who gathered up the receipt and her other papers, and they left the room.

Outside the room Teagle asked, "What do you make of that, sir?"

"Not sure. There are a number of possibilities. Let's talk to Rosie."

DC Duggan was sitting opposite Rosie and another solicitor. After the formalities the superintendent began, "Last time we met, I asked your mother about your grandfather, Mr. Ben Gladwell, not leaving a will. Do you remember?"

"Yes, Mum was upset."

"Do you know why she was upset."

"I'm not entirely sure, but she felt that Grandad wanted me to have the farm one day. Grandad talked to me about it happening but never made a will."

"Your mother now owns the farm. Can't she pass it on to you if she wants?"

"Not sure. I suppose she could, but anyway, I think Dad's got other plans. It upset me a bit after Grandad died but not anymore." She smiled at Teagle and said, "It doesn't matter now."

Teagle could feel herself blush and hoped the superintendent didn't notice. It crossed her mind that Rosie was more interested in Freddy Hawthorn than the farm.

The superintendent nodded at Teagle, who place the signed receipt in the cellophane bag on the table.

"Please don't touch it, Miss Symonds, but please read the document. The solicitor read it with her.

Rosie looked puzzled. "I don't know anything about this."

He looked at her for a few seconds and then asked, "You understand what it is? Your signed confirmation that you received a copy of your grandfather's will shortly after his death."

"Yes, that's what it says, but it's nothing to do with me. I didn't sign it. Grandad didn't leave a will as far as I know."

"How do you know he didn't?"

"Mum and Dad said he hadn't. Ravenna told them he hadn't."

The solicitor started to protest, but the superintendent intervened. "I'm going to leave you with your solicitor for a while, Miss Symonds. You can talk together about it, and I'll come back later."

He went to his office, and Teagle followed.

"What do you think, Teagle?"

"I'm puzzled, sir. Doesn't make sense; someone must be lying. It's difficult to believe that Ravenna Curlew would lie about the will. What would be her motive? Also hard to imagine that Aggie and Rosie think they can tough it out by denying they knew about the will when they've signed the receipts. Why would they want to deny it anyway? Ben Gladstone's will treated both Aggie and Rosie generously, it seems to me."

He sat back in his chair thinking. There were several possibilities, but he could only think of one with a strong motive.

"I wonder. Obtain fingerprints from Aggie and Rosie, and from Ravenna Curlew and anyone at her firm who might have touched those receipts. Explain that it's for elimination purposes. Then get forensics to check the documents for those prints.

"While that's being done, we can't have any of them talking to each other, or anyone else. How long do you think it'll take?"

"Well, I can get prints for Aggie and Rosie straightaway and then get forensics to go over the documents. Maybe in around two hours for a result on those, sir. It'll take longer to get the others. It'll mean a trip into Oxford. It's towards the end of the working day as well; they may not be there."

"OK, concentrate on Aggie and Rosie for now. Better get them to sign something as well; I want to see their signatures."

He thought for a moment before saying, "Teagle, you have to keep them incommunicado until forensics come back. Tell them we're doing some checks. Arrange refreshments. If they object let me know, and I'll come and talk to them."

Teagle was making for the door when she heard, "Do we have fingerprints for Arthur Symonds?"

She turned back. "We might have, sir. They probably would have been taken when he was arrested and kept overnight and charged."

"If we do, get forensics to check for those as well."

Less than two hours later, Teagle returned with a forensics officer.

"I think you'll be interested in this, sir."

Teagle gestured to the forensics officer to continue. "Sir, there are several sets of prints on both these receipt documents, but none of them belong to Aggie Symonds or Rosie Symonds."

"Are you saying they haven't handled those documents?"

"Not necessarily. They could have worn gloves."

"Could their fingerprints have faded away?"

"Very unlikely; in fact, no. Fingerprints on this type of paper will show up for at least forty years, and these documents are much more recent."

"What about the signatures?"

"We got both of them to sign something for comparison. I'm not an expert on handwriting, but I think it's unlikely they signed the documents. I can get that checked out tomorrow by a specialist for you."

"Anything else?"

Teagle smiled. "Arthur Symonds's prints are on both receipts, sir."

"Yes, Superintendent, especially around the signature box."

Teagle noticed the superintendent's satisfied expression. "You'd already guessed they would be, hadn't you, sir?"

"He has the strongest motive, but as you keep reminding me, Teagle, let's not jump to conclusions. Not yet at least."

After the forensics officer had left them, he said to Teagle, "We need to be cautious. You can tell Aggie and Rosie they can go home, but don't let them leave until you've brought in Arthur Symonds. We need to keep him separated. Explain it to them."

It was forty minutes later when Teagle called him.

"There's no sign of Symonds at the farm, sir. His car's not here either, so I guess he's gone out. I've tried calling his mobile phone but no answer, just the voicemail. What do you want me to do?"

"That complicates things. We can't release Aggie and Rosie until we have Symonds here. Can't risk the three of them talking together. Arrange for two officers to be on duty at the farm to arrest Symonds as soon as he returns there. Then come back, and we'll work out what to do."

When Teagle reappeared at Kidlington, she first went to see Aggie and Rosie, who were waiting in a room with DC Duggan.

"Sorry, Mrs. Symonds, but your husband is not at the farm, and his car is missing. Do you know where he might have gone?"

Aggie thought. "I honestly don't know. He doesn't go out much, especially not in the evenings. Can't imagine he'll be away for long."

"It's a problem because the superintendent doesn't want you

going home until your husband is here at Kidlington. As I said, we can't compromise the investigation by you talking with Mr. Symonds."

Rosie spoke up. "While you were out, I told Mum about Freddy. We'd rather not go back to the farm tonight anyway. If I could call Freddy, I'm sure we could go and stay the night on his family's farm near Bicester. I can call and tell our farm hands to manage the animals whilst we're away, in case Dad's not there."

Teagle thought about it. "I'll have to ask the superintendent."

She explained it to him, and he sat looking at her. "You'd better tell me about Freddy Hawthorn and how Rosie suddenly has a boyfriend."

Teagle felt embarrassed and stupid. "I think you already know, sir. I'm sorry."

"I try to know what goes on around here, Teagle. A young man arrives at HQ looking for you with a package for you to give to Rosie. You weren't here, and the duty sergeant took the package. I heard about it and asked a few questions. Seems Freddy has been to see you twice before. I noticed his name is on the list of farm visitors you got from Rosie and Aggie. So tell me."

Teagle explained all that had happened, how she'd become a go-between for Rosie and Freddy to avoid Symonds finding out: the exchange of letters, the mobile phone for them to keep in touch, and Freddy taking Rosie back to the farm in his car once.

She finished and saw the superintendent's gaze and his disapproval.

"As it happens, Teagle, you've been lucky. I don't believe that Rosie is guilty of anything. But it was a stupid risk for you to take, even if your intentions were to help her. If she had been guilty, then you'd be in trouble. You'd better hope that I am correct about her not being guilty. There's still a possibility I'm wrong."

"Thank you, sir. I'm deeply sorry."

"Yes, I'm sure you are. Learn the lesson. Now you can let Rosie make her call, and they're free to go to Bicester if they want. I'm not expecting Arthur Symonds to return to the farm, and so you'd better start looking for him. I want Symonds found and brought here very quickly.

"And I want you to visit Barry Dalby in Milton Keynes, find out what transactions he's been arranging for Symonds, what bits of the farm he's been selling. You know what to do."

A very chastened Teagle went to break the good news to Rosie and her mother. Then she went to her desk to decide what to do next. She'd let herself down and betrayed the superintendent's trust. If only she'd told him in the beginning. She needed to try and restore his faith in her somehow.

The officers at the farm reported that Symonds had not yet returned. The farmhouse was empty.

She obtained the registration number and description of Symonds's car and started a hunt for it. She also put out an alert at all ports and airports just in case. She called Symonds's mobile phone again, but it didn't answer.

She'd obtained Barry Dalby's mobile phone number during the visit to his office. Rather than wait until the morning, she called it.

"Rather late in the evening to be calling, Sergeant. How can I help?"

"Sorry, sir, but I need full details about the transactions you made for Arthur Symonds please. It's rather urgent."

"It'll have to wait until the morning; those details are at my office. If you come there tomorrow, say late morning after eleven o'clock, I'll have it ready for you. But I'll need to see a court order; it's client confidential."

"I suppose it is, sir." She had a thought. "Have you spoken to Arthur Symonds since our visit?"

The line went quiet until Dalby said, "As it happens, he did call me."

"When was that, sir?"

"Yesterday, I think."

"What did he call you about?"

"He's thinking of selling a piece of land; that's all."

"But he called you? You didn't call him? Anyway we'll be able to trace who called who."

The line went quiet again. She could sense his uncertainty.

"Actually, I think it was me who called him."

"Why?"

"Look, is this relevant? Anyway, I've told you: it was about a piece of land."

"So you called him shortly after our meeting at your office?"

"Yes, probably, I suppose so, but what of it?"

"Did you say anything about our visit?"

"I might have mentioned it; I'm not sure."

"That was very unwise, sir. I'll see you in the morning."

Teagle rang off. It looked as though Dalby had tipped off Symonds about the visit, and now he'd disappeared. She made a note to get the phone logs between the two of them.

A report came through just after midnight. Symonds's car had been picked up earlier on traffic cameras on the M25. The next report said it was on the A12 near Colchester. She guessed he was heading for Harwich for ferry across to the Hook of Holland; he was doing a runner.

Symonds was intercepted on the approach to the ferry terminal and apprehended. By 5:00 a.m. he was back at Kidlington in a cell.

Teagle was relieved and pleased. An hour or so later and Symonds would have left the country and been on his way to Holland.

She felt weary, but she needed to be in Milton Keynes. Darby had demanded she obtain a court order before he'd release the documents or discuss them with her. That wasn't going to be possible.

She wrote a brief report for the superintendent before heading off.

She entered Dalby's offices a few minutes before 8:00 a.m. He'd obviously been there for a while. He almost jumped when he saw her.

"You're early, Sergeant. We agreed late morning. I'm not ready for you."

Teagle looked around at his room. There were opened files over his desk. It looked as though he been stripping them, cleaning them up. The wastebin was full of paper. Fortunately it didn't seem like he'd started shredding things.

She smiled at him. "This is late morning for me, sir. Looks like you got up early as well. I'll give you a hand. Shall we start by putting all that paperwork back where it belongs, into the files?"

He squared his shoulders. "Show me the court order."

"Don't have it, but I'm expecting it soon. Meanwhile, you can cooperate with me, or I'll arrest you for destroying evidence and hindering a criminal investigation. Your choice. I know what I'd do in your shoes."

"Look, Sergeant, I don't want to be unhelpful. I'm only acting in the best interests of my client. Surely you understand?"

Teagle smiled at him. "I'm acting on the chief superintendent's orders, sir. I believe he understands exactly what you've done and in whose best interests you're acting."

Darby studied her while wondering what to say, but Teagle's next words made the decision for him.

"Oh, by the way, Symonds was apprehended in the night trying to board the ferry to Holland. My guess is that someone tipped him off. He's now in a cell at Kidlington."

Darby's shoulders sagged.

It was early afternoon before Teagle arrived back at Kidlington HQ. She'd spent almost four hours with Dalby reconstituting the transaction files he'd stripped. During the process he explained all he'd done for Symonds. She now had those files in her possession.

Darby was a worried man. She'd left him under no illusion

about the possible consequences facing him. He protested innocence and denied that he'd done anything unprofessional.

The superintendent listened carefully as she reported her findings.

Symonds had, with Darby acting for him, sold property, land, and investments, which he claimed were surplus to the farm's needs or uneconomical to retain. Prior to sale, Aggie had quite legally transferred these to Symonds. All was apparently properly documented, and they qualified as tax-free transfers between spouses. The proceeds of sale had been paid into Symonds's bank accounts.

"Well done, Teagle. Good work; you've achieved a lot since yesterday evening. Sounds like you found Symonds in the nick of time. Trying to flee to Holland will make it almost impossible for him to obtain bail. That'll save us a problem.

"What you've discovered at Milton Keynes is much as I'd guessed. Seems like you got there just in time as well, before Dalby had shredded the evidence."

"Tried to make amends, sir. But you've already worked out what Symonds has been doing. I've only just begun to realize."

"We're not there yet, Teagle. Still a lot to do to understand it all. Meanwhile you must be weary."

He didn't need to ask; it was obvious. Her face was strained, and she'd not changed her clothes since yesterday morning, over thirty-six hours previously.

She sighed. "I can manage the remainder of today, sir."

He smiled. "I'm sure you can, but I'd prefer you refreshed. Go home and get some rest. Symonds can sit and stew in his cell until tomorrow. It'll give me time to go through these files.

"Before you go, ask Duggan to call Aggie and Rosie and tell them that Arthur Symonds will not be returning to the farm. She's also to tell Aggie that I want to see her tomorrow—some more questions."

"Thank you, sir, I'd rather tell Aggie and Rosie myself. See you in the morning."

The following morning Aggie sat alongside her solicitor facing the superintendent and Teagle.

"I need to understand more about the situation after your father died, Mrs. Symonds. This is very important. You said last time that you had no knowledge of your late father making a will. Is that true?"

She looked thoughtful. She also looked more relaxed than previously.

"I suppose so, but it did puzzle me. Arthur said that Ravenna had called to say that Dad had not made a will. Arthur was unhappy about it, said it would cause extra cost and take a lot of time to sort out."

"Why were you puzzled?"

"Dad had spoken to me a few times. He said he wanted the farm to go to Rosie when she was older. He said he was arranging things and said that he'd make sure that I was properly looked after. I was happy about it. I trusted Dad; he was a good father."

"So you were surprised to discover he'd not made a will?"

"I was. When Arthur said there was no will, I questioned it, told him what Dad had said to me. But he got angry and said Dad was full of empty promises. I accepted it rather than have more arguments. Dad hadn't shown me any will, just said what he'd like to do."

"Just to be sure, Mrs. Symonds, can you confirm that you've never seen any will written by your late father?"

"That's right. In the end I accepted that he'd just not got around to writing one before he died. Did he actually make a will? What did it say?"

"I believe that your father did make a will, but I can't say more. Did you write this letter to Ravenna Curlew saying you intended to use another solicitor and requesting all your father's papers and other documents concerning the farm?"

Teagle placed the letter on the table. It was under a cellophane cover and had already been examined by forensics.

"Yes. Arthur told me to do it. He wanted us to use someone else, someone he knew. Someone quicker and less expensive than Ravenna."

"After probate was obtained, all your father's estate, including the farm, became yours. Did you sign other documents to transfer or sell parts of the farm?"

"Arthur asked me to sign various things. He said we needed to reorganize, to change things around. He said it would be more tax efficient."

Teagle placed some documents she'd obtained from Dalby's office on the table.

"Are these some of the documents you signed?"

Aggie looked at them, and her solicitor examined them as well.

"Yes, I did sign them. Arthur said it was necessary. I'm not sure what they were for."

The superintendent looked thoughtfully at her. Aggie might be frightened by Symonds, but she was not stupid.

"Are you sure you didn't know what they were? Didn't know what you were signing?"

Aggie stared at him. He could detect some distress, but she lifted her chin and spoke clearly.

"I am sorry, Superintendent. I accepted Arthur's instruction to sign documents and didn't argue about it. He gets so angry if I disagree. Because we were married, he said everything belonged to him as well—that was the law—so I went along with it. It was easier that way; he can get very angry. I knew in my heart that I was transferring parts of the farm to him so that Rosie could never get it. But I still did it."

She looked down, and her unhappiness was clear to see.

"All the documents have your signature witnessed by the same people. Who are they?"

She looked through several of the signature pages. "Oh, these are Harry and Pete, two of the farm hands. Arthur must have got them to witness afterwards."

"So Harry and Pete didn't actually witness your signing?"

"No, only Arthur saw me do it. Often I never saw the whole document, just the signature page. That's all Arthur showed me, but I guessed what he was doing. Poor Rosie. What's going to happen to me?"

He looked at her and then glanced at her solicitor. "I'm not yet sure, Mrs. Symonds. We have more work to do. However, I can tell you that Mr. Symonds is helping us with our inquiries and won't be returning to the farm. Meanwhile, you are free to go, but don't leave the area. I'll need to see you again in due course."

Later that day, Arthur Symonds was sitting in the same interview room alongside a solicitor. Teagle and the superintendent were facing him.

"We're still only part way through our investigation, Mr. Symonds, but I need to ask you some questions."

"You mean you've not found anything yet, so you're still looking. Still wasting everybody's time. Why have I been arrested? I've done nothing wrong, and you can't hold me here. The solicitor agrees with me."

The superintendent looked at the solicitor. "Do you agree with Mr. Symonds, sir?"

"You well know, Superintendent, that you must charge my client within twenty-four hours, unless you have grounds to apply for an extension. He was arrested during last night and has been held here since. Time is running out."

The superintendent smiled. "Let's see how we get on during this interview. Your client has already interfered with a crime scene—"

"A few old bones isn't a crime scene. That's rubbish."

"Not just a few old bones, Mr. Symonds. Rather more recent bones and evidence of murder. You tried to destroy the remains."

Symonds laughed. "You must be mad. A couple of old bones; that's all it was. I just didn't want any trouble from you lot."

"Well, you've certainly got trouble. You're my main suspect for murder."

Symonds leaned forward toward the superintendent. He gripped the table and raised his voice.

"Listen, I don't know what you're talking about. I've not committed no murder nor dumped anything in that pond. I'd have to be stupid to do it and then dig up the pond."

The superintendent smiled at him. "Sir, if murderers weren't stupid, our job would be much more difficult. I imagine the prospect of a nice government grant to clear that pond was too good to ignore. I'll bet you now wish you'd paid Danny and Karl instead of pocketing all that grant money for yourself. Greed is your undoing, Mr. Symonds."

For the first time Symonds looked uneasy but not for long. He waved his finger at the superintendent.

"What I did with that grant money is none of your business. I know nothing about your murder, and you can't pin it on me. You have no evidence for that."

The superintendent looked dismal and nodded.

"We've a lot of investigating yet to do to. This is just beginning. Let's consider your motive. Do you know Mr. Barry Dalby, a solicitor with an office in Milton Keynes?"

"I do know of him. He's done a bit of legal work for Aggie; that's all. I hardly know the man."

Symonds was surprised to see them both smiling at him from across the table. It was Teagle who placed three closely typed sheets of paper in front of him and asked, "Do you recognize these transactions, sir?"

Symonds stared at the papers, and the solicitor leaned forward to look as well.

"Look like things Aggie asked him to do. Her dad died without making a will, and she had to get probate. Dalby did it for her. Then she needed to sort the farm out, and these must be what he did for her. Nothing to do with me. I don't know anything about them."

It went quiet as the superintendent and Teagle watched and waited. Symonds sat back in his chair and folded his arms, looking satisfied. The superintendent smiled at Teagle.

She placed her hands on the papers. "Just to be clear, sir, remember you are under caution. Can you confirm that these transactions are nothing to do with you? Can you confirm that you know nothing about them, please?"

Symonds laughed. "You've got it in one. Nothing to do with me. Clever little girl, aren't you?"

Teagle smiled back. "I try my best, sir."

"Is that it then? Can I go?"

The superintendent looked sadly at him and then at the solicitor. "If only it was so simple, Mr. Symonds. Just a few more questions please. What made you decide to try and catch the ferry to Holland last night?"

"Decided I needed a holiday. Nothing illegal in that. You'd better have a good reason for stopping me or else."

"Sorry if we inconvenienced you. Sometimes we act on tip-offs. Did you receive a tip-off?"

"What do you mean?"

"Did Mr. Dalby call you to say we'd visited him and were asking about what you'd been doing together? Remember, we do look at phone records. Think carefully before you answer, Mr. Symonds."

The solicitor made to intervene, but before he could speak, the superintendent gestured with his hand to stop him. "Please let him answer, sir. It's a perfectly reasonable question."

Symonds seemed unsure what to say. His bravado was melting away.

"Now you mention it, he might have called me. Can't remember why."

The superintendent grinned at Teagle. "Strange, don't you think, Sergeant, that a man who Mr. Symonds says he hardly knows would call him after our visit? Stranger still that it happened just before Mr. Symonds felt the sudden need for a continental holiday?"

"Sounds unbelievable to me, sir—an amazing coincidence. Others might believe it was a tip-off, like a jury for instance."

Symonds scowled at her. He was about to say something but decided against it.

"Quite so, Sergeant," said the superintendent. "Anyway just a few more questions, Mr. Symonds. How did you hear that Mr. Ben Gladwell, your wife's father, had died without leaving a will?"

"Aggie told me. She said the solicitor in Oxford had called her to say there was no will."

"What did you think about it?"

"Told Aggie it was typical of old Ben. Caused us a problem. The man was useless. He should have made a will leaving the farm to me and Aggie. That's what you'd expect, isn't it?"

"It's obviously what you expected, sir." The superintendent gave him a bleak smile. "Just to be clear again, you had no reason to believe that Mr. Gladwell had made a will, nor did you ever see a will of his?"

"Why should I? The stupid sod never talked to me about it, and I never saw a will."

Teagle took the cue and placed in front of Symonds the two receipts signed by Aggie and Rosie. "Do you recognize these, sir?"

Without hesitation he replied, "Never seen them. What are they?"

"They are confirmations signed by your wife and your daughter of receiving a copy of Mr. Gladstone's will," Teagle replied.

"Never seen them. They told me there was no will. So they lied to me about it."

"We've had both documents analyzed by our forensics team. Neither has on it any fingerprint from your wife or daughter. Nor do the signatures match theirs. We believe a fraud has been committed to deny the existence of Mr. Gladwell's will. Any ideas why, sir?"

Symonds remained defiant. "How should I know? You tell me; you're the smart one, girlie."

She smiled at him again. "Let me give you a clue. There were a lot of fingerprints on both documents belonging to one person, concentrated around the signatures. Does that help you, sir?"

Symonds said nothing. Eventually the superintendent took over and addressed the solicitor.

"Those fingerprints belong to your client, Mr. Arthur Symonds. He has defrauded his wife and daughter. We're going to charge him, and then he'll go before the magistrate to plead. You'll be able to advise him.

"Until then he'll remain in custody. We shall oppose bail at the magistrate's hearing on the grounds that he poses a flight risk. His attempt to get to Holland should make that a formality, and he'll remain in custody until trial. Other charges, possibly even more serious, are certain to follow. We still have murder to investigate, and your client has a powerful motive. Anyone knowing about Mr. Gladstone's will would get in his way."

Symonds simply stared back. The superintendent caught more than a hint of defiance in his expression.

"I hope you decide to cooperate, Mr. Symonds. It'd save us all a great deal of time and effort and expense. It might also help you. Talk with your solicitor; maybe he will advise you that is your best course of action."

CHAPTER 6

Later that day the superintendent sat and reflected on the investigation. He knew precisely how Symonds had got his hands on the estate of Ben Gladwell.

It was an audacious fraud that needed knowledge of inheritance law and the legal process, as well as cunning and determination. He suspected that Barry Dalby was deeply involved. He could well understand that when Aggie inherited the farm and estate, Symonds had thought he was home and dry; he could then bully or fool Aggie into doing his bidding. He'd succeeded for years, and only the superintendent's last chance visit to see Ravenna Curlew had finally exposed him.

However, it had to be proven to the satisfaction of a jury.

The superintendent doubted Symonds would cooperate. He would deny everything.

Symonds's defense lawyers could possibly create enough doubt to get him acquitted. They could point to the legal documentation showing that Aggie had freely passed parts of the estate to Symonds. Such transactions would be quite normal between married couples. They would ask why Aggie hadn't raised any complaints at the time.

The defense could suggest that Aggie was the real fraudster, wanting the farm to herself rather than holding it in trust for Rosie. It was Aggie who had claimed to solicitor Dalby that her father died intestate, Aggie who had asked Dalby to apply for probate on her behalf, Aggie who had signed the application, Aggie who had subsequently inherited the estate. Arthur Symonds had done nothing wrong. His fingerprints on the two receipts would be a problem for the defense, but they could manufacture a possible explanation, enough to raise doubt.

It was all nonsense, of course: Symonds was the fraudster. But a clever defense might raise enough doubts in the minds of a jury. The superintendent needed to make the case watertight. He made a list of things to be done. Teagle would be busy.

Although the superintendent was confident of Symonds being convicted for the fraud, there was still no hard evidence to connect him to the murders, to the bodies in the pond.

Perhaps Symonds had discovered a copy of Gladwell's will kept at the farm—Ravenna Curlew suggested that there'd be one—or maybe Gladwell had made him aware of his intentions. Anyone then knowing about the will could interfere with Symonds's plans to get control of the farm. That could be a motive for their murder.

On the other hand, Ravenna Curlew held the will for safekeeping in her office; she was the one most likely to scupper Symonds's plan.

It was all conjecture; there was no evidence.

Anyway, the superintendent was beginning to doubt Symonds's involvement in the murders. Symonds was greedy and corrupt and very cunning, but he was by no means stupid; he would never have let anyone near that pond if he'd dumped bodies there.

It hurt the superintendent to admit it, but Symonds was probably not the murderer, although it wouldn't do any harm to keep him in the frame. There was no other suspect, and it just might encourage his cooperation. It might also encourage Barry Dalby, as his accomplice, to be more forthcoming.

If the investigation was to make any progress, he needed the identities of those remains dumped in the pond. That was not going to be easy.

It was also a busy time for the superintendent, as his responsibilities at Thames Valley Police were demanding. He rather wished he'd assigned this investigation to one of his teams in the beginning, instead of taking it upon himself. He could still, and probably should, pass it on and avoid further distraction. Unfortunately, it had now gotten under his skin. It was a puzzle he would not let go.

Consequently, he sat at his desk late into that evening wondering how he might solve the puzzle.

There was very little to identify the bodily remains. The clothing and other items found with them might yield clues and that needed following up, but it seemed a safe assumption that care had been taken by the killer to remove everything that would help with identification. Nor was there anything to indicate how they were killed.

They were all male and today would be around thirty years old according to Dr. Watson and Professor Cornelius. That was an important clue and not a coincidence.

All the bodies had been dumped in the same, hidden place, left to rot with little chance of discovery; in a place known only to few and difficult to access. Another important clue. The superintendent remained certain the killer had a link to the farm.

It all pointed to a carefully planned and premeditated crime.

He tried to imagine how best to start. He needed some information.

Teagle had enlisted DC Duggan to help fulfil the superintendent's requirements. It took them almost three weeks before Teagle felt they'd achieved what he wanted. They put it into two reports.

The larger report concerned Symonds's activities. The other contained information about missing persons.

The report on Symonds confirmed what the superintendent had deduced, and more. Teagle had gone back to the time when Symonds first appeared on the scene. Aggie had found the interviews with Teagle and Duggan difficult and upsetting, certainly in the beginning, but as she opened her heart, she showed relief.

Aggie had a happy upbringing and early life. Her parents doted on her, and she had many friends; she was a popular young woman. In her midtwenties her parents regularly indicated that it was time she became married and settled down. She was thirty-one and had become attached to one young man, ready to marry him, when Symonds showed up. He was an outsider, different and younger than her. She spent time with him. Her parents didn't approve, and she didn't heed them. Arthur Symonds was attractive and exciting.

Suddenly she was pregnant. Arthur said they must quickly marry. Her parents were against a marriage. They didn't like or trust Arthur, and nobody seemed to know much about him. Even Aggie had to admit she knew little about his background and how he made a living. So she told her parents about the pregnancy. It shocked them into accepting the situation. Aggie and Arthur married. It was a quiet, hurried wedding, not the large ceremony her parents had intended and Aggie had dreamed of, nor what their friends had expected. Arthur had insisted on a small private wedding, claimed he was uncomfortable among her friends—"those people," as he called them.

It became immediately obvious that Arthur had no means of supporting her, no regular job or home. He lived in small, rented rooms in a suburb of Oxford. The only solution was for them to live on the farm, and her father gave Arthur a job there.

It was an uncomfortable period. The birth of Rosie helped things improve; she was adored by her grandparents. Arthur, however, did little to ease the situation by remaining unfriendly and demanding.

Aggie's mother died before Rosie was five. Nothing was said, but Aggie knew that her father, Ben, blamed Arthur.

As Rosie grew up, she became increasingly attached to Ben, her grandfather, who was more than happy about it. Of course, Arthur resented their mutual attachment but used it to obtain concessions from Ben. More money, more day-to-day influence on the farm.

Rosie was popular within their society, or to be more accurate, among Ben's friends and the society he mixed in. Arthur was unpopular and hardly mixed with anyone outside the farm.

Ben and Rosie were close, and he had indicated that one day Rosie would have the farm. He'd told Aggie, who was happy to do what Ben wanted. The only person who didn't like it was Arthur Symonds. He and Ben increasingly disagreed over matters.

When Rosie was in her early twenties, Ben's health began to decline. Arthur assumed more authority on the farm. He also made it clear that he didn't want visitors. Quickly friends stopped calling, could sense they were unwelcomed. Aggie and Rosie were stopped from going out.

Arthur insisted that Ben go into a nursing home, said he'd be better cared for. Reluctantly Aggie accepted it, and her father was put into care, but he was dead within a year.

All this the superintendent either knew or had surmised. It painted an unhappy family background picture but was not much more. He needed substance, specific evidence of Symonds's wrong-doings. What Teagle discovered next didn't let him down.

Teagle had asked Aggie about how she could have missed the correspondence from Ravenna Curlew about her father's will. Aggie remembered that around that time the post stopped being delivered, and Arthur went to collect it from the sorting office. Apparently, there were staff shortages, or so Arthur explained.

Aggie said that she had received no letters of condolence either; she'd just accepted the problems with the post office as the reason. Nor had she written any letters to friends of Ben; Arthur had forbidden her to do so.

Arthur had also insisted that the phone go unanswered for a while after her father's death, said he didn't want Aggie or Rosie upset. By that time, Aggie admitted that neither she nor Rosie argued with him; they just did as he wanted.

Although Teagle was surprised and saddened at the influence

Arthur Symonds had over Aggie's and Rosie's behavior, she could well understand it. Over time his bullying had worn down their resistance; he had broken their spirit.

Teagle visited the postal sorting office and spoke to the manager. There was no record of staff difficulties disrupting postal deliveries to the farm. There was, however, a record of Arthur Symonds requesting that all mail for the farm be held at the sorting office pending his collection. The photographic file record of a request form signed by Arthur Symonds was dated the day of Ben Gladwell's death. There was a similar signed request to recommence deliveries three months later.

This was strong evidence that Symonds had deliberately set out to intercept all correspondence that might alert Aggie or Rosie to the existence of the will. Symonds's defense lawyers would try to concoct a plausible reason for his intercepting the mail, probably explain that he was simply acting to save Aggie distress. The superintendent doubted that a jury would buy it and although it was potentially damaging for Symonds defense, it wasn't conclusive evidence of guilt.

All the fingerprints on the two documents acknowledging receipt of Gladstone's will purportedly signed by Aggie and Rosie had been forensically accounted for. Neither document had any prints belonging to Aggie or Rosie. Both documents bore Ravenna Curlew's prints and some of her staff, and both bore many of Arthur Symonds's prints. The signatures on each were confirmed as fakes. This ought to confirm that both Aggie and Rosie had never seen or handled the documents, but did it prove that Symonds had forged the signatures?

Probably more importantly, Symonds's fingerprints on the receipts did prove that he knew of the existence of Ben Gladwell's will, despite his denials, and therefore had at the very least, been party to defrauding Rosie of her inheritance. Surely, this was the "smoking gun"? The superintendent wondered what Symonds's defense might be and made a note.

Teagle, with Duggan, had also visited Barry Dalby to clarify everything that he had done for Arthur and Aggie Symonds. Teagle explained that Arthur Symonds had been charged with fraud concerning the late Ben Gladstone's will and was remanded in custody pending trial. She'd explained the possibility of more serious charges, possibly murder, to follow. She'd expressed the superintendent's desire for his full cooperation. Dalby understood and explained in more detail what had happened.

Dalby confessed that he'd met Symonds long before Ben Gladstone died. Symonds had called him asking for advice. They met and talked about inheritance law: What happened to wills, and how they were handled after death. The rules on property between spouses. Who would inherit if there was no will, about the probate process, and so forth.

Dalby answered the questions but claimed he advised Symonds that it would be better if Gladstone made a will.

It was two years later when Symonds returned and introduced his wife, Aggie. She explained her father had died leaving no will and needed help. Dalby said he presumed that Symonds had not been able to persuade Ben Gladwell to make a will, despite his advice.

The superintendent stopped and thought about that. Darby's comments suggested that he and Symonds had talked about Gladstone before his death. He made a note to check that; it might be significant. He continued with Teagle's report.

Dalby then did what Aggie asked, and she inherited her father's entire estate. Subsequent instructions came from Symonds acting on Aggie's behalf, but all transactions were signed by Aggie and witnessed. It was quite normal for documents like that to be signed and witnessed at home; most client transactions were sent in the mail. What was unusual was that Symonds collected and returned all documents personally. He claimed that the postal service to the farm was unreliable. The superintendent thought about that; it would fit with Aggie's explanation that she was shown only the signature page of a document and not the transaction details.

Dalby admitted surprise at the extent of Aggie's transfers of property and investments to Symonds, but Symonds always had a plausible explanation. Anyway, all documentation appeared in order.

When asked why he'd called Symonds and tipped him off about the superintendent's investigation into Gladstone's will, Dalby denied it was a tip-off. He called simply out of duty to his client because he had discussed him with the superintendent. Symonds had not been happy to hear about it.

Teagle asked Dalby why he was stripping the transaction files when she arrived early the following morning. He denied it and said that he was simply tidying them in preparation for her visit. She said she didn't believe him and that he was really attempting to destroy evidence. He objected to her accusation and said that no evidence had been destroyed. Teagle retorted that was only because she'd interrupted him. He refused to say any more.

The farm hands Harry and Pete had been interviewed about witnessing Aggie's signatures. They each confirmed they had not actually seen Aggie signing anything, Symonds had presented documents already signed and asked them to be witnesses. Harry said that he'd mentioned to Symonds that witnesses should really see the actual signing but was told to mind his own business and get on with it. "It doesn't pay to argue with Arthur," was Harry's defense. "More than my job's worth."

The superintendent thought about Dalby and wondered how much he was holding back.

He thought that incorrectly witnessed transfer documents were probably not unusual but might create a field day for lawyers. Would it make any difference anyway? Aggie had not denied signing them. By her own admission she'd guessed what Symonds was up to.

He sat with Teagle and Duggan to discuss the report.

"Well done, Teagle. This ought to be enough to nail Symonds

for the fraud. Mind you, it'll need Aggie to testify against him; that won't be easy for her. I expect that Symonds will deny everything, and his defense is most likely to try and implicate Aggie, to present her as the real culprit, pass the blame. Either way she'll be put under huge pressure when she takes the stand and is questioned. How do you think she'll manage?"

"Well enough, sir. She'll stick to the truth. She feels—she knows—she's let Rosie down, and she also knows she let her father down. She wants justice even if it means implicating herself. Any love she had for Arthur Symonds has long gone. My worry is that because she feels guilt herself and by expressing it in the courtroom, she might help Symonds's defense. In my opinion Aggie is wholly innocent and deserves better."

The superintendent looked thoughtful. "I agree with you. Symonds's defense will most likely try to pass the buck. Anything to cause doubt amongst a jury."

"As it happens, sir, I've had a call from Mrs. Curlew. She'd like to see you."

"Fix it up for tomorrow, please, Teagle. I wonder if she might be helpful to Aggie."

"Will do. What about Dalby? I still don't think he's telling us everything."

"That's what I've been thinking as well. He's trying not to implicate himself and trying to safeguard Symonds at the same time. He will be an important defense witness for Symonds. He'll point the finger at Aggie, saying it was her who visited him and claimed Ben Gladstone died without a will, and he'll have the probate application signed by her to back it up. Dalby's evidence will make things difficult for Aggie."

All three of them sat quietly, contemplating the consequences for Aggie when she was in the witness box being questioned by Symonds's defense lawyer.

"Dalby is in this up to his neck, Teagle; we both know it. It might be worth doing some more digging. Look at phone records between him and Symonds, including before Gladwell died. Also bank accounts, both Dalby's and Symonds's. There's been a lot of money and property transferred to Symonds so that he could line his pockets at Rosie's expense. Dalby's explanations are just too convenient. You know what to look for."

"It might be difficult, sir. That would mean going back seven or eight years."

"Ask the fraud team about it and get its help if you need to. Also, probe Darby about when he first heard about Ben Gladstone. Your report indicates that Darby and Symonds talked about him before his death and before Aggie visited him."

Teagle quickly flipped through her report and found the section, "I see what you mean, sir. Sorry I'd missed the significance of that. I'll check into it."

"Do it gently. Try not to alert him to its significance."

"OK, sir. What about the murders? Do you still suspect Symonds?"

"He's all we got as a suspect, but no I don't think he did those. Anyway, my theory about him killing off any of Rosie's or Gladstone's friends who got in his way has been trashed because you've accounted for all the men on Aggie's and Rosie's list. We'll keep him under suspicion for the time being, though. We're not going to make progress on those murder victims until we know who they are, which conveniently brings us to the report on missing persons you've prepared."

"Actually, it was DC Duggan who prepared that, sir."

"Well done, Duggan. It's encouraging stuff, and I think you've given us a starting point. I want to go through it with you both, but I've run out of time today. Teagle, ask Mrs. Curlew to come here late tomorrow afternoon, and afterwards we'll look at the missing persons."

It was at 5:00 p.m. the following day when Ravenna Curlew sat in the superintendent's office.

"Thank you for seeing me so promptly, Superintendent. I need to talk to you about Aggie and Rosie if that's possible."

"Please ask away, Mrs. Curlew. I'm happy to try and answer, but you'll understand there is a criminal investigation ongoing."

"That's why I thought it best to see you. Rosie contacted me to ask if I will help her and Aggie. Asked me to represent them in fact. They've explained what has happened and are naturally concerned about the consequences for them. I want to help them but thought, in view of your previous visit about Ben Gladwell's will, I ought to speak to you first. I need to know if I or my firm is involved in your investigation in a way which might disqualify me from acting for them."

He thought carefully before deciding what to reply.

"I'm not sure that I can answer that. Let me try and explain what I can; it may assist you. Arthur Symonds has been charged with fraud concerning Ben Gladwell's will, and I expect that Rosie and Aggie have already explained to you some of the circumstances, perhaps told you what's happened. I can't say much more at this stage, but in due course a trial will take place, and evidence will be available in preparation for it. You know the process."

She nodded her understanding and waited for him to continue. He was clearly trying to choose his words carefully.

"The interaction between you, or your firm, and Ben Gladwell over his will and what happened about it after his death is crucially important in this case. However, it should be simply a matter of evidence as far as you or your firm is concerned, but that's only my opinion. I'm sure you understand?"

Again, she nodded her understanding but remained quiet.

"We shall not be charging Aggie with any crime. I expect that Symonds will deny any involvement in the fraud. He'll protest his innocence, and I imagine that his defense lawyers will endeavor to implicate Aggie, most likely present evidence to suggest that she is the guilty one, seek to pass the blame. Again, I can't say more at this stage. Aggie will be an important prosecution witness, and you can well visualize what that will mean for her in the courtroom. Rosie will also be a witness, but she is the innocent in the fraud; in fact it is Rosie who has been defrauded.

"That is probably all I can and should say to you at this point. Fraud cases are notoriously difficult to prosecute successfully. They're often too complicated for a jury to understand. Defense lawyers seek to create doubt and confusion to make it even more difficult for the jury. They will exploit every opportunity to sow doubt, as I think you understand?"

Ravenna Curlew remained quietly looking at him. She could understand very well how her friendship with Aggie and Ben's family might be twisted by Symonds's defense. In such circumstances was it plausible to imagine that Aggie was unaware of Ben's will? It might even suggest that Ravenna and Aggie were part of a conspiracy.

The superintendent watched her.

"But there is a dilemma. Ideally it would be cleaner, more straightforward, if you and your firm were not involved in the case other than to provide evidence about the existence of the will, etc. On the other hand, Aggie needs a friend, someone she can trust to help and guide her, and support her. Someone who can also protect her interests, legally and personally.

"It's a dilemma, as I said. Something to think about. Forgive me, but I've probably said too much, Mrs. Curlew."

"I'm grateful, Superintendent. As you say, it's something to think about."

"There's something practical you could do which might help Rosie. She will be thirty-one soon and under Ben Gladwell's will is to inherit his estate then. Perhaps you could get Gladwell's will enacted by the Probate Office and get his intestacy cancelled. It would stop anyone further plundering what's left of her inheritance."

She smiled at him.

"A very practical suggestion, Superintendent. I'll also see what might be done about trying to recover what's already been plundered, as you describe it, although I suspect that won't be so easy."

As soon as Ravenna Curlew had departed, Teagle and Duggan sat with the superintendent.

"We need to find more about Dalby's involvement. His evidence could make it difficult for Aggie in court. See what you can do, Teagle."

"I'll do my best, sir. Do you really think that Symonds might get away with it?"

"I sincerely hope not. Let's make our case as tight as possible. Now let's talk about your missing persons' report, Duggan."

Duggan had followed the superintendent's instructions and pulled together data from the various police forces across the UK and assembled it into her report. There were extensive statistics about missing persons, but she'd managed to distil them into a summary consistent with what the superintendent wanted.

Each year the police forces receive around three hundred thousand reports of missing persons in the UK. Three quarters of these are resolved within twenty-four hours and most of the remainder within seven days. Virtually all are accounted for in the following months.

Duggan had concentrated on those relatively few that went unresolved, so-called "long-term missing," those individuals who have remained missing for longer than one year.

There were slightly more than five thousand such cases in total on the police files. These divided roughly equally into men, women, and children. She'd included the precise numbers in the report.

Duggan had delved into the data. She sought out the males reported missing in the previous ten years who would by now be between twenty-nine and thirty-one years old. She was left with 112 individuals.

"Do you believe the bodies in the pond are amongst your 112

missing men, Duggan?" The superintendent gazed at Duggan as she shuffled her papers before replying.

"I think there's a good chance that at least some of the four bodies are, sir. I've picked out those either side of the parameters given by the forensic pathologist. If we focus just on those reported missing in the last eight years and who would be thirty today, then there are only thirty-seven individuals. Of course, these are only ones reported missing. Not all missing persons get reported. I imagine there are quite a few of those, so we can't be certain they'll be amongst this lot, but I feel it must be worth following up."

"I agree. Although I'm surprised and encouraged that there are so relatively few to work on. What's your view, Teagle?"

"I agree with Duggan, sir. We've been through it carefully. It isn't so many as we'd expected either, so it's a manageable proposition. We need to try and decide what we're looking for."

The superintendent looked at them both as he wondered how many people simply disappeared without being noticed or reported.

"There are already some links between each of the four bodies. They're all men and each the same age. That's not a coincidence. But something else must link them together."

"What do you have in mind sir?"

"Well, Duggan, you have a starting point. You know the identity of each potential candidate. Now you need personal details, background, life history even. We're looking for links between them, those who lived together or in the same town at some time, any with a family connection. Similar age suggests possibly same school, same sports team, or something like that. Check for any criminal record. Start with the thirty-seven candidates; we might strike lucky. Visit their families and get a life history on each. Teagle will help you put a plan of campaign together."

Teagle nodded and said, "It's too much for one person, sir. We need a team; otherwise, it'll take months."

"That's true, but first get a feel for it yourselves. Get a nose for what you're looking for. Show me your plan beforehand. Meanwhile I'll also have a think about it."

They both made for the door to leave his office when he added, "Well done, Duggan. It's a good report."

After they'd left him, he sat and thought about it all. It would be a slow process and he was loath to put a team on it, at least for the time being. He'd let Duggan make a start. It would be slow and tedious, but that was what most police work involved. He wanted her to get under the skin of the task, to try to get a feeling for the missing people in her list. That way, with luck, she would find what they needed.

The superintendent was all for rapid response when required, but he'd learned over many years that it was often much more effective to try to think things through before rushing to action. He'd make sure Duggan had a good plan of campaign. For the superintendent, solving a crime was an intellectual exercise—plus, an acute sense of smell for detecting untruths and a deep distrust of coincidences.

CHAPTER 7

Teagle quickly reported back that she'd visited Dalby as the superintendent had instructed, but that Dalby was now being uncooperative and evasive. He stated that he objected to being considered involved in any conspiracy with Symonds, as Teagle had implied. Symonds was simply his client, and he had nothing further to say on the matter.

Consequently, it was decided to formally interview and question him. That was why he now sat in an interview room at Thames Valley Police HQ alongside his chosen lawyer.

Dalby was formally cautioned before the superintendent spoke.

"Mr. Dalby, we need some more answers from you. So far, you've told us about some of what you've done for Arthur Symonds, but I believe you are withholding vital evidence. I'd like—"

Dalby's lawyer interrupted. "That's a preposterous allegation, Superintendent. My client has fully cooperated. In fact, from what he tells me, he has been especially open in response to your questions. Whatever you say, he still has a duty to his client, Mr. Symonds. There's nothing else he can add."

The superintendent looked at them both. Dalby appeared relaxed, comfortable to let his lawyer take any pressure off him. The superintendent addressed the lawyer. "Sorry to hear you say that, sir. My problem is that Mr. Dalby has changed his explanations as we've asked him more questions, and that makes me suspicious.

His client, Arthur Symonds, is charged with a serious crime which he only managed to commit with Mr. Dalby's assistance."

"That's another preposterous accusation. I would advise you to take care, Superintendent. Mr. Dalby has not changed his story or explanations. He has simply enlarged his answers in order to help you. Now he stands accused of deliberately obstructing your investigation. As for assisting Mr. Symonds in a criminal act, that is nonsense. He has conducted quite lawful transactions on behalf of a client. He could have no possible knowledge of any criminality."

The superintendent gently smiled at the lawyer and paused before replying.

"Let me give you an illustration of what I mean, sir. It might help. When I first visited Mr. Dalby at his office in Milton Keynes, he claimed that the first time he'd met Mr. and Mrs. Symonds was after the death of Mr. Ben Gladstone. Subsequently he has admitted to knowing Mr. Symonds well before then, years before Gladstone died. In my book that is not enlarging upon his answers; it is a clear attempt to mislead me. Don't you agree?"

"Superintendent, is that relevant? Does it really matter when they first met?"

"It certainly does."

The lawyer was surprised by the curt response and hesitated. Dalby looked uneasy.

"Perhaps you can elaborate please, Superintendent?"

The superintendent looked at the lawyer before turning to ask Dalby, "Did you discuss Ben Gladstone and his will with Arthur Symonds, or anybody, before Gladstone had died, sir?"

Dalby was certainly no longer feeling relaxed and hesitated. The lawyer intervened. "Perhaps we could take a short break before continuing, Superintendent?"

"Why? Just let Mr. Dalby answer. It's a simple question."

"I'm advising Mr. Dalby to say nothing, Superintendent. At least not until I have discussed it with him first."

The superintendent stared at them both. "We'll be back in ten minutes. That should give you enough time."

Exactly ten minutes later, the superintendent repeated the question to Dalby.

"It is possible that Symonds, my client, mentioned it to me, Superintendent. I can't recall if we actually discussed it. Symonds came to see me looking for general advice on the process of probate and inheritance law. Our discussions were not specific."

The superintendent sighed and turned to the lawyer. "This is my problem, sir. Your client, in an earlier meeting at his Milton Keynes office with Sergeant Teagle and DC Duggan, explained that he had, in fact, discussed Gladstone's will with Symonds."

"Superintendent, you've just heard Mr. Dalby say that it might have happened. Why is it so important?"

"It's important, sir, because Symonds knew well that Ben Gladstone had made a will. Gladstone had made that clear to the family and indicated that his granddaughter, Rosie, would eventually inherit. Symonds approached your client to find a way to thwart Gladstone, a way to make Gladstone's will disappear, a way to get his hands on Gladstone's estate for himself."

Dalby almost shouted, "But I know nothing about that. I understood that Gladstone had no will; he was intestate. Mrs. Symonds also said there was no will. I even checked a register; there was no record of a will for him."

"When did you check the register, Mr. Dalby? Was it before or after Gladstone's death?"

Dalby hesitated before answering. "I don't remember exactly when, but I'm sure it would have been after Mrs. Symonds's visit, after Gladstone's death."

"Well, not to worry, Mr. Dalby; we shall find out. We shall also be examining all payments you received from Symonds, both professionally and personally. We'll also be examining phone records between the two of you. It should help us to—"

Dalby's lawyer intervened. "That's outrageous. You've no

grounds for doing that. You've no evidence he's done anything wrong. You'll never get a warrant."

"We'll see. Did you know that Mr. Dalby made a phone call and tipped off Symonds that we were onto him. Luckily Sergeant Teagle managed to get Symonds arrested just as he was about to board the ferry to Holland. Sergeant Teagle also managed to stop Mr. Dalby shredding incriminating files in his office."

Darby reacted with an outburst. "I object. You are misconstruing things. I didn't know Symonds would try to leave the country, and I was just tidying-up the files as I explained to Sergeant Teagle."

"Tidying them up into the waste bin, so I heard. Anyway, with all that's gone on between you and Symonds, I anticipate a search warrant will readily be forthcoming. After that, who knows? Another warrant, an arrest warrant perhaps?"

It went quiet. As they digested the effect of what might happen, the superintendent collected his papers and rose to leave. He stood facing them both across the table. "I believe that you've got yourself drawn into a mess, Mr. Dalby. It would be stupid to go down trying to protect a man like Symonds. It'd be better to tell me all about it before it's too late."

Back in his office, Teagle asked, "What do you think Dalby will do, sir?"

"I really don't know. We're short of hard evidence of his criminality, and I suspect he's guessed that. Maybe he has only been unprofessional or negligent, and foolish, but I think it goes deeper than that. Let's try and put him under more pressure. Get a search warrant to go through his office files and other records: phone logs, bank accounts. I've made a list of what I'd like you to look for. Get his office sealed off before anything disappears.

"I also want you to go to the farm. Here's another list of what to look for there."

Teagle carefully studied the two lists and then looked back at the superintendent.

"I understand, sir. Leave it with me."

It was a week later when Teagle reported back on her progress.

"There's not much to show for a search of Dalby's client files, sir. I took away most of those concerning Symonds and the farm on an earlier visit, as you know. His accounts files tell us more and show quite a list of financial transactions for Symonds and corresponding invoices from Dalby for services rendered, which all ties in with Dalby's firm's bank accounts. No sign of any off-book payments as far as I can tell from his private bank account.

"But it is noticeable that the fees charged by Dalby's firm for this work is higher than its normal scale of charges. Thought that was worth noting, especially as Symonds is known to be mean. In fact, it looks like dealing with Symonds has been what you'd call 'a nice little earner' for Dalby."

The superintendent thought about this. "I suppose it helps confirm what we think but, in itself, doesn't help us particularly. Dalby will easily think up a plausible explanation. What else did you find?"

"There have been quite a few phone calls between Dalby and Symonds, some on their private mobile phones, which predate Ben Gladwell's death. There were some fees charged to Symonds for advice, but not specific, during the year before Gladwell's death."

"That sounds a bit more interesting. Something for Dalby and Symonds to explain to us. I wonder if their explanations will tally? What else did you find?"

"As you thought, sir, Dalby made an inquiry of the registers about Gladwell's will before his death, nearly a year before he died. His will had not been recorded."

"That is interesting. I wonder how they'll explain that. It will certainly put pressure on Dalby. Anything else?"

"Not much more of significance from Dalby's records, but I did find something at the farm. Everything to do with the correspondence from Ravenna Curlew about Gladwell's will to Aggie and Rosie is missing; presumably it's been disposed of by Symonds. But I went through Symonds's private papers. He's taken over Gladwell's old desk according to Aggie, and so some of the paperwork I found there is what Gladwell had left behind.

"I came across a copy of Gladwell's will. It's not one of the copies that was sent by Ravenna Curlew to Aggie and Rosie after Gladwell's death. I think it is the copy Gladwell would have kept for himself after he originally made the will. Ravenna Curlew mentioned that he'd probably have one in his papers. I think you'll be interested in this next bit, sir."

She smiled at the superintendent as she leafed through some papers.

"Get on with it, Teagle. You're behaving like a magician about to pull something out of his hat."

"Thought you'd like a bit of suspense, sir. Anyway, this copy of Gladwell's will has been widely handled, a lot of different fingerprints. Probably Gladwell's but also his solicitor's, old man Curlew, and some others, including the fingerprints of Symonds."

The superintendent grinned at her.

"That's more like it, Teagle. What's your conclusion?"

"A bit more to tell yet, sir. No fingerprints from Aggie or Rosie, so that helps substantiate that they've never seen Gladwell's will. I think that Symonds found this copy will in Gladwell's desk about a year before he died. Aggie says that as Ben Gladwell became ill, then Symonds took over running the farm and also took over Gladwell's desk. Shortly after that Gladwell was moved into a nursing home at Symonds's insistence, where he later died.

"In my view Symonds became alarmed, and that's when he involved Darby to contrive that Gladwell had died intestate."

"I tend to agree with you, Teagle. It'll make it even more difficult for Symonds to explain and claim he knew nothing of the will's existence. But it doesn't prove that Symonds and Dalby were involved in a plot to defraud Rosie. Dalby will say he was just advising Symonds generally on inheritance law. He'd simply searched the registers to check any existence of a will. There wasn't a record, and so he assumed Gladwell had not made one. When Aggie appeared and claimed that Gladwell had died intestate, it confirmed it, and he accepted that. He'll claim he did nothing wrong and acted quite properly."

Teagle sat and gently smiled at the superintendent before saying, "He might find that a bit difficult, sir. You see, another set of fingerprints on this copy belong to Dalby."

The superintendent laughed and asked, "Why didn't you mention it before?"

"Always save the best until the last, sir!"

"Let me see exactly what you've got."

Teagle passed various documents across the desk, and the superintendent scrutinized them.

"Is this copy of Gladwell's will identical, an exact copy, of that which Ravenna Curlew gave to us?"

"Exactly the same, sir. When Gladwell signed this will, the original was retained and held by Curlew & Williams. A copy was given to Gladwell for him to hold.

"When Gladwell died, a further copy was sent to Aggie and another to Rosie with a request for them each to sign and return a letter of receipt. Those were intercepted by Symonds when he stopped the mail being delivered to the farm, and he forged their signatures and returned the receipts to Ravenna Curlew. We can presume those copies of the will were destroyed by Symonds.

"When Aggie subsequently, at Symonds's insistence, wrote to Curlew & Williams requesting all the documents relating to her father's estate, Ben Gladwell's estate, to be passed over to her, the original will was of course included, but Ravenna Curlew also kept a copy, which we now hold as evidence.

"This copy of the will was taken at the time Gladwell signed it; I'm certain of it. It does not have Ravenna Curlew's fingerprints on it but does have those of her father, old man Curlew, who drew it up for Ben Gladwell. For some reason, Symonds didn't destroy it. He possibly forgot about it."

"We'll be able to ask him, but first let's hear what Dalby has to say about it all. Get him here for some more questioning, Teagle. It should be interesting."

It was the following day when Barry Dalby sat with his solicitor in an interview room at Kidlington.

"We've a few more questions for you, Mr. Dalby. First just a brief recap of where we left off last time.

"You confirmed that, despite earlier denials, you had met Arthur Symonds before Ben Gladwell died. You said that you had given him general advice about inheritance rules but nothing specific to Gladwell. Is that correct?"

Dalby hesitated and looked at his solicitor, who nodded.

"Yes, that's correct."

"What prompted you to make a search of the register to check if Gladwell had registered his will?"

"It's good practice. Mrs. Symonds came to me claiming her husband had died intestate. I just wanted to check and make sure that no will was registered."

It went quiet as the superintendent looked at Dalby before saying, "That's not what happened, is it?"

Dalby's solicitor intervened. "What are you trying to say, Superintendent?"

"Not trying but stating that your client's answer is not the truth. Perhaps he'd like to try again and tell me what really happened?"

Dalby looked uncomfortable as the superintendent waited for his response.

"I might have checked the register before Mrs. Symonds's visit. I can't be sure. Does it matter?"

"It matters if you did so because of your meetings with Arthur Symonds. It matters because you've just said your advice to him was not specific about Ben Gladwell. So why check the register before Gladwell's death?"

"I said that I couldn't be sure. Maybe when Mrs. Symonds made the appointment, she said it was about her father's will, and that prompted me to check."

The superintendent watched him for a moment.

"I don't have time to waste, Mr. Dalby. The fact is that you searched the register a year before Ben Gladwell died, didn't you?"

Dalby looked distinctly uneasy. He glanced at his solicitor, who took the hint and said, "Perhaps we can have a short break so that I can talk to my client, Superintendent?"

"As I said I don't have time to waste with Mr. Dalby's lies, so no you may not have a break."

"That is against the rules, Superintendent, and you know it."

"No, it isn't. Your client is deliberately trying to mislead me. Let's try something else. Mr. Dalby, you have previously said that you have no knowledge of any will made by Ben Gladstone. Is that correct?"

"Yes."

The superintendent nodded at Teagle, who pushed across the desk toward Dalby a protective transparent sleeve containing a copy of Gladwell's will.

Dalby and his solicitor studied it.

"Mr. Dalby, have you seen this before?"

Dalby looked back at the superintendent and said, "No, I've never seen it. No will showed up on the register."

"This will was written over ten years ago, when the register was only just being created, so it's not surprising it didn't show up. Nor is the register infallible as it is not a legal requirement to record a will."

"That's true, Superintendent, but it was prudent to make a check just in case."

"I think that you made the check just to be sure it had not been registered so that you could pretend there was no will."

Dalby's solicitor interrupted. "What are you trying to say, Superintendent? My client has done his best to check that Mrs. Symonds was telling the truth about her father dying intestate."

The superintendent turned again to Dalby. "Last time we met, I advised you to tell me the truth and cooperate before it is too late. What do you say, Mr. Dalby? What prompted you to check the register a year before Gladwell died?"

Dalby was clearly nervous, even agitated, and looked at his solicitor.

"Superintendent, I must insist that we have a break so that I can talk with my client."

"As I said, I've no more time to waste on this nonsense. He has been given several opportunities to cooperate and declined. Maybe this will encourage him to tell the truth."

The superintendent took hold of the copy of Gladwell's will in the plastic sleeve and held it over the table.

"Mr. Dalby has said that he has never seen this will, that he was unaware of it. But his fingerprints are on it. How does he explain that?"

Dalby rocked in his chair and went pale. His solicitor looked shocked before managing to ask, "Superintendent, please may we have a break? I really need to talk to my client."

"I agree, sir. I strongly urge you to persuade him to cooperate, to come clean and not waste any more of our time. I'm terminating this interview. If your client wishes to cooperate, then Sergeant Teagle will take his statement when you are ready. Otherwise, he will be charged with conspiracy to defraud and held here pending a magistrate's hearing. This serious crime carries a long term of imprisonment as you well know. As we continue our investigation, further charges will almost certainly follow. Interview terminated. We'll leave you to confer."

Dalby looked distraught, and his solicitor appeared anxious as the superintendent and Teagle left the interview room.

Teagle said quietly to the constable on duty by the door, "They are to remain here. Let me know when they are ready to see me."

Two days later the superintendent reviewed Teagle's report and the evidence. Dalby had decided to cooperate and had provided a full statement of his involvement with Symonds. Dalby admitted that he'd become embroiled with Symonds to pretend Gladstone had not made a will. He couldn't explain why he'd done so. It seemed what started as a possibility then become a reality, and one thing had led to another. He'd made quite a lot of money from it by charging higher fees but nothing like the amounts pillaged by Symonds. Darby had naively even convinced himself that he'd not really done anything wrong. Symonds gave him instruction, and all transactions were lawfully executed and documented; Dalby even suggested that it wasn't as if anyone was being hurt.

He called Teagle to join him.

"Well done, Teagle. I think this wraps it up, and it'll save us a lot of work."

"Thank you, sir. What will you do?"

"I think it's now a matter for the Crown Prosecution Service; it'll decide how to handle things. Dalby's confession blows a hole in any defense Symonds might have had. I expect the CPS will charge Dalby with conspiracy to defraud at the least. How do you think he'll plead?"

"Guilty. His solicitor has advised him to do so, and I think he will. Not much else he can do. They've asked for his cooperation to be taken into account."

"I doubt it'll save him from a spell in prison; he'll also be struck off from practicing as a solicitor. What a fool. What possessed him to risk everything for a man like Symonds?"

"Beats me, sir, but it happens all the time. What do you want me to do next?"

"Get everything together and pass it on to the CPS. No more we can do. The case is as cut and dried as possible; it's over to them now. I think it'll be a good result. Symonds will go down, Rosie will get what's left of the farm, perhaps not everything Gladwell intended, and Aggie will be free of Symonds. Justice will be done; it's not often we can say that."

He sat and looked at her before adding, "I think we can put aside your indiscretion over Rosie and her boyfriend."

"I'm sorry, sir. The lesson has been learned."

"Good, you've done well on this case. Now we've got to try and find who did murder the bodies in that pond. Arrange for Duggan to tells us how she's getting on."

Duggan had been working her way through the shortlist of the thirty-seven most promising candidates from the long-term missing list. It was over three weeks since she'd started, and so far, she'd covered only six candidates, despite working every day. It was a slow process. It required interviewing the next of kin, parents, or siblings or other close friends in order to try to gather a life history of each candidate up to the day they were reported missing. Despite her being thorough, there were still many gaps to fill. It took time to track them down and arrange meetings and travel to interview them. She'd begun with those closest to Kidlington, but eventually the process would become even slower the further she had to travel. Only when she'd gathered this information could she begin to look for links between candidates.

Her inquiries also created huge emotional issues. Upon contacting parents or other next of kin, they immediately assumed there was news about their missing relative. After years of nothing, hope was suddenly rekindled. Duggan had to handle it sensitively as she explained she had no news to report, but that her fact-finding mission was to try to establish possible further lines of inquiry. Their disappointment and frustration were palpable.

She felt there was little to show for all her efforts as she reported her progress to the superintendent.

The superintendent, however, was unperturbed by the slow process. Admittedly at this rate it could take six months, but the bodies had been in the pond for years. Nevertheless, he could sense that Duggan was dispirited and needed some encouragement.

"Thank you, Duggan. I know it's hard graft and tedious. Most police work is, but I'm hopeful this will be worthwhile. It's early days, but has anything caught your eye yet?"

"No links that I can see so far, sir. Nothing between these six candidates so far anyway. One does have a link to Oxford, went to Oxford University in fact. I've made a note and was going to talk to Sergeant Teagle about it. I know she went there."

"Interesting. That's quite true, Duggan, and in fact Teagle is also around thirty years old and would probably have been there at the same time."

"Not quite thirty yet, sir, if you don't mind."

"Near enough, Teagle; you'd certainly have overlapped. What's his name, Duggan?"

"Charles Henry Caterham. He was at St. John's College."

"Ring any bells, Teagle?"

"Afraid not, sir. I was at Lady Margaret Hall."

"What can you tell us about him, Duggan?"

"Comes from an influential family with homes in Surrey and Monaco, interested in sport, private schooling at Harrow. Accomplished rower in the college team and rowed in the Oxford Cambridge boat race. After graduating with a 2.2 degree in PPE, went to work in the City of London. I've yet to investigate that bit, sir. Reported missing by his family just over six years ago after he failed to turn up at work, a bank, which contacted the parents. He just disappeared. Nothing suspicious at his apartment in London where he lived alone. I've only had time to speak with his family. He's the latest on my list so far, and I'm only partway through investigating him."

"Teagle, what is a 2.2 degree in PPE?"

"Not very good, sir. Lower second class in philosophy, politics, and economics. Sort of degree you'll find many of our politicians have. It shows that he didn't do much studying. Probably only got into Oxford on his family connections."

"Careful, Teagle; you are jumping to conclusions, possibly even showing prejudices."

"Sorry, sir; please forgive me. I try to remember what you taught me and keep an open mind about anyone until I know better."

"Pleased to hear it. Remind me, what degree did you get?"

"You know very well, sir, that I got a first in modern history. You know all about me."

The superintendent smiled at her. "I doubt I know all about you, Teagle, but I try. Tell me, was Lady Margaret Hall the first Oxford College to admit women for an Oxford education?"

"Well informed as ever, sir. Founded in 1879 and didn't admit men until a hundred years later."

"Ah, I remember. Maybe that explains your poor opinion of overprivileged lazy men?"

"Not just men, sir."

Duggan listened to the exchange with barely concealed amusement. The superintendent could be a forbidding character, but Teagle seemed to be able to hold her own with him.

"Well, let's find out what he did do at Oxford if he didn't study. You can use your connections there, Teagle."

CHAPTER 8

Instead of going through the usual channels with her inquiry, Teagle decided to start by presenting herself at the porters' lodge. From her own experience at Lady Margaret Hall, porters knew most about the activities of undergraduates, especially their extracurricular activities.

She knew she was in luck as soon as she met the porter on duty: older, world weary, seen it all before, a man with a suspicious inquisitive nature and a healthy distrust of most undergraduates. He had been a porter at St. John's for nearly thirty years—a person with a long memory of those who passed before him, especially those who broke rules and caused him grief.

He was called Bacon, John Bacon. She imagined undergrads calling him "Rasher" to cause his annoyance.

"Who are you after then, Sergeant?"

"Want to know about an undergrad who was here around ten years ago, Mr. Bacon. Hoping you might remember him, Charles Henry Caterham."

Bacon grimaced and gave a snort. "Him, I thought you'd be after him one day. Charlie Caterham, bloody nuisance he was, if you'll excuse my French, Sergeant. Both him and his oppo, Yakker. What's he done?"

"You know the rules, Mr. Bacon. Not at liberty to divulge. But you remember him then?"

Bacon sighed and leaned across the counter. "Oh yes, I remember him. Member of one of those rowdy dining clubs, think they're above the law. Always manage to buy themselves out of trouble. Only here because of family influence and tradition and money. His sort usually end up running the country; makes you despair."

"He read PPE. I'm hoping one of his tutors might still be around and remember him."

Bacon snorted again. "It follows. PPE—one of those rubbish subjects in my view. Did you know that they teach ethics and morality in philosophy? Waste of time with people like Charlie; he doesn't even know the meaning of the words. Not that he spent any time studying. Spent his time rowing and enjoying himself. Mind you he did row in the Boat Race, although Oxford lost that year. Got the girls chasing after him though. Give me a minute, and I'll check if any of the faculty tutors from then are still here. I've got a feeling that Professor Plowright was around."

While Bacon disappeared to check, Teagle looked around at the college entrance. It brought back memories of her own time at Oxford. She could well imagine the antics of Charles Caterham and why Bacon remembered him so clearly.

Bacon returned after a few minutes. "As I thought, Professor Plowright was here and would have been his tutor in philosophy. Doesn't sound as if Charlie would count as one of her successes."

"Thank you, sir. You mentioned his friend, Yakker. Can you tell me anything about him?"

"Foreign student. Yakker wasn't his real name, but I remember him clearly as well. Jacob Wagner. They were both rowers. Yakker looked up to Charlie as I remember and was probably led astray by him. Something happened at the end of Charlie's last Trinity Term, just before he was due to graduate. Rumor was that it involved a woman, but it was hushed up. Even the president got involved, I heard. As I said, with money and influence, you can buy your way out of most trouble here."

"That's very interesting, Mr. Bacon. Thanks for giving me your time and assistance."

"Glad to help anytime, Sergeant. Don't suppose you'll tell me what he's done, or shall I have to wait and read about it in the newspapers?"

Teagle smiled. "You never know, sir. Goodbye."

Teagle departed, knowing she'd been fortunate to hit upon Bacon. He'd provided more information about Caterham in fifteen minutes than she'd have ever obtained from the administration or tutorial staff. He'd provided a picture of Caterham as a person. Of course, it was a prejudiced opinion but provided something to follow up. She now needed to get an appointment to meet Professor Plowright.

They met the following afternoon in her rooms at St. John's. Professor Jane Plowright was in late middle age, attentive with a lively personality.

"How may I help, Sergeant?"

"I'm hoping you can recall a student called Charles Caterham from around ten years ago."

Plowright looked thoughtful. "May I ask why you are interested?"

"I'm pursuing inquiries into Charles Caterham's apparent disappearance six years ago."

"You say apparent; does that mean you're not sure?"

"Bad choice of words, Professor. He was reported missing and has apparently not been heard of since. I wondered if you could tell me anything about him. Was he a good student?"

Plowright hesitated and seemed to be choosing her words. "It would be accurate to say that he was not a good student. Specifically he was uninterested and disruptive. He was granted a 2.2, although, in my opinion, was lucky to get that. Does that help you?"

"It fits with what we already know. More interested in rowing and enjoyment than learning, from what I hear."

"That sums it up quite well, Sergeant. Most students work hard and come here to study, to learn. Of course, they enjoy a social life as well and hopefully make lifelong friendships. Students like Caterham have a rather different agenda."

"I understand that something happened just before he graduated. Do you know about it?"

Again, Plowright looked thoughtful. "Your information is correct, but unfortunately I'm not at liberty to discuss it."

Teagle stared at her with interest. "It may be relevant to our inquiries. I could compel you to answer."

She smiled back gently. "Sergeant, I admire your tenacity, but I doubt you could compel me even with a warrant. The influence of this Oxford college reaches high into the hierarchy of the Thames Valley Police. That is not something of which I am proud, but I fear it is a fact."

Teagle was surprised at her answer and hesitated before remarking, "That must sit uneasily alongside your teaching of ethics and morality, Professor."

"A very perceptive observation, Sergeant, and one that sometimes preoccupies me."

"My superior will not be pleased to know this. He will insist that it is followed up."

"That is good to hear, Sergeant. You could try asking our president, but I wouldn't be optimistic. You may have more success with the principal of St. Hilda's. Are you familiar with Oxford colleges?"

"I was at Lady Margaret Hall."

"Were you indeed? You should have said. You'll know how these things work then."

"I didn't know, Professor, but I'm learning. Thank you for your time."

Teagle was already aware of St. Hilda's history. It was the last of the Oxford colleges set up to provide an education for women, but, after many years of debate and opposition, it had finally admitted male undergraduates just over ten years ago. This had happened around the time Teagle went up to Oxford, and she remembered how newsworthy it had been then. Undergraduates at St. Hilda's had historically been called "Hildabeasts" by some male undergraduates. This unseemly and derisory name left the women of St. Hilda's unperturbed—in fact, they happily accepted the name as a badge of honor.

Teagle was intrigued as to why Plowright had suggested this as a line of inquiry into Charles Caterham.

Before making an appointment, Teagle did some research into St. Hilda's principal. Professor Dame Mary Knight was nearing retirement after over twelve years in office. It was she who had finally driven through the introduction of male undergraduates to the college. It had been rumored that her damehood was granted in recognition of this.

"Welcome, Sergeant. It is not often that I receive a visit from the police, and my secretary said that you were mysterious about the reason."

Thank you, Professor, it was not my intention to be mysterious but simply the way we do things. It can save embarrassment and avoid confusion."

"That makes it sound even more mysterious, Sergeant. Please explain."

"I'm trying to discover more about a man who graduated nearly ten years ago from St. John's. His name is Charles Caterham. My inquiries have led me to you."

It went quiet, and Knight stared at Teagle before asking, "How extraordinary. What on earth would I know about a graduate of St. John's?"

"That is what I'm hoping you could tell me, Professor."

"Why did your inquiries lead to me?"

"As it's part of an ongoing investigation, I'm afraid I cannot tell you, at least not at present. Sorry."

"Then I am sorry that I cannot help you, Sergeant."

Teagle sat silently and detected a look of disdain from Knight.

Teagle waited, and eventually Knight spoke.

"You clearly do not understand, Sergeant. I have nothing more to say. Goodbye."

As Teagle returned to Kidlington, she felt some excitement. There was definitely something about Caterham that was being "hushed up." But was it relevant to his disappearance? That could only be decided when she knew what it was.

There was another thing she needed to check. Was Jacob Wagner missing as well? Was he on Duggan's list of potential candidates?

He was not. She checked the short list and the extended list. His name did not appear. He was not reported missing. She felt disappointed.

She explained what had happened to the superintendent and Duggan.

"I don't like the sniff of this, Teagle. I want to know what you are not being told and why. Let's do a few checks to see if anything else shows up. Look back and see if there were any suspicious reports involving Oxford students made to the police at that time; it's just possible a complaint was made. Next you and Duggan work through the list of possibilities to see if any of the other candidates went to Oxford, perhaps that's the connection we're looking for. Maybe it can be done over the telephone to the families."

"I think that's a bad idea, sir. Telephoning the families will create problems."

"What do you mean?"

"Duggan already has issues making appointments and interviewing families. They immediately assume that we have news about their loved ones. Duggan has to take time explaining that she is simply trying to follow a possible line of inquiry. They assist her, of course, but now expect us to let them know our progress. They expect results. Imagine the consequences of telephoning the extended list of 112 families to ask if their missing son went to Oxford."

The superintendent was taken aback and annoyed with himself for not anticipating this. It was obvious.

"I'm sorry, Duggan. I should have realized. Not an easy task I've given you."

"Thank you, sir. Turned out to be more difficult and slower than I'd expected. I'd not realized how much upset it would cause, but it quickly became clear. I try not to raise hopes, but that's impossible. The first thing I have to do is establish that their son is still missing. He might have shown up and not been reported, or our records might be out of date. Whatever happens, all families I've contacted now expect us bring them good news."

"I can understand the difficulties, but we've got to do it. What do you propose we do instead, Teagle?"

"Let's get a look at the university admissions records. They ought to tell us if anyone else on the list went to Oxford. That way it avoids upsetting families unnecessarily."

"Good idea. Meanwhile, I'll let the chief constable know what we're doing, because if you are correct about the shutters coming down on your inquiry, I expect she will be getting a call from the university about you meddling in things which don't concern you."

He finished explaining the situation to the chief constable, and she gave him a grin.

"You are ten minutes too late, Graham. I've just finished taking a call from the president of St. John's. He in turn seems to have received a call from the principal of St. Hilda's complaining about Teagle."

The superintendent sighed and said, "That was quick. Interesting, though: they must be worried about something they don't want us to know about. Presumably you explained that we must continue with our inquiries, ma'am?"

"Don't presume anything. However, like you, I don't take kindly to being told what not to do when following up an investigation. For your information, as if you didn't already know, the influence of St. John's College or any other Oxford college does not reach into the hierarchy of Thames Valley Police whilst I'm its chief constable."

He smiled at her. "Pleased to hear you say it, ma'am, although I never thought it would."

"That doesn't mean you can deliberately go treading on the toes of the Oxford University establishment, Graham."

"Of course not, ma'am. We'll tread carefully to find what we're looking for."

It took Teagle and Duggan two days to obtain the relevant admission records and work through both the short and extended list.

"One person on the list, sir. Robin James Scot-Wadham, he attended Keble College. Reported missing seven years ago. His time at Oxford overlapped with Caterham, but he didn't graduate; left after his second year."

It went quiet as the superintendent digested the information.

"Just the one person, Teagle?"

"That's right, sir, but remember, the list is not exhaustive; not every missing person is reported."

"Anything else about him?"

"Yes, sir, he was in the rowing club. We got that from his parents. We've yet to check with the college. Reported missing by his parents. He failed to turn up to a family gathering. They tried contacting him but couldn't. Lived alone in London, had friends apparently, but nobody seemed to miss him. He didn't work and traveled a lot. Just seemed to vanish with no trace. No trail through credit cards or bank or passport. Family wasn't worried to begin because he traveled and only had occasional contact, so they didn't report him missing for a while. He could have disappeared earlier."

"It's too much of a coincidence. Both at Oxford at the same

time, both in the rowing club, both missing, and both fit our victim profile. Follow it up, Teagle. Make inquiries at Keble and St. John's. Find out all about their time at Oxford. Duggan, can help you and leave aside the list for the time being."

"Yes, sir. Incidentally, I've found nothing yet to connect to Caterham to any official police complaint."

"Keep looking and sniffing around. I'll bet there'll be something. Go along to Oxford Central. Speak to the old hands or anyone else there at that time. They'll remember."

Oxford Central, an abbreviation for Oxford City Centre Police Station in St. Aldates, is surrounded by Oxford colleges. Any complaint or misdemeanor involving students finds its way there. Oxford Central liaises closely with the colleges, and some residents claim it favors those connected to the university.

The relationship between citizens of Oxford and the university—town versus gown, as it is known—has a centuries-long volatile history, including rioting and violence. Even today resentment lingers through a perception that the gown enjoys a privileged status at the expense of the town.

Teagle remembered Professor Plowright's remark about St. John's College's influence and wondered if it extended into Oxford Central. The superintendent would know; she added Oxford Central to her action list.

Teagle decided to visit Keble and find out if the porter there could be as helpful as that at St. John's.

With Duggan, she visited the porters' lodge. She showed her card and asked about Scot-Wadham.

"Before my time, Sergeant. I've only been here for four years. Sorry, can't help you."

"Are there any porters who might remember him?"

"I can try for you. Perhaps you can write the details, and I'll see that it's passed to all the porters."

Teagle wrote out the details and included her telephone number.

"It's urgent. Please ask anyone who can remember him to contact me."

"I'll see what I can do, Sergeant. Maybe you should try the administration office; they might be able to help you better."

The administration office couldn't provide more than was in the official records. Scot-Wadham read modern languages, specializing in French. He didn't return after his second year, for reasons unknown. His tutor at the time had moved on; it was thought he may be abroad. It seemed that nobody could remember him or suggest anyone who might be able to help Teagle with her inquiries.

At the rowing club, it was the same. Records showed that he had been a member but he otherwise couldn't be remembered despite Teagle asking around. It was ten years ago, after all, she was told by the club secretary.

They went back to St. John's, and by chance Bacon was on duty again.

"Hello, Sergeant. What brings you back here again?"

"Pursuing the same inquiries, Mr. Bacon."

Bacon smiled at her and glanced at Duggan.

"Not sure I can tell you any more, if you get my meaning, Sergeant."

Teagle looked at him. He still had a faint smile, a knowing smile. Teagle got the message.

"I'm beginning to think I do get your meaning, Mr. Bacon. That explains my fruitless morning at Keble."

Bacon shrugged and said, "Sorry, Sergeant, but you know how it is when the shutters come down."

"Thank you, Mr. Bacon, I'm beginning to realize how it is. I wondered if you could tell me any more about Jacob Wagner? Yakker you called him, Caterham's friend, or most likely his partner in crime, perhaps?"

Bacon chuckled. "Well put, Sergeant. Unfortunately, I've

already told you all I can. Nothing more to tell. You could try the administration office."

"I don't imagine that'll help me very much."

"Don't imagine it will either."

Bacon was clearly enjoying the exchange. She believed the canny old porter could tell her a great deal more. He'd been warned off but was trying to give her some hints.

"Did you come across an undergraduate called Robin Scot-Wadham, at Keble, the same time Charlie Caterham was here?"

Bacon grinned at her. "Can't say I like the sound of the circles you mix in, Sergeant. I suppose it goes with the territory?"

"So, you do know him?"

"I didn't say so. You're putting words in my mouth. I simply made a remark. Sorry, my memory is not as good as it was."

"Not as good as it was a few days ago, that's for sure. Anyway, thanks for trying, Mr. Bacon. Should your memory miraculously return, please let me know."

He chuckled again. "You'll be the first to know, Sergeant. Good hunting."

On the drive back to Kidlington, they discussed it. As Bacon had implied, the shutters had come down. But why? Why could the antics or bad behavior of a few undergraduates be so important?

Duggan asked, "Why don't we just get a warrant and bring them in for questioning under oath, Sergeant?"

"It might come to that, Duggan. Meanwhile we still got some other lines of inquiry, including Oxford Central. First, though, I want to have another talk to Professor Plowright."

Teagle called St. John's but was unable to connect with Plowright despite several attempts. She sat wondering what to do next when her phone rang. It was the front desk.

"I've got Jane Plowright on the phone, Sergeant. Shall I put her through?"

"Yes please."

"Sorry I couldn't take your calls earlier, Sergeant, but I think by now you'll guess why."

"I'm getting the picture, Professor."

"Better I'm not known to be talking to you—better for me, that is—but I'd like to hear about how you've got on. You've certainly put the wind up the president. He's made it very clear that you are off limits."

"So I've discovered. Actually, I've not made much progress. The principal of St. Hilda's terminated my interview. It seems she complained about me to your president, who in turn complained to the chief constable. But I'm still investigating, and I've now been shown the cold shoulder at Keble as well as St. John's."

"Interesting that you've made the connection with Keble. I suspect you are now even more inquisitive than ever?"

"Not finished yet, if that's what you mean."

"That's good to know. From what I hear, you are very resourceful, Sergeant. You have made considerable progress and connected the three colleges to this matter."

"You mean St. John's and St. Hilda's and Keble."

"I can only talk obliquely. More than my job's worth as one might say in the vernacular. You'll make little headway using official channels, but being at Lady Margaret Hall around the same time this happened opens other avenues for you. The undergraduate or alumni grapevine perhaps?"

Teagle digested this. It seemed a tortuous route to get what she wanted.

"You know what happened, Professor. Why not just tell me?"

The phone went quiet. Teagle could sense that Plowright was thinking it through.

"I don't know all that happened. I know some, and I've deduced a lot from subsequent events at the time. Whether or not it has a bearing on your missing-person case, I don't know. But I believe that what happened here ten years ago should be investigated. An innocent person suffered a grievous injustice. I really must stop now, Sergeant. Good hunting."

The line went dead. Teagle put her handset down, wondering what to do. That was the second time she'd been wished "good hunting": first Bacon and now again by Plowright, who had given her clues and encouragement. Plowright also left the impression that she'd checked up on Teagle.

Bacon had implied a connection between St. John's and St. Hilda's and Keble, and Plowright had confirmed it. What did a grievous injustice mean? Did it have a bearing on the missing persons? Was Plowright trying to use Teagle to settle an old score? Was the rowing club connection important? She decided to talk to the superintendent.

He sat and listened carefully to everything she said.

"It's quite typical of the Oxford establishment, Teagle. It believes there are things we shouldn't get involved in, things which should remain within the university network. It's usually because it simply doesn't want us nosing about. Maybe it just wants to protect the reputation of some undergraduates who behaved stupidly and might cause embarrassment to the college.

"But we won't know if it's relevant to this inquiry until we find out what it is. I think it's time we went to see the president of St. John's."

It was the following day when they headed to St. John's for an appointment with its president. The superintendent briefed Teagle on the way.

"I'm not expecting the president to open up with us, Teagle. We may be lucky, of course, but that's unlikely. It'll be more a question of what he won't say that I'm interested in. He may try to provoke us, but don't rise to the bait. By the way, why do the heads of colleges have such different titles? Presidents or principals or wardens or provosts and so on makes it confusing."

"Don't know, sir. Historic reasons, I imagine, but it is peculiar, I agree. Pompous as well, like their regalia."

They were shown into the president's room and greeted by a tall, stooping elderly man standing behind a large desk.

"Welcome, Chief Superintendent; take a seat." He pointed to chairs opposite his desk and sat down.

"Thank you, sir. This is my associate, Detective Sergeant Teagle."

He looked keenly at Teagle and simply nodded at her and returned his gaze to the superintendent.

"Thank you for meeting us, sir. I'm hoping you can help with an investigation into missing persons. One of them is a graduate of St. John's, Charles Henry Caterham. I believe you've already heard his name, and I believe you were president during his time at St. John's."

Teagle noted that the superintendent had done his homework on the president.

"I have heard that his name was raised by Sergeant Teagle, but otherwise I don't think I can help you. He went missing after he left St. John's presumably?"

"Quite correct, sir. He was reported missing six years ago, around four years after he left St. John's."

"There you are. I don't see how I can help."

"It's possible that something happened during his time here that may have a bearing. We have heard that Caterham was involved in an incident at the end of his last term, just before he graduated."

The president stared at the superintendent and eventually asked, "Where did you hear that?"

"In the course of investigations, sir. We heard that you became involved and that it was hushed up."

The president continued looking at the superintendent and glanced at Teagle before eventually speaking. "What an extraordinary observation, Superintendent. I suggest that Sergeant Teagle is misinformed or misunderstood some comment. Easily happens when unfamiliar with Oxford University ways."

The superintendent smiled. "I'm certainly unfamiliar with Oxford ways as you call them, but Sergeant Teagle has firsthand experience of them from her time at Lady Margaret Hall."

The president sat back in his chair and smiled. "That would explain it. Lady Margaret Hall is a relatively new college. Did you know that it was originally set up for women only? Lots of gossip there, Superintendent."

"I did know it was set up for women about 140 years ago. I agree that's recent compared to St. John's, which I think can trace its history to the dissolution of the monasteries by King Henry the Eighth, 1555. Originally, as I understand it, St. John's was intended to provide educated Roman Catholic clerics to support the Counter Reformation; and I know that St. John's is a rich college, possibly the richest in Oxford, due in large part to ancient endowments of real estate. If I remember correctly, St. John's only accepted women undergraduates in 1979, which was the same year that Lady Margaret Hall admitted men. Quite an interesting coincidence, but is it important to this inquiry, sir?"

The president looked expressionless. Teagle imagined that he'd just realized that the superintendent was no fool.

"I am surprised; you are well informed, Superintendent. I believe that our history is relevant. St. John's—more properly the College of St. John the Baptist—is steeped in long tradition and historically has policed its own affairs. That works very well and avoids unnecessary embarrassment. I accept that our academic privilege, influence, and great wealth can create envy amongst the newer colleges, and even the townsfolk, which is only to be expected. It encourages a tendency for them to look for shadows where there are none."

The president smiled at Teagle. "I hope that I've not caused offence, Sergeant, but I'm sure you can see my point?"

Teagle looked inquiringly at the superintendent.

"Well, what do you think, Sergeant?"

"I wouldn't want to disagree with the president; I can understand his point of view, sir. However, we still have to try and solve
the disappearance of Charles Caterham. His family will expect us
to leave no avenue unexplored."

"Good point, Sergeant. You'll understand, sir, that we must follow this up and inquire into the incident involving Caterham in
his last term, last Trinity term as I think you call it, just before
he graduated. It may have a bearing upon his disappearance. We
shall, of course be careful to try and avoid causing the college unnecessary embarrassment."

The president looked thoughtfully at the superintendent before replying.

"I know Charles Caterham's father, Superintendent. He would
not thank you for prying into the events you refer to. You can take
it from me that they have absolutely no bearing upon Caterham's
disappearance."

The superintendent gently smiled as he absorbed these words.

"I understand, sir. Thank you for confirming things for me.
Unfortunately, the job of the police is to pry. It would be best if
you explain exactly what happened, then we can decide if it is
relevant."

It went quiet. Teagle could sense that the president was struggling to control his exasperation.

"We'll have to disagree, Superintendent. It has no relevance to
your investigation. We cannot assist you further. There is nothing
more to discuss."

On the return to Kidlington as they sat together in the car, Teagle
noticed that the superintendent appeared happy and relaxed.
Teagle felt intense annoyance; they'd hit a brick wall, and she felt
slighted.

"Tell me, Teagle, what would you have preferred to say to the
president?"

She took a deep breath.

"Not wishing to cause offence to you, President, but most folks at Oxford, both undergraduates and townsfolk, are already too familiar with the patronizing attitude of St. John's College and its ilk."

He chuckled. "Very restrained of you in the circumstances, Teagle. Nevertheless, I'm glad you bit your tongue. You handled it perfectly, and he gave us what we wanted. Well done."

"But we got nowhere, sir. He gave us the brush-off."

"He did indeed, but remember what he said. He didn't deny that something happened involving Caterham, and, thanks to you not rising to the bait, your reply encouraged him to confirm that there was an incident and one which we should keep our noses out of. He admitted he knew Caterham's father and effectively told us that things had been hushed up. Since he has refused to help us, we can only but continue to pry."

She looked at him as she thought back to the meeting.

"Sorry, sir, I was so annoyed at the president's attitude to me and women generally, I wasn't thinking carefully. He's not as clever as he thinks he is. Not half as clever as you, sir."

"Don't underestimate him, Teagle, and don't overestimate me. Remember, he may be correct that it has no relevance to our investigation. If so, we shall end up looking very foolish or worse. But I don't think it'll come to that."

"You're enjoying this aren't you, sir?"

He smiled at her. "It doesn't pay to tweak the noses of the so-called great and good of the Oxford establishment. But sometimes the opportunity is too tempting to resist.

"But let's not rise to that temptation until we know some more. Oxford Central should be next on our list. I'd be surprised if someone there wasn't involved in this cover up.

"Anyway, that's all we've got time for today. There's other Thames Valley crime to occupy us. This'll wait for a bit, and I also need to think about what we do next."

It was three days later before the superintendent had thought about what to do.

"I had time to read through the reports and think some more about these skeletons, Teagle. I sense that the rowing club connection might be important. Do you remember Professor Cornelius remarking that each of the four skeletons belonged to men of above-average height, and probably strong men?"

"Vaguely, sir, but why is that important?"

"Oarsmen, competitive oarsmen, tend to be taller, stronger, and heavier than average. We know that Caterham and Scot-Wadham belonged to the rowing clubs. I think we should keep it in mind. The other two men could also be oarsmen."

"I see. What do you want me to do, sir?"

"Not sure yet. It would help if we could get a better idea about what it is that the colleges are so determined to keep quiet about. Get in touch with Oxford Central and try to find someone there who was around ten years ago and might remember something. There may even be something tucked away in the records."

It didn't take Teagle long to discover that none of the current officers at Oxford Central served there ten years ago. Nor did the old records show any incident involving Caterham or Scot-Wadham.

"They did suggest that a retired sergeant, William Jenkins, might remember, sir. He retired about four years ago. I got his address, lives in Jericho."

"Of course, Bill Jenkins. I should have remembered. He's always lived in Jericho. Come on, let's see if he's at home."

Jericho is a historical part of Oxford only a fifteen-minute walk from the city center and the nearby canal. Its streets are of mostly Victorian workers' cottages, and it has more recently become a sought-after part of Oxford in which to live. Jenkins's home was a typical terraced small house.

He was at home.

"Good to see you again, Chief Super. Let me make some tea."

The superintendent sat quietly in the small front room. It was only a few minutes before Jenkins appeared carrying a tray with teapot, cups, and milk.

"Sorry I can't offer any cake. I don't expect visitors these days."

"I was sorry about Brenda; very sad, Bill."

"Thanks, and it was good to get your letter. We had three lovely years after I retired. I'd not expected it, not realized she was so poorly. Still getting used to it."

"Have you thought of moving?"

"Crossed my mind, but this place suits me fine. Been here so long it'd be daft to move. I know everyone, and it's walking distance to everywhere I go. It's a good place to live; I like it. Anyway, you've not come to pass the time. What can I do?"

"Hoping you might help us with a case, Bill. Something happened, an incident, ten years ago involving an undergrad from St. John's and possibly others. It was hushed up. Involved a student called Charles Henry Caterham at St. John's and would have happened in May or June that year, shortly before graduation. Thought Oxford central would have known about it."

Jenkins looked glum. "Happened all the time, as you probably know. Generally, students committing minor misdemeanors are simply given a warning. If it's more serious then sometimes their college gets involved to try and help. Try to sort things out quietly. Sometimes students didn't give their names when we took them in, just gave us their college—arrogant lot some are. The college would send someone along to get them off 'scot-free' if they could. They usually managed it somehow. St. John's got a reputation for doing that, if that's any help. It always annoyed us, but that's how it was."

Jenkins went quiet, obviously thinking, and they waited until he was ready.

"Can't say I remember the name Caterham. There was a serious incident which got hushed up, though, long time ago, maybe ten years—can't be sure when. It upset our station inspector. He'd gone and arrested some students and locked them up overnight for questioning and was ready to charge them. The chief constable got involved and told him to drop it and release them without charge. Wouldn't have happened with your present chief constable, from what I've heard about her, but it's how it was in those days.

"Anyway, our station inspector was deeply upset about it. He left soon afterwards. I think he went to a force in the north of England."

"Can you remember the charge?"

"I wasn't on duty at the time, but word got around until we were warned off. Serious sexual assault apparently. The inspector believed all four should be put in prison, but nothing was done."

The superintendent leaned toward him.

"You said four were involved, Bill?"

"Yes, that's what I heard. Four men, all undergraduates, went on the rampage after one of those dinner parties they hold in the last term."

"Was St. John's involved?"

Jenkins hesitated while he tried to recall. "Can't be sure. You could try looking in the incident book if it still exists for then."

Teagle spoke. "I tried that but couldn't find anything."

"Hmm. As I said, it was hushed up. Someone had powerful influence. All the officers involved in the arrests got transferred."

The superintendent sat quietly, thinking about what he'd heard.

"Thanks, Bill; that could be helpful. If you remember anything else, you know where to find me. Much appreciated. Nice to see you, and take care of yourself."

"Happy to help, Chief Super. You take care too, or you'll find yourself in the north of England as well."

He smiled at Jenkins. "That could be the least of my problems."

The superintendent said nothing on the journey back to Kidlington. He sat alongside Teagle in the back of the car thinking about what he'd heard from Bill Jenkins.

When they arrived back, Teagle followed him into his office.

"I think it's starting to add up, Teagle. Too many coincidences. I'd like to talk to that inspector, find out who he was and where he is now.

"By the way, what are these dinner parties that Jenkins referred to?"

"I'm sure you already know, sir. There are formal college dinners all year around but more frequently around the end of the academic year. Also balls, but these are usually coordinated and shared between colleges. I imagine that Bill Jenkins was referring to those college society dinners, which are little more than drinking clubs. You'll have heard of the Bullingdon Club, sir?"

"I have, Teagle. A bunch of hooligans who create mayhem."

"Hooligans who then go on to run our government, sir. Some other societies also behave outrageously after their dinners. Not so long ago one held a misogynistic fox hunt. Ran around the streets of Oxford dressed like huntsmen chasing female undergrads, thought it was fair game. It caused some outrage and has now been stopped."

"Not a surprise the townsfolk get fed up with the university."

"Most societies behave quite properly; it's the stupid few who spoil things as usual. As it happens, rowing societies hold dinners, and they've been known to get out of hand."

"Interesting; worth keeping in mind. Find that inspector for me, please."

It didn't take Teagle very long. Inspector James Marsden was in the far north of England with the Northumbria Police and based in Newcastle. He was now a chief inspector.

Later that day the superintendent spoke to him over the telephone. After the introductions he asked, "I'm hoping that you can help me with a missing persons case, Chief Inspector. About ten years ago, there was a serious incident when you were at Oxford Central involving four male undergraduates. You arrested them, but charges were later dropped. Can you remember anything?"

The line went quiet for a few seconds.

"If it's what I think you are referring to, then I'm hardly likely to forget it, although I'd prefer to."

"Can you please explain what happened? I believe it could be relevant."

There was a laugh from Marsden. "I'd have thought that you already knew; it happened on your patch."

"It was before I joined Thames Valley, and I can't find any record of it."

"Sir, I don't want to be unhelpful, but it was made clear to me, in no uncertain terms, that I was never to discuss it. The chief constable ordered me to forget it and drop all charges. That's why I'm up here in Northumbria. Why don't you speak to him?"

"You're quite right. I shall do that. Thames Valley has a different chief constable now; do you know where he went?"

"Sir, I'm very sorry to seem unhelpful, but I know you can easily find him. When you do, please make it clear that I refused to talk to you about this. Otherwise, my next posting might be the North Pole."

"A sad situation. I may yet want to talk again with you."

"Worse than sad. I call it criminal. Take care sir."

The phone went dead. The superintendent sat and considered what he'd just heard. He would talk to the previous chief constable, but before that, he decided to obtain some ammunition. He needed to connect what happened at Oxford Central ten years ago to the dead bodies somehow.

The following day they met Professor Cornelius and Dr. Watson.

"We've got two missing persons which fit the profile you gave me," the superintendent explained. "Both male, thirty years old as of today, reported missing in your time frame of death. Both oarsmen, rowers, so would probably be above average height and weight. Could you check if they are two of the dead men from the remains you have?"

Cornelius and Watson looked thoughtful before Watson answered, "Presumably you know the identities of the missing men and have spoken to their families, Superintendent?"

"That's correct, Doctor."

"We've struggled to get accurate DNA from the remains, but we could try to match what we've got with the parents' DNA. It would also help if you could obtain dental records. We have skulls with teeth remaining. I think that would be the starting point; don't you agree, Lionel?"

Cornelius nodded. "I do agree. In addition, if you could obtain physical characteristics—height, weight, shoe size, that sort of thing—it would assist even if it was only the process of elimination. I seem to recall that oarsmen, competitive oarsmen, have the boat adjusted to fit them, so there may be some records of leg length. Were they competitive?"

"One, at least, rowed in the Oxford and Cambridge boat race."

"There you are. I'd expect there'd be something about his measurements in the records."

"We can try that, but let's concentrate on the other things first. Please tell us what we need to do."

On the drive back to Kidlington, Teagle asked, "You don't want me to follow up about them at the boat clubs, sir?"

"No, not yet anyway. I don't want to alert the colleges that we're still investigating until I'm surer of our facts. You and Duggan get together what we need from their families. Don't mention the Oxford connection. Let each think that you are only investigating one missing person, their son. Tell them we need this information to help with an elimination."

"It'll still raise their hopes, sir. They'll ask questions."

"You know how to handle things. Actually, if you can obtain what Watson and Cornelius require, I think we'll have a match for two of the bodies."

"You're that confident, sir?"

"I am, Teagle. Not entirely sure why. Too many coincidences I suppose."

CHAPTER 9

I t was ten days later that the superintendent visited the laboratory in Oxford.

Doctor Watson and Professor Cornelius were waiting for him. Teagle and Duggan were also there. They'd gathered the information Watson had requested and arranged for James Scot-Wadham's parents and Charlie Caterham's mother to give DNA samples. Caterham's father was unavailable, being abroad on business.

Watson began proceedings.

"Well, Superintendent, we've got a result for you. I think we can say, with considerable certainty, that you've identified two of the bodies in the pond. Fortunately, both had regular visits to a dentist during their lives, and so we have dental records. Those together with DNA samples, physical descriptions, height, etc., and even shoe size have helped."

Watson walked across the room where the four skeletons were laid out. He stood alongside one of the skeletons.

"Meet Charles Henry Caterham."

He moved to another skeleton. "And here is Robin James Scot-Wadham."

He stood smiling at the superintendent and continued, "Your approach to the problem has paid off. Teagle and Duggan have explained your novel method of analyzing the missing-person reports, and I must say both Lionel and I were impressed. I wondered

127

why you'd not been hassling me during these weeks for more information; it makes a pleasant change. Anyway, well done."

"Teagle and Duggan are too modest; they did the work, but you both gave me a pointer, and we had a bit of luck."

"Clever deduction in my opinion, Superintendent." It was Cornelius who spoke. "Do you have any idea about the other two? According to your theory, presumably they are also connected to the university?"

"Mustn't jump to conclusions, as Doctor Watson is always reminding me. But yes, I'm confident they are all linked to an event at Oxford. Your identification of Caterham and Scot-Wadham convinces me. All I now must do is lift the veil of secrecy imposed by the Oxford College establishment, and I expect we'll be able to identify all four bodies."

Watson exclaimed, "Ah, one of those situations, is it? Lifting that particular veil might be a bit more difficult, Superintendent, as we all know."

"Indeed, Doctor, but you've given me some ammunition. Thank you."

It was time he brought the chief constable up to date.

"So you've come mob handed, Graham?"

"Hardly, ma'am. I wanted Teagle here because she's been subjected to the Oxford mafia at first hand, and she was an Oxford undergraduate at the time this all happened. She is fundamental to this investigation. I hope that's OK?"

"No problem; only my little joke. I presume you are likening the Oxford academia to the mafia. Is that wise?"

"That's just my little joke, ma'am, although it might be more apt than we imagine."

"Ok, Graham, get on with it. Bring me up to speed."

The chief constable listened without interruption. He kept his report brief and factual and complete. They'd worked together for eight years. She expected clear, concise reporting. She could work out the implications without him needing to elaborate.

As he talked, she made brief notes. When he'd finished she sat quietly, thoughtfully, before eventually responding.

"Not very pretty—in fact, outrageous. I understand why you used the term 'mafia.' What do you intend to do next?

"I want to know what happened on that night—why it was covered up and how. I intend to get those involved to talk. When I try there will be squeals of protest. You will be put under pressure to call me off. Last time you received a complaint from the president of St. John's about us. You indicated that I didn't have your permission to go deliberately treading on the toes of the Oxford University establishment, as you put it, ma'am. I'd like to tread upon some toes please."

She looked at him. Teagle noticed the beginnings of a smile on her face.

"Tread away, Graham. In the past, you've caused squeals of protest, as you put it, from a prime minister, a foreign secretary, the head of the secret service, and a commissioner of police, amongst others; I imagine that we can easily withstand protests from the Oxford mafia and my predecessor. On your way, and keep me posted, although I suspect news of your activities will quickly reach my ears. Good hunting to you both."

As they left the room, Teagle reflected that the chief constable was the third person to wish her "good hunting."

Later in his office the superintendent instructed Teagle to notify the parents of Caterham and Scot-Wadham, as their next of kin, that the remains had been identified. She was to set up an interview with each set of parents so that he could explain the circumstances and question them.

The coroner would be notified as legally required and would formally open an inquest to establish the suspicious circumstances of death. The inquest would then be adjourned while the criminal investigation continued.

The inquest would hit the news, and it would be the end of

keeping things out of the public gaze. The circumstances surrounding the four bodies, or their remains, discovered in the pond would attract a great deal of attention and interest. It should also cause some consternation among those involved in the cover-up ten years previously and whoever had committed the subsequent murders.

The superintendent hoped to use this to his advantage.

As instructed, Teagle had arranged their first interview with the parents of Robin Scot-Wadham. They'd traveled from Exeter.

Scot-Wadham's parents were in their midfifties and looked anxiously at the superintendent as he outlined the situation.

The father asked, "So you're sure it's Robin? There's no doubt?"

"We're almost certain, sir. I don't want to distress you unnecessarily. We have a skeleton which dates from the time Robin was reported missing by you. From the information you've provided and dental records, the pathologist is almost certain. You'll understand that after all this time, identification is difficult. However, there are other circumstances which convince me that we have identified your son."

"What circumstances, Superintendent?"

"That's what I want to talk to you about. Robin was at Keble. I understand he was a keen rower."

Father and mother exchanged glances and she replied, "It was his passion. He rowed for Keble college and hoped to make the varsity team for the boat race next year."

"What happened?"

"We're not sure. He came home at the end of his second year and said he didn't want to go back. Didn't seem his usual self. We tried to have a discussion, but he wouldn't talk about it."

The father continued, "I got the impression there'd been a falling out of some sort. Anyway, he didn't go back. He went off and took an apartment in London. Said he wanted to travel. We've always traveled around as a family; we have a place in the south of France, and Robin speaks fluent French. We didn't see much of him after that."

The mother took over. "Of course, I kept in touch as much as I could. We were upset that he'd dropped out of Oxford and gone away. As time went by, he became more remote, although he always assured me that he was happy. It became a struggle to persuade him to come and see us. He always had something else happening, and he traveled abroad a lot. Then we didn't hear from him at all, and I couldn't make contact. I tried all the time, and I became so worried and reported it to the police. He'd vanished, just left us."

She started to weep.

"What happened to him?" asked the father.

The superintendent looked at them both before explaining, "I'm afraid that his death is suspicious. We're in the middle of our investigation, but I believe that his death is connected to something which happened at the end of his second year, an incident in which he was involved and the reason he didn't return to Oxford."

It was quiet as both parents looked at each other. Teagle noticed that they were holding hands.

"Are you saying that Robin was murdered?"

"I believe that is very likely, sir. Because it happened seven years ago, we're struggling with the evidence. Anything you can remember about why he didn't return to Oxford may help."

They looked at each other before the mother spoke. "He was ashamed of something. He wouldn't tell us, but I knew. I don't know what he'd done, but I knew it was something wrong, something bad. He'd mixed with some unpleasant, nasty people, I could sense it. We went there once and met some of his friends at the rowing club. I didn't like them."

"Can you remember their names?"

"Not sure I can; they seemed to use nicknames. As I said I didn't like them."

"There are the photographs, darling. We took pictures at the college regatta. There was one also from Keble, but the other two went to different colleges."

"Was another college St. John's, sir?"

"It was, I remember. It was that one from St. John's that we took most dislike to. He seemed to mock us."

"We'd like to see those photographs please."

"Do you think they are involved in Robin's death, Superintendent?"

"Not directly, but I need to follow it up. Sergeant Teagle will be in touch about any photographs which could help us identify his friends. There were three friends, you said?"

"I think so. There may have been others, but these three we remember because we disliked them."

"Try to think back during the next few days about that time. Anything you remember which you think might help, please let us know."

The mother asked, "Can we please see Robin?"

There was silence as the superintendent considered his reply. He'd anticipated this and prepared for it.

"Of course. But I must tell you that we only have Robin's skeleton. There are some remains of clothing, but that is all. Do you still want to see him?"

She gripped the father's hand and sobbed, "Yes please."

"Sergeant Teagle will take you. Thank you for your help."

Teagle escorted Mr. and Mrs. Scot-Wadham to Oxford to view the remains of Robin, their son. In the viewing room was the laid-out skeleton and what few pieces of clothing and personal effects could be attributed to it, and which may be identifiable.

They were both silent and shocked by what they saw, until his mother gasped as she saw the remains of a jacket. She clung to the father and quietly sobbed. "It's Robin's jacket; I know it."

After they'd set off on the journey back to Exeter, Teagle went to see the superintendent. She told him that the mother had recognized the remains of the jacket.

"Good, that's another confirmation. I want to see those photographs before we interview Caterham's parents. Can you get down to Exeter tomorrow and collect them and see if they've recalled anything else?"

"Already arranged to do it, sir. They're expecting me there at ten tomorrow morning."

The following afternoon Teagle placed two photographs on his desk.

"Here you are, sir. I've ringed the four faces on each one. This is Scot-Wadham, and here's Caterham." She pointed to the two. "It was Caterham who Scot-Wadham's mother especially disliked, but she said all three were a bad influence. Of the other two, this one was at Keble with Scot-Wadham, and this fourth one, we don't know which college."

"Excellent. Who are the others in the photos?"

"Members of rowing teams apparently, all wearing club blazers, which might help with identification."

The superintendent studied the photos and then picked up a magnifying glass off his desk and studied them closely.

"This fourth man is wearing the same badge on his blazer as Caterham."

Teagle took the magnifying glass and looked. "That's right, sir. It looks like the St. John's rowing club badge."

"Good. Now let's see what Caterham's parents can tell us."

Caterham's parents were also in their midfifties. They lived just outside London near Walton-on-Thames in Surrey.

After the introductions the superintendent continued, "Thank you for coming, and my apologies for the brief delay. I was waiting on some information which might help us. As you've been told, I'm sorry to inform you that we've identified the remains of your son, Charles."

Caterham's mother looked distressed. His father asked, "Where did you find him?"

"Not far from Oxford. His remains were found on a farm. We

believe his body had been left there from before the time you reported him missing."

"When you say his body was left there, do you mean he was
murdered?"

"Most likely, sir, in my opinion. The evidence points to it. We
don't yet know the cause of death."

Caterham's mother sat silently, looking shocked.

"But why would anyone kill him?"

"I believe it's connected to an event, an incident, which occurred at Oxford just before he graduated. I'm hoping you can
help by telling me what happened then."

Caterham's father hesitated, his features hardened, and he
leaned toward the superintendent. "Nothing happened that I am
aware of."

The superintendent turned toward the mother. "Can you remember what happened, Mrs. Caterham?"

She dropped her gaze and shook her head. She was gripping
her handbag, which rested on her knees. She remained silent.

He turned toward the father again. "He was arrested for involvement in a serious sexual assault."

The father looked angry. "No charges were brought, and the
case was dropped. It was nothing, just a group of undergraduates
in high spirits."

"Ah, so you do remember something, sir?"

The father was clearly angry and pointed his finger as he
spoke. "Look, Superintendent, I'll not have you trying to damage
the good character of my dead son with your innuendo. Nothing
happened. Have some respect for God's sake. My son did nothing
wrong, and it can have no bearing on his murder. Just leave this
alone. Don't go digging into things which don't concern you."

The superintendent looked impassively at him and then the
mother. She remained sitting with her head down and gripping
her handbag. She was quietly sobbing. The superintendent turned
to Teagle, and she handed over the two photographs.

"You mentioned a group of undergraduates, sir. Perhaps you can identify them? Are they in these photographs?"

He slid the photos across the table. The father glanced at them. "Apart from Charles, I've no idea who the other three are."

"How about you Mrs. Caterham? Have you seen any of them before?"

She raised her eyes and sat looking at the photos for some time before looking down and shaking her head. "No, sorry."

The superintendent recovered the photographs and looked directly at the father. "A pity, sir. If you believe that what happened on that night in Oxford is not connected to your son's death, then why not tell me about it so that I can eliminate it from our investigation? That would be the easiest way to protect your son's reputation."

The father stood, ready to leave. "Because you will only misconstrue things. I'll not have you prying into it."

"It's relevant to my investigation. I need to know what happened, sir."

"I intend to put a stop to it."

"That won't help find the murderer of your son."

Caterham's father turned to his wife. "Come on; we're leaving. We've nothing more to say."

She remained seated and simply said, "Can I see Charles please, Superintendent?"

"Of course you may, Mrs. Caterham. But I must warn you that we have only his skeleton; decomposition was far advanced. But it is Charles. There are some remains of clothing. Sergeant Teagle will take you."

"Thank you, Superintendent."

Caterham's father looked at his wife and then turned to Teagle. "How long will this take?"

"We have to go into Oxford, sir. I imagine about an hour or so before we get back here."

He hesitated and then spoke to his wife. "You go to Oxford

with the sergeant. I'll follow in my car, and then we'll go home from there."

When Teagle returned from Oxford, she reported what had happened.

"On the journey there, I felt Caterham's mother wanted to talk. I asked her if Charles had been happy at Oxford. She said he had. She knew something had happened just before he graduated but neither he nor his father would talk about it. I asked if she'd recognized any of those in the photos. She just said that she couldn't be sure and apologized."

"What did his father do?"

"His car followed behind us to Oxford. He has a driver, and I think he spent the time on his phone. Anyway, he joined us to view Caterham's remains. The mother thought she recognized the remains of a belt and a jacket; the belt had a distinctive buckle. She was distressed; the father said nothing. They left together in his car. What shall I do next, sir?"

"Let's leave it for the time being and see what happens. I'm expecting that our chief constable will shortly ask to see us."

Later that day the chief constable took the call from Paul Rigby.

Rigby was the chief constable of Greater Manchester Police. She knew he'd moved from Thames Valley just before she was appointed in his place. They'd not met, and their paths had never crossed. She did know that he was about to retire.

They briefly exchanged pleasantries before he got to the point.

"I need a favor from you. Chief Superintendent Barnes is stirring up a bit of dust. You're probably not aware, but he's digging into something which was shelved ten years ago. It's not relevant to anything, and we'd like him to let things alone. It'd be much appreciated."

"Can you be more specific about what it is?"

"A group of students, drunken students, did something stupid. The college authorities handled it, wanted to save reputations.

The complaint was withdrawn, and no charges were laid. Case was closed—not that there ever was a case. It didn't get that far."

"Did it involve four men, serious sexual assault?"

"So you do know about it. Stuff and nonsense really. The girl was drunk as well. She made no complaint. No harm done."

"Do you know the names of those involved?"

It went quiet before he replied. "Look, does it matter? No records were kept, so the names are not on file."

"Well, it is a murder investigation, and it's necessary for the superintendent to decide whether it matters or not."

"Who's been murdered?"

"So far, the superintendent has identified two victims. They are two of the men involved in that sexual assault. He understandably believes the matter is relevant and wants to know more. I agree with him, and I imagine that you'd also agree and want to help him."

There as a long pause before he replied.

"Look, this is getting us nowhere. Barnes should just leave things alone."

"Why are you so anxious about this? Why not leave him to get on with it? If it's not relevant, he'll soon know, and there'll be no harm done."

"If he continues, he will upset some influential people, powerful people. I'm sure you understand?"

"Not sure that I do understand. Who are these influential powerful people who want to stop this murder investigation?"

"This is stupid. I'd heard you can be a difficult person to deal with, but I presumed that you'd at least understand how things are done. Don't forget that I did try to warn you."

"Thanks for the warning."

She put the phone down. She wondered whom she'd hear from next.

It didn't take long. An hour later the permanent secretary to the Home Office called her. They were known to each other, so he wasted little time before getting to the reason for his call. It was as she'd guessed.

"We've had a complaint that Chief Superintendent Barnes is inquiring into a sensitive matter. Do you know anything about it?"

"I think so. Is it about an event at Oxford ten years ago?"

"That's what I'm told. No relevance to his investigation and will cause serious reputational damage if he continues. The usual reminder of repercussions if he persists."

She gave a gentle laugh. "I not sure that will worry him, as you already know. However, he has kept me fully informed, and I believe that he should follow it up. It has a direct connection to a murder investigation. It was hushed up at the time and very improperly from what we know so far. Can you tell me who has complained?"

"Not sure I should, at least not until I know some more about it."

"It involves four undergraduates who were originally arrested for a serious sexual assault and taken into custody. The case was quickly dropped on the orders of my predecessor at the time and apparently handled by the colleges concerned. Two of the undergraduates involved have subsequently died in suspicious circumstances, almost certainly murdered. That is what Graham Barnes is investigating."

"Ah, so Paul Rigby is involved?"

"Yes, he called me about it just over an hour ago. I wondered who'd call me next."

"Very interesting. Rigby and the Oxford University establishment—that's reminded me of something. Which colleges are involved?"

"St. John's, Keble, and St. Hilda's so far."

"That's interesting too. Well, I'd better leave Superintendent Barnes to get on with it."

"You haven't told me who complained."

"Another time maybe."

"Are you an Oxford man?"

"Cambridge, thank goodness. An Oxford man would be telling you not to get involved."

She spoke to the superintendent alone.

"Some news for you, Graham. I had a call from Paul Rigby. He was chief constable here ten years ago."

"Your predecessor, ma'am. He had the charges dropped against Caterham and Scot-Wadham and the other two."

"That's right. He called wanting me to stop you investigating it. But he confirmed that it involved four undergraduate men and a girl. He suggested that the girl was drunk and subsequently withdrew her complaint."

"Was the girl an undergraduate?"

"He didn't say, just referred to her as a girl. Sorry, but I didn't ask either."

"Pity. I'm guessing she was. I'm also guessing she was at St. Hilda's, which would explain why Teagle was pointed in that direction."

"I've also had a call from the Home Office. Somebody had complained—don't know who—also wanting to stop you."

He looked questioningly at her. "What happened, ma'am?"

"Home Office asked to know what you were doing. I explained the circumstances. You've been left to get on with it."

He looked at her with surprise. "Does that mean I have the Home Office's approval?"

"I believe so, for the time being at least; it knows what you are doing. Make the most of it while it lasts."

CHAPTER 10

It was late that day when he found time to think things over and summarize them in his mind.

Four undergraduates, including Caterham and Scot-Wadham, sexually assaulted a girl ten years ago. Was she really a girl? Paul Rigby had said she was drunk, so probably a young woman.

Caterham and Scot-Wadham were subsequently murdered and left in the farm pond. Were they murdered because of the assault? That was the obvious conclusion.

Who are the other two bodies in the pond? Possibly the other two undergraduates committing the assault. Are they in the photograph provided by Scot-Wadham's parents, part of his group of friends?

Who is the victim? Maybe an undergraduate, perhaps at St. Hilda's college. Why didn't she make a complaint? What has happened to her?

Who knows what happened ten years ago? The president of St. John's; Paul Rigby, chief constable of Thames Valley at the time, now in Manchester; Inspector James Marsden, now in Newcastle; Caterham's father; probably the principal of St. Hilda's; perhaps the warden of Keble at the time.

All of these have refused to talk. James Marsden would probably like to talk but so far won't.

Why are they so determined to cover it up?

Who has tried to help the investigation? Professor Jane Plowright of St. John's, Caterham's tutor, has provided clues and is encouraging the investigation. Why? John Bacon, St. John's porter, also initially helpful; he could

NBR3QVWZ3EIH4QDLBY7FWAURDFG3F7YGSFF5KGQWMYTH4B65W6YH6FEHM3UZ63XKHZKKSVZV2W2AAVVP4AB2ZSYAW2MTV4GGGB7BXPA

FUHCSY4TTPJ4N6G4YASSHWQTQAAWTB4J2MG5OXO6CK5RE24HX4ZL5BUJPNXNOJJCQ3KQZF5LRTOR6IMY4MHQ72XE3BTTFAJOXOBBXQ

SCGI3AK5QDPT5ON5DJR3Q2PCAGCRXCYSEE25LPT2PTGMT2JXZ56TNVAQWL7ANUA3E3DXJD35LT4A6PNT3FV2QWEADCPAFZ3CUBAXPI

YHDR77V6JF36QUGKTRQJFHR6EHIBPCF427SM7BY6JB6HQ2KMTDU6ATVL2SOO4SWP72AWB3TPPHJ6JGDWX5IHX4BR6TXI2RGXXBJ6GA

Ian Ellis

perhaps identify the undergraduates in the photograph. Scot-Wadham's parents have told what they know.

Of course, the victim would know what happened ten years ago.

Who else might know? Possibly some witnesses; the police officers involved in the arrests; the victim's family perhaps; maybe she required medical attention.

Who committed the murders? What was the motive? How was it done? How and why did the bodies get dumped in the farm pond?

Was it certain that the events of ten years ago were connected to the murders?

There were too many unanswered questions. During the night he imagined various scenarios. To get to the truth, he'd need to outwit those who were determined to stop him. It was almost dawn before he managed to sleep.

He sat with Teagle later that morning and explained what he wanted to do.

They visited the porters' lodge. Teagle had made sure that Bacon was on duty. She introduced the superintendent.

"Good to meet you, Mr. Bacon, and thank you for helping us."

Bacon looked uneasy. "Don't think I've helped anyone, Chief Superintendent; just passed the time of day with Sergeant Teagle."

"Nonsense, you've been a great help, and I've got a few more questions."

Bacon now looked alarmed. "Now look, the Sergeant knows I can't help you, and I'd appreciate you forgetting anything I might have said inadvertently, if you get my drift."

The superintendent smiled at him. "Not to worry, Mr. Bacon. You are going to do something which will put you in favor with your masters. Trust me."

Bacon relaxed and gave a wry smile. "I've always been wary of trusting anyone who says, 'Trust me.'"

"I don't blame you; so have I. But make an exception this time; you'll enjoy it."

"What do you want?"

"Here's a photograph of some undergraduates. I want to know about what they did ten years ago. Just tell me if you recognize anyone."

Bacon studied the photograph. He looked at Teagle and then shrugged. "Not sure I do, Superintendent. Just look like undergraduates to me."

"Take a closer look at the four we've ringed. Two have St. John's blazers, and the other two are wearing ones for Keble college. You previously talked about them to Sergeant Teagle. Would a magnifying glass help?"

He took the magnifying glass from Teagle, but it was obvious he didn't need it.

"Now you mention it, I can recognize Charlie-boy and Yakker."

"You mean Charles Caterham and Jacob Wagner?"

"You know I do; you're just playing a game."

"That's right. What about the other two?"

Bacon didn't even look at the photograph before replying.

"Scotty, Scot-Wadham, and Big-Mac or Robert McClennon, to use his proper name. All partners in crime, as your sergeant called them. What's this all about? You already know who they are."

"Just wanted to set the scene for you, nothing more. Now I think you should report to your president of St. John's that I have been to see you about these four undergraduates. Say that I asked about their activities ten years ago, end of Trinity Term. Emphasize that you refused to tell me anything."

Bacon gave him a smile. "I know your game. You said I'd enjoy it. You want to stir up a hornets' nest. Anything to oblige the Thames Valley Police. Mind you, expect to get stung, Superintendent. These particular hornets can be vicious."

"I'll bear it in mind. Many thanks, sir, I'll be back."

They sat together in the back of the car.

"OK, Teagle, that went well. He's given us all four names. I should have guessed one would be Jacob Wagner."

"I'm the one who should have guessed. It's obvious now. Anyway, well done, sir."

"He also gave us their nicknames. Do you remember Mrs. Scot-Wadham talking about nicknames?"

"I do remember, sir. Charlie-boy, Yakker, Scotty, and Big-Mac. Rather juvenile in my opinion, but that's what boys do apparently."

"Hmm, not only boys, Teagle. We'd better get busy before the drawbridge comes down."

They were quickly at Oxford Central police station, and it was not long before Professor Jane Plowright arrived. She was shown into a meeting room.

"Thank you for coming, Professor. I'll try not to make things difficult for you, but I do need to ask you some questions."

She nodded. "I'll try my best to help, but I am constrained as I've told Sergeant Teagle."

"Let's see how we get on. I'll endeavor to talk generally. Ten years ago, around the end of Trinity Term, four undergraduates committed a serious sexual assault on a young woman. University colleges intervened, the woman's complaint was apparently withdrawn, the charges against the men were dropped, and the whole affair was hushed up. Do you recall anything like that happening?"

"I do."

"Two of the undergraduates were from St. John's and two from Keble. Are you aware of that?"

She hesitated. "That's what I'd heard."

He smiled at her. "The young woman, the victim, was an undergraduate at St. Hilda's. Did you know that?"

She remained quiet but continued looking at the superintendent.

"Sergeant Teagle told me that you claimed there had been a serious miscarriage of justice. Was it against this young undergraduate?"

She continued looking at the superintendent but said nothing.

"Do you know her identity?"

Again, she remained quiet.

"Apart from the four men, and the young victim, I believe there were other witnesses to the attack."

Still, she remained quiet.

"Is anything that I've described incorrect?"

Again, no response.

"Would you like to assist us try to correct this injustice?"

"Very much so, Superintendent. I am sincerely sorry that I am too cowardly to do so."

"You have helped. Silence speaks volumes. It will also help if you report this meeting to the president of St. John's. Tell him that you were required to attend at Oxford Central police station because you were Charles Caterham's tutor. Tell him all that I have said. Emphasize that you refused to answer my questions. Will you do this for me?"

They could see that she was initially puzzled, but then understanding dawned on her face. She gave a slight smile and nodded.

"Yes, I certainly will, Superintendent."

"Thank you. Please do it without delay."

The car was driven to St. Hilda's college, and they were shown into the principal's office. Professor Dame Mary Knight didn't look happy to be seeing them.

"I must say, Chief Superintendent, I'd not expected another visit from the police. Sergeant Teagle said you have disturbing news."

"I do indeed, ma'am. When you previously met Sergeant Teagle, you said you wouldn't help us."

"I believe I said that I couldn't help because I didn't know to whom she was referring. Is this all you've come about?"

"Ten years ago, four male undergraduates were arrested for a serious sexual assault against a young woman in Oxford. Do you recall the incident?"

"Continue, Superintendent."

He studied her carefully and detected defiance in her expression.

"Two undergraduates from St. John's and two from Keble. Their victim was a female undergraduate at St. Hilda's."

She was about to speak but hesitated and remained quiet.

"Ma'am, do you recall it? You were principal of St. Hilda's at the time."

"There was an incident, but nothing became of it. No complaint was made, and no charges were laid."

"That's not true, is it?"

She checked herself and then quietly asked, "Could you elaborate please?"

"A complaint was made by the victim. The four men were arrested and taken to Oxford Central to be detained and charged. That's what happened, isn't it?"

She looked warily at the superintendent.

"It was an incident which was exaggerated. There'd been an end-of-term party, stupid behavior by some students who'd drunk too much. The girl overreacted—that's all. The police were heavy handed, and for the sake of those involved, the college authorities decided to handle it themselves. The police agreed."

"Thank you, ma'am. That's more helpful. I now need to know how the college authorities handled it. What did you do? What happened to the victim? How did you persuade her to withdraw her complaint?"

"Superintendent, since it was not a police matter, it is none of your business. I have nothing more to say."

He smiled at her. "Unfortunately it has become my business, ma'am. The events of that night and what happened subsequently are now part of another inquiry."

"I have already been informed of what you are trying to assert. You are wrong, Superintendent. It has no connection to your investigation. Your murders are simply a coincidence."

"I've not mentioned murders to you, ma'am. Who's told you that?"

She looked angry.

"I have nothing more to say. Please leave, Superintendent."

He stared at her face for a few seconds and then rose from his chair and nodded to Teagle.

"As you wish, ma'am. I am disappointed that you, of all people, have something to hide. I'm relieved that I didn't entrust a daughter of mine to your care."

She visibly shook with indignation.

"How dare you. I have nothing to hide."

He smiled at her, "Ma'am, you have plainly demonstrated that you are hiding a great deal."

He'd reached the doorway before she spoke again.

"You are out of your depth, Superintendent. My advice is to let this alone."

He didn't turn or respond but kept going with Teagle following behind. He almost ran down the staircase and marched out of the building. Teagle struggled to keep up, but when she did finally get alongside, she noticed satisfaction on his face.

They reached the car, and it set off for Kidlington.

He smiled at Teagle. "I'll bet you're glad you didn't go to St. Hilda's?"

"The undergrads are OK, sir. It's the principal who isn't."

"Beware the overambitious Oxford don."

"Do you think that's why she got involved in the cover-up?"

"We'll find out eventually. Meanwhile we're making progress at last. Your next task will be much easier now, thanks to Bacon."

The car arrived back at Oxford Central, and Teagle got out. Duggan was there waiting for her.

It was late in the afternoon when Chief Inspector James Marsden arrived at Kidlington HQ, having traveled from Newcastle.

"Thanks for coming, Inspector."

"I didn't have much choice, sir."

The superintendent smiled at him. "I don't suppose you did. Time to put a stop to all this nonsense, don't you think?"

"Didn't feel like nonsense at the time. Almost cost me my career. I hope you know what you're doing, with all due respect, sir."

"I need to know what happened ten years ago. I'll tell you what I know, and you can fill in the gaps."

"I can do better than that."

Marsden reached into his briefcase and removed a folder of documents.

"I was ordered by the chief constable to remove all the records and pass them to him. I did so but only after I'd made a copy. These are the copies."

The superintendent looked surprised and then nodded approval.

"Was the chief constable called Paul Rigby?"

"That's right. It was a direct order and, he claimed, authorized at the highest level. I objected, but he told me it would be stupid to ruin my career. Afterwards, I couldn't face staying in Oxford. He arranged my transfer to the Northumbria force. Warned me to keep my mouth shut."

"Why did you make the copy?"

"It was spur-of-the-moment thing at the time. I was angry about a very serious crime being covered up. I thought it might help me if later things went wrong. Anyway, I've hung on to it. When you see what's there, you'll understand why."

He picked up the folder and carefully studied its contents. Marsden sat watching him and could see his features harden.

When he'd finished reading, he sat quietly thinking. After a few minutes he looked at Marsden.

"This is not good. It's a pity you didn't show me earlier."

"I wanted to, sir, but I wasn't entirely sure where you stood in all this. Whose side you'd be on."

"That's disappointing to hear. You're saying that you didn't know if you could trust me?"

"Sorry, but yes. I wasn't sure."

"What changed your mind?"

"I asked around, not only about you but also your chief constable. The word is that you are straight, so when you summoned me here, I decided to take the risk. Just hope I'm right."

The superintendent felt close to despair.

"Thank you for taking the risk. Let's talk about these records. There's incomplete information."

"That's simply because things were shut down before we'd had enough time."

"How did you come to be at the crime scene so quickly?"

"We'd received a complaint about behavior at a party. Keble College rowing club event in a marquee near the boat house. I was on duty and set off with three officers. As we drew close, there was an urgent call about a disturbance in the boathouse. We were there in a few minutes. The victim was lying unconscious, clothes torn off and bleeding. It was obvious she'd been assaulted and raped; you can see from the photos."

"How did the witnesses come to be there?"

"Both couples had been at the party. It was late. They were leaving and walking away when the victim ran past and then four men also ran past chasing her and shouting. The witnesses recognized them from the party. It was these men's behavior that caused the original complaint.

"They'd all run towards the boathouse, and the witnesses decided to follow them. They saw the lights in the boathouse switched on, then heard shouts and screams. One of the witnesses rang 999 on her mobile. That was relayed to us in the car, and we were on the scene in minutes. The witnesses were there, and the two young women were trying to help the victim. One of them knew her and told me who she was. The four men had run off."

"Did anyone actually witness the attack?"

Marsden looked directly at him and nodded. "The witnesses arrived together and found one of the four men in the act of raping the victim. She was fighting to resist but being held down by two of the men. The other man was shouting encouragement to the rapist.

They saw the victim punched on the side of the face. The witnesses apparently shouted at the men and tried to stop them. There was a scuffle and shouting, and the men ran off, laughing together."

"What happened next?"

"We did what we could for the victim until the ambulance arrived. I questioned the witnesses. They knew the identities of the four men; they have a reputation. The ambulance arrived, and the crew tended her. She regained consciousness and was able to confirm her identity before she went in the ambulance to the John Radcliffe Hospital. I took the names of the witnesses and instructed them to attend Oxford Central in the morning to provide formal statements. Then I set off to arrest the four men."

"So you didn't set up a crime scene?"

Marsden grimaced. "No sir. I wanted to get on and arrest the gang. I didn't want to lose them. We knew who they were, and there were witnesses. The victim had gone to hospital. I normally would have; sorry."

"OK, so you set off to get them."

"It was almost midnight when we got to St. John's. A porter accompanied us to their rooms. Caterham refused to open his door; we could hear him talking on his phone. The porter provided a passkey before we broke down the door. We arrested him. Wagner's room was close by, and he was also arrested. Caterham told Wagner to say nothing and not to worry.

"They were handcuffed and taken to Oxford Central. We then set off for Keble to arrest Scot-Wadham and McClennon. We had all four in custody by just after 1:30 a.m., as you can see from the record."

"Did you formally charge them?"

Marsden hesitated. "No, sir. They'd each been cautioned, of course, and at the station I tried to question Caterham and Wagner. Both remained silent. Caterham obviously found it amusing. I decided it would be best to hold them until I'd got the witness statements and taken a statement from the victim."

Marsden sighed. "I was just leaving to visit the victim at the hospital when the bursar from Keble arrived with an executive officer from St. John's. They requested to take over the matter. Said it happened on college property, concerned undergraduates, and the colleges would deal with it."

"What did you do?"

"I refused. Told them the matter was far too serious, a vicious sexual assault. They seemed taken aback and went outside to make phone calls. They came back and advised me to await instructions before doing anything else."

"Did you tell them the victim was an undergraduate?"

Marsden hesitated again and thought back. "Might have done. I maybe mentioned St. Hilda's but not sure if I gave her name, sir."

The superintendent asked him to continue.

"I waited and began to write up the records, more or less what you have here."

"Who took the photos?"

"One of my officers. He was wearing a camera, a bodycam. About an hour and a half later, I received a call from the chief constable, Paul Rigby. Ordered me to release the men and drop the matter. I objected, told him it was a vicious rape, and the victim was in hospital. He asked me about the victim, and I told him. He replied that she would be taken care of. He repeated his direct order, then instructed me to report to him the following day. Word had got to the two college officials who were waiting. They came and escorted the four undergraduates away."

"Then what did you do?"

"I finished writing up the records and then decided to go and visit the John Radcliffe to see how the victim was doing and to try and take a statement. I thought a statement might change the chief constable's mind. It was after 6:00 a.m. when I arrived, but she had been discharged, apparently taken by private ambulance somewhere. The staff nurse showed me the discharge papers signed by an official of St. Hilda's, but they didn't describe where she'd gone."

"Why hadn't you sent an officer to the hospital with the ambulance?"

"I wanted to keep the officers with me for the arrests. The ambulance crew said they'd look after her and where she'd be. Sorry, sir."

"I don't think it would have made any difference, as it happens. Carry on."

"I was due to go off duty but decided to stay on until the witnesses arrived at Oxford Central to give statements. Despite what the chief constable had said, I still intended to get statements.

"Unfortunately, I received another phone call from the chief constable. Somehow, he'd heard I'd visited the John Radcliffe. He demanded to know why. I told him that I'd been to inquire about the victim, to see how she was. He wasn't pleased and repeated his order for me to drop things. He also told me to be at Kidlington to see him that afternoon and to bring all the records with me.

"The witnesses turned up at 9:00 a.m. as requested, and I informed them that the matter had been dropped by the police, and the college authorities were handling it. They were surprised and unhappy. I obtained their names and college details so they could be contacted if required. It's in the records.

"I collected the original records to give to the chief constable but made the copy you now have. The chief constable ordered me to forget all about it. I voiced my objection, said they should be charged and prosecuted, said they were brutal thugs, etc. He threatened me, and you know the rest."

The superintendent sat thinking, and Marsden sat quietly watching him. His face gave no expression while he contemplated it all.

"So, Inspector, it's true to say that the police never received a complaint from the victim, the witnesses never gave a statement, and the four men were never interviewed or charged. Nor is there forensic or medical evidence to support a charge of rape and assault. Is that correct?"

Marsden grimaced and then sighed. "You make it sound as if it never happened, that I've meddled where I shouldn't. Just like bloody Chief Constable Paul Rigby. Thank you for nothing, sir!"

"I certainly didn't intend that, and I don't think it. I'm certain it happened just as you've described. If you'd not been stopped, those four undergraduates would have gone to trial. But you know that it's important to look on the downside. It's what a defense lawyer will say."

"Sorry, sir. I'm annoyed with myself for not doing more."

"In my view you did well, very well. Just let me think for a minute."

Eventually he looked up and asked, "Did you give the chief constable everything in this folder, including the photographs?"

"Yes, sir."

"Did you also include the details of the witnesses?"

Marsden hesitated before answering, "I did. It seemed best not to hide anything, and anyway, I expected him to ask about them. He did ask, wanted to know who they were and wanted me to confirm that all records had been removed from Oxford Central as if the assault had never occurred."

"Did you ever have contact or see any of the four culprits, or the victim or the witnesses again?"

"No, sir. I was given some leave and transferred from Oxford within weeks. I know that the other three officers who attended with me at the scene were also moved out of Oxford Central. They'd also been told not to discuss the matter."

"Is that all? Is there anything else you want to tell me?"

Marsden looked directly at the superintendent as he replied.

"I've told you the truth. I'm ashamed about us—the police, that is—giving in time and again, to the so-called Oxford ruling class. It is not right. They do what they like, and never pay the price, if you understand me, sir."

"Do you mean this is a regular type of occurrence?"

"Come on, sir. You know what goes on. Been going on for decades, centuries probably, in Oxford. It'll still be going on. Oxford Central police station was set up to facilitate it, to make sure the reputations of misbehaving Oxford students and academics were protected. It's thought that your present chief constable is not as amenable to us showing a blind eye as her predecessors were, but she'll not stop it happening."

The superintendent couldn't remember when he was last stunned by what he heard, but he was certainly astonished by Marsden's words. He also felt stupid and naïve, and bewildered. He didn't know what to reply. He could see Marsden watching in puzzlement.

"What do you intend to do, sir?"

"I'm not sure yet, Inspector. I need to think."

"It'll be known you called me here to see you; word will get around. I've only got two years until retirement, Superintendent. Please don't mess that up for me."

The superintendent looked disappointed. "I understand. It's a sad day when it comes to this, when police officers can't trust each other and need to watch their backs. However, I'm very grateful for your copy of the records and glad you saw fit to make it; the original will have long ago been destroyed, I imagine. I shall use it; if there are any repercussions for you or if anyone contacts you about it, then you let me know."

"Nothing I can do about it now. I'm entirely in your hands. I hope you nail the bastards, all those involved."

After Marsden had left, the superintendent made careful notes about their meeting and reviewed the copy of the records again. He wondered about the unfortunate victim: where had she been taken to from hospital, how had she been persuaded to drop any complaint, where was she now. Her name was Amelia Sheridan, undergraduate of St. Hilda's.

He now had the names of the four witnesses, all undergraduates. Where were they now? One of the women was at St. John's, and she knew Amelia Sheridan. The other was at Lady Margaret Hall, Teagle's old college; did they know each other? Both the men were at Keble.

The records also identified the three officers who attended the scene with Marsden. What had happened to them?

He summoned Teagle and Duggan and gave them further instructions.

That evening he carefully summarized it all into a report for the chief constable. In it he explained his next course of action.

CHAPTER 11

The following afternoon he was summoned to the chief constable.

"Come in, Graham; take a seat."

He sat across her desk.

"I've just finished reading your report about the Oxford affair. It has upset and annoyed me. I believed that Thames Valley Police Force was better than this."

"It was ten years ago and specifically events at Oxford Central, but it's also upset me."

"Not just Oxford Central, my predecessor, Paul Rigby, was in the thick of it, and it's probably still going on, according to your report. Is that true?"

He sighed and looked directly at her. "There have been enough clues to tell us, but I've misread them and accepted it all as the peculiar ways of the Oxford establishment. Showing the cold shoulder, refusing to assist, even telling us to go away and mind our own business, calling on higher authority if we don't comply. I feel that I've gone along with it and been pussyfooting around searching for scraps of evidence."

She laughed. "I'd never have imagined you pussyfooting around anything."

"Well, it certainly feels like it. I'm weary of not being able to get a straight answer to a question; it makes me very suspicious. In fact, I'm beginning to believe that this whole business has been covered up to hide something even more sinister. I don't think it's just to protect some thuggish undergraduates. This cover-up is about something else."

"Do you think that's the motive for the murders? You obviously think the skeletons belong to all four undergraduates involved in the assault?"

"I'm almost certain we'll discover that all four in the gang were murdered and dumped in the pond. No idea yet how they were killed or how they got there. Two possible motives occur so far: either retribution for Amelia Sheridan or to keep some other crime from being exposed."

"I can understand the revenge motive, especially reading about what happened to her. But what other crime could it be covering up?"

"Don't know, ma'am, but whatever it is involves the president of St. John's and the principal of St. Hilda's and your predecessor."

"Yes, I've been wondering about Paul Rigby. Extraordinary to think that knowing what happened, having seen this file, these photographs, he'd do such a thing."

"Even more extraordinary to know that he actually managed to do it and got away with it, ma'am."

They sat quietly looking at each other and considered what had been done.

Finally, he said, "The bigger question is what motivated Rigby to do it? What did he get out of it? It doesn't ring true that he'd take such a risk just to protect some rotten undergraduates from the law."

"The Home Office permanent secretary made some enigmatic comments when he called me, after he'd received complaints about you sticking your nose in. I told him about Paul Rigby had already warned us off, and I mentioned the involvement of St. John's and Keble and St. Hilda's; it was as if he wasn't surprised. It seemed almost as if he relished the fact that you were digging away. I asked him if he was an Oxford man, and he replied, 'Cambridge, thank goodness. An Oxford man would tell you not to get involved.' I'm beginning to think he knows more about what's going on than me, and that's a very uncomfortable sensation to have."

"Anyway, ma'am, my pussyfooting has come to an end. Teagle and Duggan are armed with warrants to make sure they gather the information we need about the victim and the witnesses, and anyone else connected. I'm going to rattle the cages of the so-called Oxford establishment. I expect you'll hear all about it very soon."

She smiled at him. "I envy you. I'm going to scrutinize exactly what's been going on at Oxford Central."

She heard about it sooner than she'd expected. Within two hours of the superintendent leaving her, she was listening on the telephone to the permanent secretary to the Home Office.

"I'd not expected to be talking to you again so soon, Chief Constable, but Superintendent Barnes seems to have been busy. He's certainly caused some consternation."

"I met with him only a couple of hours ago. He's hardly started yet, so I expect that consternation will quickly become panic."

She heard a light chuckle on the telephone line. "I hope he's got his facts straight because the message coming to me is that he's fishing for information simply to suit his case. His police size-twelve boots are raising clouds of dust in hallowed places, if you'll forgive my metaphor."

"Is this a warning, Permanent Secretary? Are you now wearing the cap of an Oxford man?"

Again, there was some laughter on the line. "Good heavens, surprised you could even think such a thing. No, just interested to know if this is likely to become a scandal. I'm picking up a whiff of something nasty, so I'd like to be prepared."

She thought about what to reply.

"I think you should become prepared, sir. What I've seen and heard is very nasty. I'd suggest you wait, and if panic sets then, perhaps we should meet."

There was silence on the line for a moment.

"As bad as that, Chief Constable?"

"It's bad enough already, but it could get even worse, unfortunately."

"Are the same players still involved?"

"If you mean Paul Rigby, the president of St. John's, and the principal of St. Hilda's, and possibly the warden of Keble, then yes. Perhaps also a man called Caterham, if that means anything to you, sir."

Again, the line went quiet. She detected the permanent secretary digesting what he'd heard. She also thought she detected a sigh.

"Diligent fellow, Superintendent Barnes. It sounds like he's got a full house. I expect we'll be in touch again soon."

"Do you know what this is all about, Permanent Secretary?"

"What on earth makes you say that?"

"A sensation that I've picked up from what you've said, or to be more accurate, what you've not said. Superintendent Barnes doesn't buy any of the explanations he's so far been offered, believes there's a sinister motive behind the cover-up. I just feel you know something you're not telling me."

"An extraordinary thing to say. I look forward to our meeting before long, Chief Constable."

He rang off, and she sat thinking about the conversation. She rather liked and respected the permanent secretary, but he'd left her puzzled for some reason. She decided there was something he was keeping back, and the mention of Caterham, Charlie's father, seemed to be significant.

Meanwhile the superintendent had an appointment to keep at St. Hilda's.

He was shown into the room where the principal, Professor

Dame Mary Knight, was seated behind her desk. She remained seated as he entered and looked displeased.

"Chief Superintendent, your demands to see me at short notice are becoming irksome. I told you on your last visit that I have nothing more to say."

He remained standing and looked directly into her face. "Thank you for seeing me again, Professor. I'd like to show you something."

He reached into his document case and laid a folder on her desk. He withdrew a photograph and placed it in front of her.

"This is a photograph of the young woman who you told me had overreacted when we last met. She was attacked by four men, undergraduates, held down and stripped of her clothes before being raped and knocked unconscious. This is the scene when the police arrived."

He watched the principal's eyes staring at the photograph with a shocked expression, which quickly turned to anger before she looked up and glared at him.

"What sort of cheap trick is this? You are a disgrace. I shall report you to the chief constable. Get out! Leave at once."

She pushed the photograph away. He picked it up and held so that it was still visible to her.

"She is called Amelia Sheridan, an undergraduate of St. Hilda's. Her attackers ran away laughing when bystanders came to her rescue. After being treated at the scene, she was taken by ambulance to the John Radcliffe Hospital."

She remained glaring at him as he continued.

"But you know all this, don't you, Professor?"

"I know nothing of the sort. Leave my office at once."

She picked up her telephone and shouted into the handset, "Veronica, call security and have this man removed from my office."

She put the handset back. The superintendent was unperturbed and took another document from his folder.

"During the night Miss Sheridan was removed from the John

Radcliffe and taken by private ambulance elsewhere. This is a copy of the authorization to release her, signed by one of your officials. You can clearly read his name."

He placed the document in front of her. He noticed she almost flinched away. The door to the office was opened and two uniformed security men entered. She pointed to the superintendent. They advanced to either side of him and gripped his arms.

"Come on. Don't struggle and come with us, sir."

The superintendent didn't move but simply said, "If you don't remove your hands, then I'll have you arrested for assaulting a police officer. I shall also have you arrested, Professor, for aiding and abetting them."

He felt the grip on his arms loosen and could sense the uncertainty of the guards. The principal said nothing, and the guards eventually released their grip.

The superintendent turned to face the two guards and produced his warrant card to show them. They both stared at the card before one quietly said, "Sorry, Chief Superintendent, I didn't realize. Nobody told us."

"Please leave me alone with the professor."

They left the room, and the door closed.

"I will discover where Miss Sheridan was taken and what happened to her. You will save me time and help yourself if you tell me everything you know."

She sat looking at him. He sensed she was about to say something but hesitated. Eventually she lowered her gaze and quietly said, "As I've already explained, there is nothing I have to say. Please go."

He sighed. "That is unfortunate. I shall also discover why you behaved so reprehensibly and why you have conspired in the cover up of an appalling crime. That is a very serious charge which carries a long prison sentence."

She remained silent. It was as he anticipated. He had one more message to give her.

"At some point my officers will come to arrest you. You will be taken into custody for questioning, and you will then almost certainly be charged."

She looked up, and he sensed her defiance.

"You can't prove I've done anything wrong. You have nothing with which to charge me. We know that you are simply on a fishing expedition."

So, they still thought he was fishing. That should change when she told them about this meeting.

He smiled at her and gently shook his head. "Wishful thinking on the part of you and of your accomplices. But if that is true, then you have nothing to fear, Professor. My advice is don't believe anything they tell you."

He gathered up the photograph and documents and returned the folder to his case. He left the room without another word.

He sat in the back of the car on the return to Kidlington reflecting on the meeting. The professor was obstinate and arrogant; she still refused to grasp the reality of the situation. But she was shaken by the photograph, he was sure of that. Nevertheless, she was determined to deny it and grasped at the possibility that it was a fake, a "cheap trick" as she put it. That should change when word got to Paul Rigby. Even if he'd long ago destroyed the records from Oxford Central, he'd remember the photographs. The authorization to release Amelia Sheridan from the hospital should also stir things up. Teagle had somehow dug it out of the hospital records. It confirmed James Marsden's story of events. It also showed the name of the official at St. Hilda's who had attended.

He'd leave the professor to pass on the news of his visit and wait for the reaction. He didn't expect it would be a long wait. Meanwhile he'd check on Teagle's progress.

Teagle and Duggan reported what they'd done. They had initially met with resistance by the colleges. Teagle served the warrants and explained that if cooperation was not forthcoming, then a team of police officers would be attending to conduct searches. After some hasty phone calls, the college departments concerned decided that cooperation was the best alternative. Even so, it had taken time to delve into the records from ten years ago.

"To summarize, sir, we have the last known addresses for all four you called witnesses, but these have not been updated since they graduated and left and so may be the home addresses of their parents."

"Did they all graduate that same year, just after the assault?"

"Yes, within days they had all gone down, left Oxford, I expect. Interestingly, Elspeth Robertson was at St. John's and read PPE."

"That is interesting, I knew she was at St. John's but not that she'd read PPE. She would have known Professor Plowright then?"

"That occurred to me too, sir."

What about Fiona Mathews, another witness? She was at Lady Margaret Hall; did you know her?"

"Sorry, her name is not familiar, sir."

"Pity. What about the three police officers who attended the scene?"

"All transferred from Oxford Central shortly after it happened but are still in the Thames Valley Force; details also in our report, sir. We've also got the last addresses of Jacob Wagner and Robert McClennon, the other two of the gang, but these also have not been updated since they left Oxford. Wagner's address is in Switzerland. They both graduated just after the assault, like Caterham. As you know, Scot-Wadham was a second-year student but didn't return to finish his degree.

"Amelia Sheridan, who you said was the victim, was also a second-year undergraduate. She was at St. Hilda's, and she also didn't return for the final year. Unusually, very unusually I'm told, she was awarded her degree 'in absentia' on the recommendation of the principal of St. Hilda's and supported by the president of St. John's. We managed to obtain her address, but, again, it's not been updated since she left, sir. We did try to see if there were more up-to-date addresses for anyone on the alumni register. The colleges all maintain one; it's used to keep contact with graduates, but there's nothing recorded for them."

He sat thinking about it. All those connected to the assault left Oxford almost immediately afterward. That was convenient. Teagle interrupted his thoughts, "What do you want us to do next, sir?"

"Before anything else, I should tell you what happened on that night in Oxford. It's quite dreadful and extremely sensitive, as you'll hear."

He explained the events in detail to them both. That sat and listened with rapt attention. Duggan was astonished by it; Teagle had guessed part having been more involved with things but was taken aback by the reality of what had happened in the boatshed and the cover-up.

Neither said a word as he spoke and sat looking shocked as he finished. Eventually Duggan asked, "Sir, what do you think happened to the poor woman, Amelia Sheridan?"

"I don't know, Duggan. We need to find out."

"I now understand why you were so keen that I searched for her release authorization from the John Radcliffe Hospital."

"That's a vital piece of evidence, Teagle. It substantiates Inspector Marsden's narrative of events that night. Anyway, there's a great deal to do, and we need to prioritize things.

"First thing, get those three officers who attended at the scene to Kidlington, and we'll take their statements about that night and what happened to them subsequently. That should add more substance to what Inspector Marsden told me.

"While you are organizing that, check out the address for Amelia Sheridan. I just want to know if it is current. Do the same for all the other addresses. Don't let any of them know that it's a police inquiry."

The following morning the superintendent, with Teagle present, interviewed the three officers in turn.

Initially each was reluctant to talk, explaining that the then chief constable, Paul Rigby, had ordered them never to discuss the events of that night. He'd said the order came from the highest level and that the matter would be dealt with confidentially.

The superintendent showed each the photograph of the scene in the boathouse showing the unconscious Amelia Sheridan after she'd been assaulted and raped.

"You attended this scene. It is now a criminal investigation. There was no high-level clearance given to cover it up. I want chapter and verse about your role."

They each gave similar accounts confirming Inspector Marsden's statement of events. After accompanying Marsden to make the arrests, they helped Marsden write up the report. They were aware of the visit of the college officials and the intervention of the chief constable. Marsden was very upset, angry. They'd each gone off shift and returned home, leaving Marsden at Oxford Central. It was the last they saw of him.

Later that day they'd each received phone calls at home ordering them to Kidlington. The chief constable, Paul Rigby, saw them together in his office. He was accompanied by a superintendent. All three officers were ordered to forget what had happened and never to speak about it. They were told that they would be transferred from Oxford Central and to return home on leave until then. They were ordered not to return to Oxford Central.

Afterward, Teagle and Duggan took written statements from each of the officers.

That afternoon the superintendent read through the statements. It was difficult to believe that Paul Rigby could shut down the investigation so easily and so effectively. Only Inspector Marsden had put up resistance, but even he had quickly been compelled to fall into line, albeit very reluctantly and not before he'd made copies of the records. It demonstrated a rotten culture at Thames Valley Police Force. He hoped it was confined only to

Oxford Central. He hoped it was also confined only to Paul Rigby's tenure, but he was beginning to doubt it.

He recognized the name of the superintendent accompanying Rigby at the meeting. He'd been promoted to chief superintendent and retired at the time Rigby became chief constable of the Greater Manchester Force, shortly before Barnes joined Thames Valley. He made a note; at some point that retired chief superintendent would be interviewed.

He was interrupted by the telephone.

"Hello, Chief Superintendent; Marsden here, to let you know that I've had Paul Rigby on the phone. Very angry, accused me of giving you information. He knew I'd been to see you. I told you word would get around."

"What did you say?"

"Said I couldn't help him. He swore at me and threatened dire consequences if I didn't keep my mouth shut."

"Did he say what information?"

"He did. Mentioned a photograph and a discharge document from the John Radcliffe. Told him I didn't know anything about it. Funny that, there was no discharge document in my folder."

"You're right, there wasn't. I'll tell you about it another time. Meanwhile, thanks for your call and please let me know if anything else happens, and don't worry."

"Best of luck, sir."

He put the phone down. Clearly news of his meeting with Professor Mary Knight at St. Hilda's had reached Rigby. He wondered who else had heard about it. He soon discovered. The chief constable knocked and opened his door.

She sat down and asked him to bring her up to date. He told her everything that had happened since they last spoke.

"It gets worse, Graham. What do you think will happen next?"

"By now they must know that I'm not on a fishing expedition as they call it. Or at least Paul Rigby must know; he saw the original file and photographs. It worries me that he knows of Marsden coming to see me. I'm guessing that he'll soon know that I've also taken statements from the three police officers.

"Anyway, I expect they'll now try again to get the investigation shut down."

She smiled. "They already have. The Home Office has called me. It has detected a sense of panic from whoever is complaining about you. Apparently, you are fabricating evidence to try and suit your purpose. The principal of St. Hilda's is distressed about what you are falsely alleging."

He smiled. "So, what do you think will happen next, ma'am?"

She smiled back at him. "I can tell you exactly. You are coming with me to the Home Office. The permanent secretary wants to know what you've been doing. My car leaves in thirty minutes."

They were ushered into the permanent secretary's office in Westminster nearby the Houses of Parliament. Also in attendance was an undersecretary.

The permanent secretary smiled and waited until they were all seated.

"Well, Chief Superintendent Barnes, you are upsetting the good citizens of Oxford. Are you going to uncover something unpleasant that I should want to know about?"

The superintendent hesitated briefly before replying.

"I very much doubt that I am upsetting the good citizens of Oxford, sir."

The permanent secretary smile broadened. "Point taken, Superintendent. Perhaps these are not-so-good citizens. But please, tell me."

"I have discovered something unpleasant, sir. A cover-up by the Thames Valley Police of a serious crime ten years ago."

His smile had disappeared. "Is it going to cause embarrassment to the Home Office?"

"If it becomes publicly known, then it almost certainly will."

"Will it become publicly known?"

"The investigation of a crime has been suppressed for ten years, and it is now fundamental to a multiple murder investigation. If the murders result in a trial, then it will become public knowledge. I imagine that is why you are under pressure to shut down my investigation."

The permanent secretary sat looking at him.

"Would exposing it serve any practical purpose in solving your murder investigation? If this has been hidden for ten years, why not let it alone?"

The superintendent now sat staring at the permanent secretary.

"Forgive me, sir, but with all due respect, my job is to uphold the law and to investigate crime. A crime has been covered up which affects my investigation, and I want to know why because it has a bearing. It may be the motive for murder."

"Chief Superintendent, that's all very well, but there are wider issues to be considered."

"My remit is narrow, sir. It doesn't allow me to consider wider issues. The day that I stray from the law to allow for the so-called greater good is the day that I should resign"

"But will your investigation succeed, Chief Superintendent? Will the embarrassment caused by exposing something that happened ten years ago be worth it?"

The superintendent sighed. "Sir, nothing is certain. I may not succeed in solving the crime, but I shall do my utmost. Sorry, but I can't answer about the embarrassment."

The permanent secretary was silent. It was clear that he was trying to imagine the possible consequences, but the superintendent decided to continue. "Sir, again with respect, I believe we are missing the point. Ten years ago, a serious violent crime was not investigated and was covered up by the police; dealing with that will almost certainly be damaging to Thames Valley Police, and perhaps for my chief constable even though it preceded her appointment. But to ignore it would be a greater crime, in my humble opinion. It should properly be reported to the IOPC, the independent office for police conduct."

The permanent secretary looked at the chief constable. "Have you thought through the consequences, Chief Constable?"

"I have, and I don't relish what may occur, but the superintendent is correct."

He nodded at her and turned and asked, "How do you want to handle this, Superintendent?"

"I'd like to continue my murder investigation, sir. There is a long way still to go. In the meantime, because the police cover-up is intertwined with my four murders, I would appreciate the IOPC not being involved until I've finished. That should give a better chance to find out the real reason behind the cover-up."

"Yes, the chief constable told me that you didn't believe it was to safeguard the reputations of the four undergraduates."

"No, sir, I don't believe that. It is something else, I'm sure."

"Maybe I can help. We've done a little research since this cropped up. The chief constable told me the names of the players involved, and it rang a bell. Apparently, there was some unease ten years ago about property development involving St. John's. It died away, and nothing further was done about it. It might be worth following up on it."

"Thank you, sir. That's very interesting. Greed is usually the motive for many a crime. Do we have your approval to continue?"

"Of course. Sorry if I caused you any doubt. Is there anything else I can do to help?"

"It might help if next time you receive complaints about me from those not-so-good Oxford citizens, you could say that I am struggling with my investigation but that it must be left to play out, sir."

The permanent secretary looking quizzically at him and then smiled. "It'll be my pleasure, Chief Superintendent."

On the journey back to Kidlington, they discussed what had happened.

"That went well, Graham. You got what you wanted. Although I don't think the permanent secretary was ever going to interfere; he was just testing you."

"Thank you, ma'am. He's also given me a clue; money could make sense as a motive for the cover-up. Will all this create difficulties for you?"

"I expect so. Eventually, Paul Rigby should go to prison, and then I'll probably have to resign."

"That sounds harsh. It happened before your appointment. Why should you resign?"

"I didn't spot it. There was always something odd about Rigby's leaving. Meanwhile, I need to discover what's been going on at Oxford Central since. I've been wondering if I should bring Marsden back from Newcastle; I suspect he'd know what to look for and how to clean things up if necessary."

Teagle reported the progress that she and Duggan had made.

"As we thought, sir, the addresses we obtained from the colleges were out of date, except for Amelia Sheridan, the victim. We've been able to verify that she still resides there. It's in Dorset, southwest England.

"We've obtained up-to-date addresses for all four witnesses. But we've had no luck with the other two in the gang of four. Wagner's address was that of his parents in Switzerland; McClennan's was also his parents' home address at the time, but his parents have since separated and remarried. We have their new addresses, but we've not made contact yet. What next, sir?"

"The next step is to visit Amelia Sheridan. We need her to talk to us. I imagine it will be a delicate subject, but there's no avoiding it. I'm wondering how best to approach it."

"It may be better if I visit with Duggan, sir. It would be less intimidating without you appearing, and I've also got something in common with her, having been up at Oxford around that time."

"It had been my thought as well, Teagle, although at some point I will need to formally interview her. Meanwhile you and Duggan can break the ice and prepare her and hopefully persuade her to talk to you."

CHAPTER 12

It was the following morning when Teagle with Duggan approached the house set in extensive grounds overlooking the sea, the English Channel.

The imposing door was opened by a housekeeper. Teagle and Duggan introduced themselves and asked if this was the home of Amelia Sheridan. The housekeeper nodded and invited them into a hallway and asked them to wait.

After a few minutes another woman approached them and introduced herself as Carol Reynolds. She looked around forty years old, had a pleasant face, wore spectacles, and was neatly dressed. She asked if she may help them.

"We really need to talk to Miss Sheridan herself," Teagle explained.

"You've come a long way, from Oxford, Sergeant. It would have been better if you had telephoned first. However, let us sit and talk. Perhaps you can tell me about the purpose of your visit."

Reynolds led them both into a reception room and asked them to sit.

"I don't want to be unhelpful, Sergeant, but one of my roles is to protect Miss Sheridan. It will be necessary for you to tell me why you have come unannounced to see Miss Sheridan before I can let you see her."

The door opened, and the housekeeper entered carrying a tray of coffee.

"Thank you, Sarah. I imagine that after your journey, you would both appreciate some coffee." The tray was set down, and the housekeeper left the room.

"Please help yourselves to coffee and tell me why you are here. It will be best, I assure you."

Teagle gathered her thoughts. This was not what she expected.

"Thank you, ma'am. This is a very grand house, and from what we know, it was Miss Sheridan's address before she was at Oxford. Can you provide some background for me?"

Reynolds looked at Teagle and thought about how much to tell. The Oxford connection worried her.

"Miss Sheridan was orphaned as a child; her parents died in an air crash. She was brought up by her elderly spinster aunt, whose house this was. The aunt died four years ago."

"How long have you lived here? I presume that you do live here with Miss Sheridan?"

"I've lived here for nearly ten years. I was employed by Miss Sheridan's aunt and have stayed on in my role."

"What exactly is your role?"

"Miss Sheridan is in a delicate state. I am her companion, but I also protect her and ensure her welfare. Her aunt employed me to do that and left provision for me to continue after her death. I am in fact Miss Sheridan's legal guardian."

Teagle was surprised but began to understand the situation.

"Why does Miss Sheridan need a legal guardian?"

"Her mental state is fragile; she is vulnerable."

"Miss Sheridan was an Oxford undergraduate. When did this become necessary."

Reynolds stared at Teagle and said, "Why don't you tell me why you are here?"

"I'm sorry, ma'am; I'll try. It's about an incident which happened in Oxford ten years ago. We believe that Miss Sheridan was the victim of a serious assault. We're trying to discover what happened and would like to interview Miss Sheridan."

Reynolds sat silently and expressionless before speaking.

"That is not going to be possible, Sergeant, for several reasons. Miss Sheridan's mental state is a direct consequence of that incident, and she is in no condition to answer any questions about it. To try and do so would almost certainly cause her trauma.

"Another reason is because the police, your Thames Valley Force, refused to investigate at the time, and Miss Sheridan and her aunt were pressed into withdrawing any complaint. Before your visit today, I was prewarned of your possible approach and reminded about a legal undertaking. As her legal guardian, neither can I help you, much as I would like to."

Teagle was astonished. It was unbelievable. She wondered what to do.

"I'm desperately sorry to hear that, ma'am. It is a terrible situation, and I would desperately like to help. Can you at least tell me some more about why you, at least, can't answer our questions?"

Reynolds hesitated. She wondered how far she might go without compromising her position.

"I will try. Immediately after the attack—yes, it was a vicious assault—Miss Sheridan was in hospital. Her aunt then had her brought here and arranged further nursing care. In the weeks which followed, it became clear that Miss Sheridan's mental health had been affected. She became delirious at times, had nightmares, would not leave her room. She has not been away from this house and its grounds in the ten years since.

"Her aunt was bitter about the injustice of the situation. She wanted to take the matter to court, but the college authorities continued to press her to let the situation alone. They said that it would serve no purpose to force a prosecution. It would be Miss Sheridan's word alone, and it would also be a traumatic experience for her.

"During this time, the aunt was becoming increasingly concerned about the future. The medical prognosis was that Miss

Sheridan would require special care for a long time, maybe even for the rest of her life. The medical advice was that Miss Sheridan would be best off in these surroundings, somewhere she was at ease with, where she had grown up. Although well off financially, the aunt was elderly, and the cost of funding such care, in this house, for perhaps sixty or seventy years was beyond her means.

"In the end, the aunt, in desperation, accepted a settlement with the college authorities. In return for a lump-sum payment to support Miss Sheridan, the aunt made an agreement not to prosecute nor to divulge what had happened. The aunt was by then Miss Sheridan's legal guardian.

"I had already been appointed as a companion to Miss Sheridan. When the aunt became too frail, at her request I was appointed as legal guardian in her place. In due course, I will have to arrange for someone to replace me. I would like to help you, and to right an injustice, but my hands are tied."

Teagle and Duggan sat quietly, digesting what had been said. Teagle's mind was racing. There were so many questions she wanted to ask, but she decided that now was not the time. Eventually she just asked, "You said that you were prewarned about our visit today. Who did that?"

"It was a solicitor. It was to remind me of the aunt's agreement not to divulge information about the attack. I was told that agreement now extends to me as legal guardian. Any breach of it could cause an action to recover the funds provided for Miss Sheridan's care. I can't take that risk."

"Who was the solicitor representing?"

"St. John's College."

"Thank you for explaining. I'll report it to Chief Superintendent Barnes. He's heading this investigation, and I expect he'll want to see you."

She'd watched them through the window when they had arrived earlier. Two women who stepped from the car. The younger, slimmer, dark-haired one seemed about her own age. Both were dressed in formal dark clothes, and she imagined they might be accountants or solicitors come to see Carol.

Now she watched them leave. As they got into the car, she could clearly see their faces. The younger one looked familiar somehow; she felt sure they'd met before. She'd ask Carol.

The superintendent listened to Teagle's report about the visit to Dorset. He shouldn't have been surprised; he should have antic-ipated something like this. The fate of the unfortunate Amelia Sheridan made him even more determined to extract justice for her.

Her misfortune had played into the hands of those responsible. Had Amelia Sheridan not been so traumatized by what happened, he doubted that the cover-up could have succeeded. It also left unanswered questions: How was it possible to keep the witnesses quiet, for example? Where had Miss Sheridan been between leaving the John Radcliffe Hospital and then transferred to the home of her aunt? What had happened to her in that period? Was she receiving the best treatment to try to cure her? He doubted that those responsible would want to have her cured.

He thought about the settlement agreement. It sounded as though it was between St. John's College and the aunt. Could it legally also apply to Carol Reynolds? Would St. John's realistically sue for breach of agreement bearing in mind the unwelcome publicity? He needed to see that agreement, and then he needed legal advice.

In addition, he had yet had to identify two of the bodies in the pond. He expected they were Wagner and McClennon, but he had to prove it. Then he had to find the murderers and discover how the bodies came to be in the pond.

All the while his mind kept wondering about why there had been such an elaborate and audacious attempt at cover-up.

The following day he was outside the house in Dorset with Teagle. She had telephoned and alerted Carol Reynolds to expect them.

It was as Teagle had described, a large, impressive house with extensive, well-maintained grounds—no doubt expensive to run before the added costs of care for Amelia Sheridan. He could well understand why the aunt had been anxious about funds for her niece's lifetime care.

It was Carol Reynolds who greeted them at the front door and led them to the reception room where coffee was already waiting.

"Thank you for agreeing to see me, Miss Reynolds. Following your meeting with Sergeant Teagle, there are some questions I need to ask."

"As I told the sergeant yesterday, for various reasons I'm legally restricted in what I can say."

"So I understand. Perhaps we can clarify that first. Can you show me the agreement which restricts you?"

She hesitated, "Actually, I can't. I don't have it. In fact I've never seen it."

"So how do you know about it, ma'am?"

"Well, I know there is an agreement. I remember the fuss about it. I was working here then. The aunt spoke to me about it. She was very unhappy at having to accept it but said it was a practical arrangement to help Miss Sheridan. I explained the reasons to the sergeant."

"So you've not seen any agreement but still believe you are bound by one?"

"As I explained, that's because a solicitor contacted me some days ago to inform me about it, and to warn me about your possible visit."

"Who was that solicitor?"

"I'm sorry, but I didn't make a note. He said he was acting for St. John's College in Oxford."

"Presumably the aunt would have retained a copy?"

"Yes, I expect it's held by the solicitors who acted for her. They still act for the estate and act as its trustees. The aunt left her entire estate to be held in trust for Miss Sheridan. They are based in Dorchester; I can give you the address."

"We'll need that before we leave. Can you tell me which hospital was looking after Miss Sheridan following her attack and before she returned here?"

"I'm sorry, but I don't know, Chief Superintendent. I wasn't employed until after that."

"Does Miss Sheridan receive specialist medical care?"

"She does have a specialist who visits regularly. I think it was arranged by the aunt. It continues still, although Miss Sheridan doesn't enjoy the sessions. I have wondered about the benefit of it. I've been meaning to speak the family doctor about it; she also visits periodically."

"Are drugs given to Miss Sheridan?"

"Yes, unfortunately. The specialist says they are necessary."

"I'd like the name of that specialist and of the family doctor before we leave, please. Does Miss Sheridan receive any visitors?"

"Nobody comes these days. Her parents were killed in a plane crash when she was young. Her only relative was her aunt, who took her in and eventually adopted her. There were a few visitors to see her years ago, but none recently. She lives a lonely existence; I would like her to have some friends, but the specialist recommends against visitors if possible. It has proved difficult, as you can imagine."

"The visitors who came before, who were they?"

She hesitated. He sensed a problem for her. Finally, she answered, "I can't really remember; sorry."

He looked at her and could see she was uneasy. He wondered why.

"Did any of the witnesses to the attack on Miss Sheridan ever visit?"

She was clearly uncomfortable.

"I'm sorry, Chief Superintendent, but I don't think that I should discuss the attack. The agreement, you see."

"No reason why you can't tell me, ma'am. We know who the witnesses are, and we'll be questioning them later."

She looked anxiously at him before replying, "I hope you are right. Anyway I want to help. Her aunt had no idea that there were witnesses until one called about two years after the attack. Miss Sheridan couldn't or wouldn't discuss what had happened to her or couldn't remember. The aunt managed to piece together most of what had taken place, and there were also the nightmares when Miss Sheridan relived it and screamed out at her attackers.

"When the witness turned up and explained everything, we were horrified. Had the aunt known, she would never have made the agreement to keep things quiet. The aunt became increasingly angry and even more bitter about things. It seems that the witnesses had been somehow persuaded to forget about it for the sake of Miss Sheridan."

"Who was that witness?"

"Elspeth Robertson"

"Were there further visits?"

"There were, over a period of two or three years I suppose. Another witness called as well sometimes—Fiona Mathews, I think that was her name. They spent time with the aunt together. Then they stopped coming. They saw Miss Sheridan, but she couldn't remember them, or had somehow blotted them from her mind."

The superintendent decided not to ask any more questions on this visit. There was a lot to think about and much do from what had already been said.

"Thank you for your help, Miss Reynolds, and don't worry. I'm going to stop there for the time being. I want to obtain the agreement to study it. Can you please obtain those names and addresses before we leave?"

"Of course. By the way, Sergeant, I think your warrant card gives your first name as Alice. Did you go to Oxford university?"

"I did, Lady Margaret Hall. Why do you ask?"

"Miss Sheridan saw you arrive and leave yesterday and thought she knew you. Told me she thought your name was Alice."

Teagle hesitated and looked at the superintendent. She tried to remember the photograph of the crime scene. She hadn't recognized the face of Amelia Sheridan in it.

"How odd. Did she say where she knew me from?"

"She thought she'd played against you at tennis. Do you play tennis?"

"I played for my college."

"Miss Sheridan played for St. Hilda's. Could you have met?"

"I suppose so."

"Would you like to meet her? I promised I'd ask you."

She looked at the superintendent. He nodded his approval.

"Yes, please, if that's all right."

"I've told her that you came from the accountants; they visit regularly. I didn't want to mention the police, and I hope you won't ask any questions."

"I understand. Thank you."

"I'm afraid you'll have to wait here, Chief Superintendent; I hope you understand?"

Teagle followed her with some apprehension across the hallway and into a drawing room comfortably furnished and with easy chairs. It overlooked the approach to the front of the house.

A slim, pale, pleasant-looking woman her own age stood up and smiled.

"I thought it was you, Alice, when I saw you leaving yesterday."

Teagle stared at her and then smiled back at her. "Bunny, how lovely. How are you?"

She walked toward her, and they hugged each other.

"You only just beat me in that final, but it was a good match, Alice. A long time ago."

"Over ten years ago, but I'll not forget it. We had a party afterwards."

181

"A good party. They were fun times."

"Do you still play, Bunny?"

"Afraid not. We have a nice court here, but I've not played for a long time."

"Can you show it to me?"

Bunny hesitated and looked at Carol Reynolds. Teagle saw Reynolds nod and smile back. "Why not show it to Alice? Have a stroll together."

Reynolds watched them disappear together chatting about tennis. She hoped she'd done the right thing; she'd not seen happiness in Amelia's eyes for a long time. She went to gather the details the superintendent had requested.

"This is a pleasant surprise. I never realized your proper name. You were always known as Bunny, not Amelia."

"I know; we all had funny names at my school, and somehow the names carried on to university."

"This is a lovely place to live, super grounds. Look at the view. Do the grounds go all the way to the seaside?"

In the distance across the fields was the English Channel.

"They go to the coast. It's a cliff, but we have a walkway down to the beach. I used to go there and swim in the summer, but I don't go anymore. We have a nice pool here which I use. Look, here's the tennis court."

It was a well-maintained grass court. It was freshly mowed, the net was in place, the lines were newly marked. Alongside was a small pavilion.

"Does anybody play on it?"

"I don't think so, but it's looked after just in case someone wants a game. It's the way my aunt used to like things."

"Your aunt sounds very nice."

"She was. She looked after me; she still does, I suppose. I miss her a lot. Carol looks after me now; she's a good friend."

"I ought to be getting back, Bunny. I'll be coming again. There are still some things to sort out with Miss Reynolds."

"Why don't you call her Carol?"

"I think it would a bit too familiar—professional etiquette and all that."

"When do you think you'll come again?"

"A few days, I imagine. I could bring my tennis kit, and we could have a game."

Bunny laughed. "I'll be rusty, well out of practice, but why not? It could be fun."

After saying goodbye, Teagle returned to explain to the superintendent and Carol Reynolds what had happened.

"I'm uncomfortable about you misrepresenting yourself, Teagle. It will cause problems later."

"If I'd said you are police officers, she may well have panicked. At least this way, Superintendent, you've broken the ice. She was more animated with the sergeant than I've seen her in a long time. It was an extraordinary coincidence, worth taking the chance surely?"

"I hope so, but I'm concerned too, sir. I think that on my next visit I must find a way of saying who I am. It's too much of a risk otherwise."

They sat together in the car to Dorchester to visit the family solicitor. It was on the way back to Kidlington, and Teagle had called to check that the partner they wanted was there.

"What are you thinking, sir?"

"Another set of coincidences, Teagle, and you know that I don't trust them."

"I agree the tennis is odd but that's all. I've just looked at that photograph again, and I can now see that it's Amelia, or Bunny, as I knew her, but it simply didn't register with me, and it's not a good likeness, unsurprisingly in the circumstances. I never knew her as Amelia Sheridan."

"I can accept that, Teagle, but it's the coincidence of the witnesses showing up that bothers me. Their first visit two years after the assault and then more visits for three years before they stopped."

"I agree it's a pity they didn't visit sooner. Things might have turned out differently if the aunt had known there were witnesses. But they visited and only talked with the aunt, who then became frail and subsequently died, so they ceased to visit again. Seems logical to me, sir."

"Those two witnesses turned up at the aunt's house not long before the first murder was committed and stopped visiting just after the final murder. That's the coincidence that bothers me."

Teagle grinned. "Bit of a stretch, sir. Are you suggesting the aunt and the two women witnesses are the murderers?"

"I'm not suggesting anything, but the coincidence bothers me. I also don't like that specialist continuing to treat Amelia Sheridan with drugs for ten years unchecked. That can't be correct."

"You don't know he is unchecked, sir. Perhaps the family doctor checks."

"We'll soon know because it's your next task; here are their details. Now let me get my thoughts straight for this family solicitor."

Thirty minutes later they were sitting in front of the family solicitor, a partner in the practice based in Dorchester. He was in his early sixties, professionally attired in a black three-piece suit with a crisp white shirt and a plain necktie. He was clean shaven with spectacles.

The superintendent outlined the purpose of the meeting, and the partner confirmed that he held the agreement signed by the aunt and called for it to brought to him.

"Do you know the circumstances of the agreement, Chief Superintendent?"

"I understand that it is to provide funds for the ongoing care of Amelia Sheridan in return for nondisclosure of what happened to her. Paid off to keep quiet, in other words."

"Very clearly expressed by you. It is precisely that."

"Who are the parties to the agreement?"

"Miss Sheridan's aunt, who also adopted Miss Sheridan as her daughter, is one party. I presume you know that history. The other party is St. John's College Oxford in the person of its president. The aunt agrees to nondisclosure in return for monies from St. John's."

"How much?"

"If you mean how much did St. John's pay, then in total £5,750,000. It was a hard-fought negotiation. St. John's pressed for the settlement, but the aunt was initially not disposed to one. Then she became concerned by the prognosis from a specialist about Miss Sheridan's care. The aunt was wealthy, but the lifetime costs and care for Miss Sheridan to continue living in the house would be demanding on her estate. The aunt also required that damages be paid for the harm done to Miss Sheridan; she insisted on some recognition by St. John's for what had happened, an acknowledge-ment of liability, if you like. We obtained an expert opinion, and that was accepted by St. John's."

"Is the aunt the only signatory to the nondisclosure?"

"She is. She signed in her own right and then also for Miss Sheridan as her legal guardian. Miss Sheridan was adjudged unfit to enter the agreement."

"So does the agreement bind Miss Sheridan?"

"It is unlikely it could be enforced against her if she is adjudged unfit, in my opinion. If she is later judged to be of fit mind, then again, in my view, it would also be difficult to enforce. It is but a nasty, grubby contract."

"The aunt is dead, so what does that mean?"

"I'm not sure. St. John's was quiet on the death of the aunt and remained so until very recently. It has now written and made clear that it expects the nondisclosure to bind Miss Reynolds, who succeeded the aunt as legal guardian. I have not yet responded; I need to take advice."

"Did you know that Miss Reynolds has received a call from a solicitor representing St. John's warning her of her obligations under this agreement. She is concerned not to hazard Miss Sheridan's ongoing care funding."

"I didn't know, Chief Superintendent. I shall contact her and give support and reassurance. As I said it is a nasty, grubby contract forced upon the aunt by a nasty, grubby Oxford college."

"Are you an Oxford man, sir?"

"As it happens, I am. Worcester College. The aunt later told me what she subsequently discovered had happened to Miss Sheridan, and I find the behavior of both the Thames Valley Police and St. John's College outrageous and unlawful. The aunt was unaware of it at the time of signing the agreement, and she simply sought a practical solution to try and mitigate against the misery heaped upon Miss Sheridan."

The superintendent felt ashamed. He also felt a deep anger at what had happened.

"I can fully understand your feelings, sir. Did Miss Sheridan inherit her aunt's estate?"

"In its entirety, to be held in trust for her benefit. I and my partner are trustees of both that and the settlement fund paid by St. John's."

"Presumably you, as trustee, discharge the running costs of the estate, pay wages, bills, etc.?"

"Yes, although it is managed by a firm of accountants with an estate manager on our behalf, but we are fully aware and control the outgoings. Similarly, we employ financial advisors to manage the estate's investments but under our control."

"Please tell me about the medical treatment Miss Sheridan receives. Do you organize that?"

The partner hesitated and looked puzzled. "Actually, we don't.

I know a specialist attends Miss Sheridan. He has done from the beginning. I understand that he is retained by Oxford university for this purpose. We don't pay fees to him. I've not met him."

"I find that surprising, sir."

"Yes, perhaps I should meet him. But surely, you're not suggesting anything suspicious, Chief Superintendent?"

"My job is to be suspicious, sir, and, as you've said, you are dealing with a nasty, grubby Oxford college. You say that he's an Oxford university appointee who has attended Miss Sheridan for ten years. Has he ever produced a report on her condition?"

"Not that I'm aware of."

"Do you know that he administers drugs to Miss Sheridan?"

"No."

"Is he authorized to do that without permission from her legal guardian, or another doctor, or from you as her trustee?"

"I'm not sure. Your comments have perturbed me. I shall inquire about it, Chief Superintendent."

"That would be wise, sir. Tell me please, do you know which hospital Miss Sheridan stayed in after her attack and before she was brought home by her aunt?"

"I did know; it was a private nursing clinic in or near Oxford."

"Is this it?"

The solicitor read the address on the document shown by the superintendent. It was the address of the specialist provided by Carol Reynolds.

"Yes, that's it."

"Thank you, sir. When the aunt subsequently discovered the details of the attack, did anything happen? What was the aunt's reaction?"

"She was bitterly angry and upset. She wanted me to sue Thames Valley Police and St. John's. College. She wanted those who'd committed the attack to go to prison. She wanted justice done. We discussed it and considered the possible consequences. Nothing could undo the damage already done to Miss Sheridan.

"Eventually she accepted that it would be a traumatic and public process. It would be costly with no guarantee of success; and it could jeopardize the funding agreement. I know she felt deeply upset that she'd somehow failed her niece. Later, towards the end of her life, she seemed more content. I think she realized that she'd done all she possibly could in the circumstances."

The superintendent looked more closely at him. "Is that all? It strikes me that she was a determined lady, unlikely to let an injustice go unpunished."

"Well, she was old by then, and perhaps tired. There was one odd thing which has always stuck in my mind. She asked me for the name of an inquiry agent, said she wanted to track down some relatives she'd lost contact with. We use an agent from time to time, and so I passed on the name. I asked her what had happened, but she never told me, said it didn't matter."

Teagle could sense the superintendent's interest and saw a slight smile cross his face.

"I'd like the address of that agent please."

They sat together in the back of the car. The superintendent had told his driver not to set off; he wanted to think things through.

"What are you thinking, sir? I think you caused the solicitor some consternation."

"I suspect he's competent and usually thorough, but he's kicking himself now. He should have checked on that specialist.

"I'm just beginning to realize the cunning of the St. John's president. I've underestimated him, Teagle."

"Do you want me to check out the specialist now?"

"I want him stopped from attending Amelia Sheridan until we've seen him. You can do that on the way. We're going to visit the inquiry agent. Address is in Newbury; it's on our way to Kidlington, and after that we'll go and surprise that specialist at the clinic near Oxford."

The address was near the center of Newbury. They got out of the car near a narrow lane and walked along to the doorway of a shabby building. It was a multioccupancy office building with six floors according to the name plates. "Universal Private Investigations. 4th Floor" was proudly displayed by the doorway. They were lucky; the inquiry agent was getting ready to go out as they arrived at his office.

"Don't often get a visit from a detective chief superintendent. What brings you here, sir?"

"Heard that you might be able to help me and just happened to be passing by."

"Pull the other leg. Who said I could help?"

"Can't tell you that. Just asked around, and your name came up."

"A likely story. So how can I be of service to Her Majesty's constabulary?"

The superintendent placed a piece of paper in front of him. It contained the name and address of the aunt.

"You made some inquiries for this lady. I imagine it was about eight years ago."

"Don't think so. Don't recognize the name. What did she look like?"

"An old lady."

"Sorry, can't remember. An old lady would be unusual. Any more details? My clients often avoid using their real names, and I promise discretion, if you know what I mean, Chief Superintendent."

"It was to try and track down some people. Possibly four men who'd previously been Oxford students."

The agent sat looking at the superintendent before answering, "I can sort of recall something. You're right, maybe seven or eight years ago. Not sure, but there wasn't an old lady involved."

"Come on, stop wasting my time. Tell me about it."

"Hang about, Chief Superintendent. Client confidentiality,

discretion, that sort of thing. My reputation depends on it. Anyway, what's in it for me if I tell you?"

"The gratitude of Thames Valley Police. If you don't, then I'll rustle up a search warrant and go through your files. How will that do?"

"Look, there's no need to get heavy. I just thought there ought at least to be something in it for me, that's all. It's hard to make a living at this job."

"It should be reward enough to know that you are helping the police with their inquiries. Now stop wasting time."

"OK, OK. It wasn't an old lady; it was a young woman. I'm certain. Can't describe her because she wore a headscarf, a Muslim scarf around her face, could only see her eyes. She gave me her name, but it'll mean nothing. She gave me a list of four names, men. They'd all been at Oxford University."

"Have you got the names?"

"It'll be in my files. Wait a minute."

He went to a row of filing cabinets along the wall of his office and started looking into various drawers until he exclaimed, "You were right, over seven years ago."

He removed four wallets and put them on his desk.

"It's come back now. Two were easy to find; they were in London area. The other two were difficult, took a longer time, gone abroad to Africa."

"Give me those files please."

He reached for them. He and Teagle looked at the names: Charles Caterham, Jacob Wagner, Robin Scot-Wadham, Robert McClennon.

"How did you find them?"

"Asked around like you do. Tricks of the trade. You don't want to know, Chief Superintendent. Lay out a bit of money in the right hands, and it's surprising what you can find out."

"How did you get paid?"

"Cash. It's quite usual in my profession. Lady gave me a deposit.

She telephoned me regularly to ask how I was getting on. If I'd been successful, I gave her the details. If I said I needed more money, she came in and paid me some more cash."

"Did you note the number she called from? It'd be on your logs."

"Don't do that kind of thing. Discretion guaranteed."

"We could look through your logs."

"You could indeed, Chief Superintendent, but I doubt you'd find anything useful. Seven years ago, and I get a lot of calls; anyway this woman was careful to make sure I couldn't identify her, so I doubt she'd leave you a telephone trail."

The superintendent thought about it. The agent was right: this had been carefully thought out.

"Very well. We'll take these files with us. Sergeant Teagle will give you a receipt. Thank you for your help. If you remember anything else, you know what to do."

"Always pleased to help, Chief Superintendent. For what it's worth, she was very well spoken, nice accent—posh, in my opinion."

They sat in the car as it was driven toward Oxford and the private nursing clinic.

"Well, Teagle, now what odds will you give me on the elderly aunt being behind the murders?"

"You already knew, sir. You'd worked it out before today's visits."

"Not really, but your report of yesterday's visit contained the clues. Too many coincidences and convenient circumstances. Let's find out what that medical specialist has been up to."

"I telephoned and told him to expect us, so he should be waiting."

"I'll bet you the president of St. John's already knows were on the way."

They were shown to a consulting room and were soon joined by the medical specialist.

"How can I help you, Chief Superintendent?"

"You've been treating Miss Amelia Sheridan for ten years; can you tell me why?"

"You know that I can't tell you that. Patient confidentiality."

"Ah, yes. But did she consent to be your patient?"

"Can't answer that either; again, patient confidentiality."

"I'll presume that she hasn't consented then, in which case I'm instructing you to stop treating her."

"I'm sorry, but you can't do that. This is none of your business."

"I've made it my business as a result of what I've discovered."

"What have you discovered?"

"You've not rendered any fees for her treatment nor provided any medical reports or explanations about the treatment."

"I certainly have. My services are paid for by the university; my invoices and reports go there."

"That's unusual. I can perhaps understand the university paying for the treatment, but your medical reports should go to her family doctor or otherwise her legal guardian or her trustee. What part of the university?"

"Look, Chief Superintendent, I don't want to be unhelpful, but mine is a private arrangement with the university, which has instructed me not to speak to you. Maybe the university passes on my reports to the family doctor."

"I need to know what happens to your reports. Who do I ask about it?"

He hesitated before replying, "I'm not sure that I should tell you that."

The superintendent smiled at him. "I can easily find out by looking at your invoices and patient records. I can also check who you telephoned since Sergeant Teagle made this appointment—your mobile phone or the clinic's logs will show that—but it'll delay things by a day, that's all. You did telephone to report this visit, didn't you?"

He looked embarrassed but said nothing.

"Sir, I strongly suspect that you have behaved unethically—most probably unlawfully. We'd better put you under caution. Sergeant, do me the honors please."

"You do not have to say anything, but it may harm your defense if you do not mention when questioned something which you later rely on in court. Anything you do say may be given in evidence."

"Thank you, Sergeant. Do you understand that, sir?"

He just nodded.

"Now, sir, you have two choices: you can cooperate now and save time, or I'll arrest you and take you to Kidlington for an interview in the presence of a solicitor. The choice is yours."

He looked dejectedly at them both and spoke quietly. "OK. I'm retained to treat Miss Sheridan by St. John's. I telephoned the president about your visit just before you arrived."

The superintendent looked grim as he spoke. "Thank you, sir. I have many more questions for you, but we'll do that formally in the presence of a solicitor. Sergeant Teagle will be in touch to arrange for that.

"Meanwhile you are to cease treating Miss Sheridan. Sergeant Teagle will remain here and collect details of the treatment you've given so far, and we'll notify the family doctor so that alternative arrangements can be made. Is that clear?"

He looked unhappy and simply said, "Yes."

It was nearly two hours later when Teagle returned to Kidlington. She'd used a taxi from the clinic.

"Did you get everything, Teagle?"

"All here, sir. He's paid well for his services, and the medical reports are brief, but he claims that more detailed reporting is given verbally to the president."

"All very unsatisfactory. Take copies for me and get the reports and anything else medical to the family doctor. Explain the situation to her and Miss Reynolds and the family solicitor. Before you do that, brief Duggan about getting forensics information on

Wagner and McClennon so that our pathologist, Doctor Watson, can discover if they match the two unidentified bodily remains from the pond. I'm confident that all four bodies will belong to that gang of four who assaulted Miss Sheridan, but we need to be certain."

"It might be difficult information to get, sir, and could take time."

"We need it, or else we need to find those two alive to rule them out. Maybe we should hire the inquiry agent?"

"You're not serious, are you?"

"No, Teagle, but get Duggan on to it. There's just too much to do, and I need time to think. I'll send for you when I'm ready. Don't approach the four witnesses yet."

CHAPTER 13

He'd spent the night and most of the following day analyzing and thinking it all through before he called for Teagle.

"I'm still convinced that all four of the gang who attacked Amelia Sheridan were murdered and dumped in that pond."

"I agree it points to that, sir. Have you worked out who did it?"

"No, but I'm increasingly sure the aunt orchestrated it. Her way of getting some retribution for what happened to her niece, her adopted daughter, Amelia. She'd been hoodwinked by St. John's and the police into thinking it was a lesser assault, probably drunken behavior which went wrong—no witnesses and difficult to prosecute. Then two years later she discovers there were witnesses who come and tell her the whole story and name the culprits.

"She's outraged but had by then signed the agreement, been duped into taking blood money from St. John's for the sake of her niece in return for keeping quiet; that's the way she would have seen it. She wanted revenge."

"I can understand that she'd want revenge, sir, although I can't imagine how she could have committed the murders."

"I agree. There's no way she could do it by herself, but she was determined and resourceful and clever. She found a way of discovering where they were. That inquiry agent was very effective, maybe even more so than us. Perhaps that was luck."

"You're assuming that whoever went to the inquiry agent was acting for the aunt."

"I am, but it seems the most plausible explanation."

"OK, sir, but that's the easy bit. How does she then get them murdered and dumped in a pond near Oxford?

"That's where I've come unstuck. I don't know. Those four culprits were in very different places, and at least two were abroad. Who did it, how, and where were they killed, and how come they all ended up in that pond, I don't know. There are no clues that I can see except for the connection of the aunt to two of the witnesses."

"Each murder was at a different time, sir."

"Agreed, and that's a clue as well. I expect we'll find that they were murdered in the order that the inquiry agent discovered each whereabouts, if you follow me."

"Do you think that might give us a lead?"

"It might do, but I'm not sure how. It's possible the inquiry agent's files might hold leads, but I've not found any yet. We might have more luck by going through the aunt's bank transactions; she probably had to pay someone to do the murders."

"She might not have been involved in the murders, sir. You did jump to the wrong conclusion before about the farmer, Symonds, being responsible. Maybe St. John's is responsible for the murders as well, part of the cover-up. It discovered what the aunt was doing, perhaps she told them she had discovered the identities of the culprits, and so it arranged the murders to stop them talking. It must be a possibility sir, don't you think?"

He stared at her and sighed. "You've just shot a hole in my theory, Teagle. I agree, it is another possibility. The fact is, we just don't know. But I'm convinced there must also be a connection to the farm; it's the only way to explain the pond being used. That's another puzzle, surely: only someone familiar with the farm could possibly know about that pond.

"Anyway, let's talk about the cover-up instead. A huge sum of money has been paid to keep things quiet. Nearly six million pounds to care for Amelia Sheridan and to avoid the aunt talking. Presumably others have been paid off as well, including, I imagine, Chief Constable Paul Rigby. That can't be simply to protect the reputations of four undergraduate thugs, can it?"

"I suppose if one of them was royalty or was someone special, it's possible, sir, but we've not come across anything like that."

"The president of St. John's is pulling the strings. I've underestimated him; he is particularly evil. I expect we'll find that the so-called medical specialist was put in place by him to make sure that Amelia Sheridan was kept out of the way and didn't cause any trouble."

"It's almost impossible to believe that he could manage to do that and is still doing it. I know that Paul Rigby cooperated with him, but even so."

"That's what's on my mind, and we don't know the motive, the real motive."

"What are you going to do, sir?"

"We're going to keep digging away until we find out. The permanent secretary gave me a hint, something about an old property development issue at St. John's, suggested we follow it up. Property development can involve a lot of money, and St. John's owns a lot of property.

"Charles Caterham's father also interests me. He is involved somehow. President knows him. Both want us off the case. I'd like you to find out about him."

"I'll get on to it, sir. Is it all right for me to go to Dorset tomorrow and see Amelia Sheridan? I need to visit about the medical reports. I spoke to the solicitor and the family doctor and Carol Reynolds as you instructed, and I've sent the reports to the doctor. All three want to speak to me about the situation. Amelia will expect me to see her, and I'll take my tennis kit as I promised."

"You must tell Amelia you're a police officer. You'll have to decide how much you say after that; it'll depend upon her reaction. Visit the family doctor beforehand and take guidance."

"Understood, sir. I never discussed what I did or why I was there when we met, so I haven't misled her."

"But we both know Carol Reynolds misrepresented you. Admittedly it was to avoid distressing Amelia, but nevertheless… important you don't let it continue."

"What do you intend doing next, Graham?"

He spent nearly an hour briefing the chief constable about the case.

"We'll keep digging away. Eventually we'll find the answer. It might take time. I'd like to bring Paul Rigby in and question him. I'd like to examine his finances; he'll have been on the make, been paid for his trouble."

"You know the rules. That's for the IOPC. You can't go arresting a chief constable. But you've now got enough to get IOPC involved if you want to."

"That can come later. He's unlikely to know the real reason for the cover-up. He's just in the pocket of the president of St. John's and maybe others. Involving the IOPC at this point could be counterproductive."

"Who else is involved, do you think, the principal of St. Hilda's?"

"Thought about that, ma'am. Interestingly, and despite her bluster, I think she was genuinely shocked to see the photograph of the scene in the boathouse showing Amelia Sheridan after the attack. I am beginning to think that she didn't know what had really happened. She refused to accept what I showed her, said I was pulling a cheap trick, implied I'd somehow faked the photo. Maybe like the aunt, she was misled and believed it was just an incident which got out of hand, fueled by drink. From her viewpoint, there was no formal complaint, and the police didn't make any charges. Instead, Amelia, her undergraduate victim, was looked after by the president, and he even endorsed her degree award despite her not completing the final year."

"That's no excuse for her the principal's behavior, and why

did she send an official to move Amelia from the John Radcliffe to that private clinic if she thought it was a minor incident? Why doesn't she cooperate in answering your questions if she's nothing to hide?"

"I agree with you, ma'am, but she might have another reason for her actions. Anyway, I don't believe she's a main player, that's all."

"Pity. So you'll just keep digging?"

"There is someone else who might stir things up for me, help things along. Do you recall Eddie Wiggins?"

"He retired soon after I took over here. A recently promoted chief superintendent but not up to the job as I recall."

"That's correct, ma'am. He was Rigby's assistant in this. He was present when the case was closed, and the officers involved were reassigned from Oxford Central. Got promoted by Rigby just before you took over. I imagine that he also had his snout in the trough of St. John's College. Anyway, I'm going to find out."

"Hello, Eddie. Not sure if you'll remember me. I'm Graham Barnes. You retired very soon after I joined Thames Valley at Kidlington."

The was a brief hesitation on the line before a reply. "Yes, I do remember. What can I do for you?"

"I'm hoping that you can help me. I've a murder inquiry going on. It involves four undergraduates who got into trouble ten years ago in Oxford. You were involved in getting the case dropped and having the officers involved reassigned. I expect you'll remember."

"Vaguely. The chief constable handled it mainly. Not sure I can help, sorry."

"I've got some questions. Can you get to Kidlington HQ to see me today or tomorrow?"

"Sorry, Barnes, I can't help, and I'm busy. Need to be on the first tee in forty minutes."

"Ah, golf; meeting friends there, I imagine. Where do you play?"

"The Oxfordshire."

"I've heard of it, near Thame; they say it's a good course, fine clubhouse. Anyway, I'll not interfere with your game today, although I do need to see you quite urgently. Probably best if I come over to your home tomorrow morning, say 9:00 a.m., save you the trouble of coming to Kidlington. Best of luck. Hope you have a good round."

He put the phone down before Wiggins could reply. He smiled to himself. That should have unsettled him enough to spoil his golf. Having learned something about Wiggins and his habits, and his friends, maybe he could unsettle him some more. He did a calculation: tee in forty minutes, eighteen holes of golf, drinks in the bar afterward. He called the traffic division.

As soon as the superintendent had terminated the call, Wiggins cursed aloud. He immediately called Paul Rigby in Manchester to tell him. Rigby told him not to mention the connection between them both, said he was keeping clear of Barnes and told Wiggins to do the same. Instructed Wiggins to "play dumb"; it would blow over, Barnes' investigation was struggling and would soon go away. He then cut the connection just like the superintendent had done. Wiggins was left holding a dead handset for the second time in less than fifteen minutes.

He cursed again. By now he was running seriously late to meet his tee time. He drove fast to the golf club and rushed to the locker room. His two playing partners were ready to go.

"Come on, Eddie, you're cutting it fine. We'll see you on the tee. Don't be late, or you'll forfeit the match; that'll cost you."

They laughed and left Wiggins to get ready. He got to the tee with a minute to spare. He put his golf ball into the proffered hat, which already contained two balls. One of them reached in and blindly drew a ball.

"It's yours, Eddie. You go first. Usual rules."

Wiggins was still breathing heavily from the exertion of rushing. He felt unsettled. He grasped his driver, placed his tee peg into the turf, and tried to balance his ball on it. His hand shook, and the ball fell off. Behind him was laughter.

"You don't seem your usual happy self today, Eddie."

Wiggins got the ball to balance on his next attempt. It went quiet as he attempted a practice swing. It felt all wrong. He could sense them smirking behind him. He moved up to address the ball, made the backswing, and then swung down on the ball. He connected. He looked up and saw the ball arcing in a slice to the right, and he watched with dismay as it disappeared into the out-of-bounds rough.

His partners exclaimed, "Oh bad luck, Eddie." "You've not done that recently." "That's two shots gone." "You'll have to play another ball."

Wiggins tried to smile as he again pressed a tee peg into the turf and balanced a new ball on it. With the penalty for going out of bounds, this would count as his third shot before he'd even got off the tee box. He stood for a minute trying to calm down and gather his wits.

"Don't hang around too long, Eddie, or we'll hold up the next group."

He grimaced, addressed his ball, swung, and knew it was a poor hit, but at least the ball went toward to fairway, if only for a hundred yards or so.

He heard an insincere "Well done, Eddie. Good recovery."

He stood unhappily alongside the tee box and watched his partners each drive off, quietly willing them to make a mess of it.

Instead, he watched glorious drives almost three hundred yards down the center of the fairway. He forced himself to say, "Well done; good shot." He said it twice.

He had an awful round. His mind kept going to his brief conversation with Rigby. He had sensed that Rigby was rattled; there was no confidence in his voice.

His partners, by contrast, played very well.

"Not your day, Eddie. We can see there's something worrying you. Come on, you can buy the drinks and tell us all about it."

They walked into the spike bar and ordered drinks on Wiggins' account. They took their winnings from him. He began to feel better after a couple of drinks. His partners left him to it and went home.

Wiggins stayed in the bar drinking alone and contemplating his bad luck, until the bar steward suggested he'd probably had too much and would he like a taxi called to take him home?

"No need, Harry. I'll manage OK. Not a problem for me."

He made unsteadily for the door. Harry assisted him and said, "Take care, Eddie," and received a slurred, "Thanks, see you soon, Harry."

The superintendent received the call around seven in the evening. It lasted only a few minutes. He put the phone down and made a few notes.

Thirty minutes later he went to an interview room. He watched from outside through the one-way glass window. He could see Wiggins and two police officers. One was a sergeant whom he recognized from traffic division. The other was a chief inspector from Kidlington HQ. He listened to the conversation.

"...sorry, sir, but I can't release him without charge. You know the rules."

"Don't be so stupid. You know this man was a chief superintendent here before he retired. You should not have breathalyzed him. Just delete the result and forget it. He's not caused any harm. Take him back to his car and let him get home."

"But, sir, he's way over the limit. He can't be allowed to drive."

"You are a fucking pain, Sergeant. Sorry about this, Eddie. I'll get someone else to take you. You can clear off, Sergeant. I'll sort you out later."

He watched the sergeant hesitate and then say, "This isn't right, sir."

"Just go, get out."

As the sergeant made to leave the interview room, the chief

inspector lifted a telephone and spoke into it. The sergeant left, closed the door behind him, and then noticed the superintendent standing looking through the glass. Together they watched and listened.

"All sorted, Eddie. I'll take you along to the front desk, and we'll get you on your way."

"Thanks, Norman, appreciate it. You need to sort that idiot sergeant out, both him and the officer with him. They knew who I was when they stopped me, and I told them, but they still went ahead and tested me. Bloody fools; makes me look a laughingstock."

The door opened, and they emerged to be confronted by the superintendent and the sergeant.

The superintendent was the first to speak.

"I'd not expected to see you so soon, Mr. Wiggins. Why don't we all go back into the room, and you can tell me what all this is about?"

The chief inspector answered, "No need to waste your time, sir; it's all sorted. Just a small misunderstanding by the sergeant. Easily been put right."

The superintendent stared at him. "Not from what I saw and heard it hasn't. Come on, tell me about it."

They reentered the room. Wiggins looked angry, and his face was flushed. The chief inspector and the sergeant appeared apprehensive.

"OK, sergeant what happened?"

"I was on patrol, sir, and we noticed a car driving erratically. We pulled it over, and Mr. Wiggins was driving it. We asked him to get out. He was unsteady on his feet, and he smelled of drink. I called my guv'nor, and he told me to breathalyze him. He was more than three times over the limit, so I called my guv'nor again and was told to bring Mr. Wiggins here and charge him."

"Do you normally call in before you breathalyze a driver?"

"No, sir, but it was Mr. Wiggins. There's a sort of understanding, if you know what I mean."

"Really, you surprise me. So then what happened?"

"Well, we put Mr. Wiggins's car in the golf club car park and then brought him here for processing as instructed. He got very angry and demanded that I speak to the chief inspector, which I did. He came and told me to drop it."

"Why did you do that, Chief Inspector?"

"It's a general rule, Chief Superintendent. We don't breathalyze our own. The sergeant knew that."

"Did you know that, Sergeant?"

"Yes, but I don't agree with it, sir. Anyway, I'd got new instructions not to apply the rule in future without checking in first, so that's what I did, and I was told to breathalyze Mr. Wiggins."

"When did you get these new instructions?"

"Today, sir."

"Why were you on patrol near the Oxfordshire golf club?"

"We'd been instructed to patrol there, sir."

"That was a bit of bad luck for Mr. Wiggins. Well, Sergeant, you must continue to process him and charge him. If he cooperates, he can then call for a taxi to take him home. Otherwise, keep him in a cell here overnight. Do not return his car keys; I'll give them to him when we meet tomorrow. I'd like to see you in my office, Chief Inspector."

Wiggins could not contain himself. He almost screeched the slurred words, "You bastard, Barnes, you'll pay for this."

The superintendent remained impassive and spoke quietly. "I'll see you at nine tomorrow morning, Mr. Wiggins, when hopefully you'll have sobered up."

Wiggins had decided to be cooperative and was released later that night. The superintendent arrived at his home at nine the following morning. It was a handsome property, in the affluent market town of Thame.

Wiggins still looked angry as he stood in the doorway.

"You've got a nerve, Barnes. I've got nothing to say. Just give me my car keys and clear off."

"I can take you back to Kidlington if you'd prefer."

They stood looking at each other until Wiggins invited him inside.

"You set me up. I'll lose my license now. It'll be bloody inconvenient and makes me look a fool. Why do it to me?"

"You did it to yourself. Now I'd like your answers to my questions."

"You must be joking. Anyway, I can't help you."

"I'm sure you can. You can start by telling me why you are an accomplice to covering up a serious crime ten years ago. You know what I'm talking about."

Wiggins was quiet for a moment, obviously thinking how to reply.

"You know how it works around here, Barnes. The Oxford colleges call the shots where their undergraduates are concerned. Makes sense: they bring a lot of money to the area and don't want reputations trashed just because of a few unruly youngsters. We just turn a blind eye from time to time."

"No, I don't know how it works, but I'm beginning to find out. So for how long have we been destroying evidence of very serious crime, closing down investigations, ordering police officers to ignore the law, and transferring them elsewhere if they don't comply?"

"Get real, Barnes. It's not usually like that. I admit, that particular case went a bit far, but the college was very keen to keep it under wraps. Anyway, no real harm was done."

"You couldn't be further from the truth. Why did you really do it? What was in it for you? You went to a great deal of risk because the college—St. John's, I presume—was very keen, as you put it."

Wiggins glared at him. "What do you mean 'What was in it for me'? I just did what seemed best in the circumstances."

The superintendent smiled at him. "Eddie, don't try to play the innocent. I expect that when we start digging around, then we shall see what you've been doing. Take what happened last night as a warning; that'll just mean you can't drive that nice expensive car of yours for a while.

"Imagine what might happen when we get to work on your finances over the years. It'll probably mean no car, no home, no golf club, and no friends but instead, a long stretch locked away at Her Majesty's pleasure. Don't expect convivial cellmates; prisoners take a definite disliking to bent ex–chief superintendents, but you don't need me to tell you that. You might be better off thinking hard about how you can help me."

Wiggins sat quietly, saying nothing.

"Another thing to consider, Eddie. If you harbor any hopes that your so-called friends in high places will come to your rescue, forget it. What happened to you last night demonstrated that you've been cast aside. You no longer have any friends in high places nor amongst the Thames Valley Police.

"I imagine that Paul Rigby has already been in touch and told you not to talk to me and that I'll soon be off the case. Don't believe a word of it. Rigby's only interested in trying to save his own neck."

Wiggins still remained quiet, but his earlier defiance had vanished.

"You've got forty-eight hours, Eddie. Give me chapter and verse; otherwise, I'm coming with a warrant to go through your affairs. You know where to find me."

He stood to leave and took the car keys from his pocket.

"Here you are: the keys to your car as promised. Be careful how you go."

On the way back to Kidlington, he thought about it. He was certain that Wiggins had been on the take; he was corrupt. With luck Wiggins would cooperate; he'd decide to try and save his own neck. The superintendent only hoped he knew enough to help things along.

The chief constable was going be unhappy about the events of the previous evening outside the Oxfordshire golf course. It suggested that it wasn't only Oxford Central which needed sorting out.

Wiggins meanwhile was on the telephone, talking again to Paul Rigby and explaining what had happened.

"Look, Eddie, I told you yesterday, don't get involved with Barnes. He's thrashing about trying to find something. He's putting you under pressure, that's all."

"That's all very well for you to say, Paul. I'm the one who'll lose my driving license. I'm the one he's going for."

"Just make sure he doesn't find anything. Don't talk to him, and don't involve me."

"But, Paul, you got me into this. You need to get Barnes off my back."

"You went into it willingly, Eddie, and did well out of it. Now you've just got to sit tight until Barnes decides to piss off. Don't drag me into it"

The handset went dead, and Wiggins cursed. It was just as Barnes had said: Rigby was only interested in saving his own neck. Well, two could play at that game.

Amelia Sheridan had been eagerly looking forward to Teagle's visit.

"Thanks for coming, Alice. I'm glad you could make it. Been ages since I had any friends here."

"I've been looking forward to it, Bunny, and nice to get a break from work. Is it OK to call you Bunny, or would you prefer Amelia?"

"I don't mind Bunny, although nobody else uses it these days."

"Why were you called Bunny?"

"I was shy at school, rather timid. Initially people said I was like a frightened bunny rabbit. Then I got called Bunny, and the nickname stuck."

"I think Amelia sounds a lot nicer. I'll call you Amelia."

They had a fun game of tennis. Both were out of practice, but soon their skills began to return, and they played some good long rallies.

Afterward they sat alongside the court in the sunshine. The housekeeper had laid out cold drinks and a light lunch. Carol Reynolds joined them.

They chatted together about their childhoods. Amelia seemed relaxed, and Teagle decided it was time to take the plunge.

"Amelia, after I graduated, I joined the police force."

Amelia hesitated and looked surprised.

"That's a funny thing to do. But Carol said you were an accountant, didn't you?"

"I know I did. Just didn't want to worry you. Sorry."

"Why should it worry me?"

It went quiet until Teagle said, "I've been investigating what happened to you ten years ago."

They both watched as Amelia stared in shock and then collapsed and seemed to go into a trance. Her eyes were closed but suddenly she began to convulse, and the words tumbled from her lips.

Why did I go there with Charlie? He's so awful, embarrassing. Him and his cronies so rude and pawing at me, people watching. Must get away.

Oh no, they're coming. I can hear them shouting, "Find the little hildabeast for me. Come on, boys, she'll be good sport, fun for us all."

I must get away.

"Hildabeast, hildabeast we're after you."

I must run faster, need somewhere to hide. There's the boathouse, can hide there.

Quick, must get in the shadows, out of the way, so they can't see.

They're close. I can hear them, can hear Charlie.

"Where are you, hildabitch, where are you? Come to Charlie. Find the fucking light switch, someone."

Lights come on, must get hidden away, out of sight, mustn't let them find me. Someone's close, hear breathing noises.

Suddenly grabbing hands and shouting.

"Got her, Charlie; she's here."

"Well done, Yakkers; you've got the second go. Get her, boys; bring her over here."

Dragged across the floor, hands all over me. Oh no my clothes being torn, no, no, get off me. Go away. Please, please don't do this to me.

"Hold her down, you two. She's my hildabeast, my turn first."

Can feel his weight on me. I can't move. Must get away.

"Come on, Charlie, hurry up; my turn next."

Must get him off me. He's so heavy, so strong. Must push him off.

"Hold the bitch still. Can't get at her while she's struggling."

He's on me. The pain—please no, don't do this to me, please.

"Come on, Charlie stop buggering about. Let me have a go."

No, no, no, it hurts so much. Must stop him...

The words stopped. Amelia lay unconscious in Teagle's arms with sweat running down her face and breathing heavily, but her body was calm.

Teagle whispered to Carol to call for the doctor.

After a while Amelia became awake. Her eyes opened, and she looked up at Teagle.

"What happened? Was it my nightmare again?"

"Yes, I'm sorry I upset you. Just lie still."

"You didn't upset me, Alice. I remember now what happened. It was awful. Charlie and his gang—why did they do it to me?"

"Let's try and take you inside. Lean on me; we'll take it slowly."

Teagle helped Amelia to her feet. They walked toward the house and were met by the family doctor, who'd just arrived.

Teagle sat waiting. The doctor and Carol Reynolds had taken Amelia to her room. It was nearly forty-five minutes later when the doctor entered.

"How is Amelia, doctor?"

"Thanks for waiting, Sergeant. I think it's going to be all right.

For the first time she has remembered what happened to her. She talked to me about it, and I believe the whole episode today has been liberating for her. A good start to her recovery, I'd say, thanks to you."

"That's a relief. I thought I may have done harm."

"Quite the opposite. Amelia trusts you and likes you. Somehow what happened today appears to have released her from her demons. She wants to see you before you go. She needs more company, more visitors.

"But before then I need to discuss that medical specialist from Oxford. Since we met earlier, I've studied his records which you sent me and taken another opinion about his treatment of Amelia. In short, the treatment has been very unsatisfactory and has done nothing to help her—quite the opposite, in fact. He prescribed doses of a mild sedative which simply kept her quiet and compliant, and he also advised against her leaving this house and against having any visitors. That's just kept her in a state of limbo."

"It supports what we believe, Doctor. His job was to keep her from causing any problems, not to cure her. But wouldn't sedatives for ten years cause an addiction?"

"It's often a consequence, but fortunately not, it seems, in Amelia's case. She didn't like the pills and admits that she often avoided taking them, secretly threw them away. I think she's going to be fine. It'll take some time because what she suffered was very traumatic, but I'm confident she'll eventually get over it."

"It's a pity you weren't able to spot what was happening."

"To my shame, I've let down both Amelia and her aunt. I should have inquired into things, I should have taken more notice of what was happening, I should have insisted on another opinion, but I failed. It won't happen again."

Teagle went to see Amelia and was pleased and relieved that she was smiling and up and about. Carol Reynolds was with her.

"I hope you're feeling better. Good to see you smile."

"I feel fine, Alice. Thanks for being here. You will come again, won't you please?"

"Of course, I will. Sorry that I can't stay longer today, but I need to get back to Kidlington."

"How about coming this weekend? You could stay the night if you want. Unless you have other things on, of course."

Teagle hesitated; she was free but ought to first report back and get the superintendent's approval.

"I'd love to do that, but I need to check if I'm off duty. I'll give you a call after I get back to the station if that's OK?"

Teagle arrived back and went straight to see the superintendent. Duggan was with him.

"Come in, Teagle. You've got here at just the right time. Duggan is about to tell me how she's got on." He nodded to Duggan to continue.

"Partial progress, sir. I've managed to get most of what is required about Robert McClennon and passed it on to Doctor Watson. He says it'll take a day or so. McClennon's parents are separated, as you know, but they are both now very concerned. As for collecting information about Wagner, I've made little progress so far.

"The inquiry agent tracked Wagner down to a safari camp in Africa. I've made contact with the camp, which confirms he was a ranger there. Anyway, it seems he left the camp over five years ago. They think he was heading back home, and he was expected to return to the camp but didn't.

"Unfortunately, I've no idea where he is now, and I've not yet managed to contact his parents in Switzerland. Sorry. They seem to be away from home. But I did talk to the camp's manager about Wagner; he was generally popular and capable, got on well with the guests, a bit too well with some of the ladies, according to manager. The manager also told me that Wagner's middle name is Yakabu. It's an African name and apparently it was given because his grandfather was African; that was his story anyway. Thought that might interest you, sir."

The superintendent thought about. He remembered something but couldn't quite place it.

"Thank you, Duggan. That is interesting, and presumably it's why he was called Yakker? Keep at it and let me know as soon as Dr. Watson comes back about McClennon. OK, Teagle, tell us how you got on in Dorset."

Teagle explained all that had happened on her visit.

"I count that a success, Teagle. I'm happy for you to spend the weekend with Amelia. You can decide if it's an appropriate time to discuss any more about what happened to her. Meanwhile there's a lot left for us to do.

"Tell me how far you've got finding out about Caterham's father?"

"Sorry, sir; not much to report yet, but I'm on to it. I can tell you that he's a financier and into property development in a big way amongst other things. He's also very rich—billionaire status—but keeps a low profile. Peter Joseph Caterham, fifty-eight years old, married for thirty-five years. Charles was his only son; he has a younger married daughter. Only basic stuff so far; it's all there's been time for. Shall I make it a priority?"

"Yes, and also try to find for me his link to St. John's apart from his son Charles; why does the president know him? That reminds me, whilst you're doing that, find out if Professor Plowright remembers Elspeth Robertson. Watch her reaction carefully."

Teagle looked puzzled and then realized his meaning. "You think Elspeth talked to Professor Plowright about Amelia, don't you, sir? That's why she's keen for us to investigate."

"It's a thought. Charlie-boy Caterham and Elspeth Robertson both read PPE at St. John's. so both knew Professor Plowright. Elspeth was a witness to Charlie's rape of Amelia. He gets away with it, she tells Plowright, and they are both appalled at the injustice. Suddenly you appear, ten years later, inquiring about Charlie, and the professor sees the chance to right a wrong but daren't say too much, so she gives you a few clues to follow. Something like that; as I said, just a thought."

"You're too smart for me, sir. I should have spotted that possibility. It sounds like a dead cert. Do you think that the professor is still in contact with Elspeth?"

"It's also a thought, Teagle. We'll have to bear in mind that possibility when we interview Elspeth. Maybe you should ask the good professor. Specifically, ask her when she last spoke to Elspeth."

The superintendent turned to Duggan.

"We need to interview the four witnesses. Duggan, you get that arranged. Give the two men a choice of coming here, or we'll go to them locally if they'd prefer. Arrange it for next week if you can. But I want to see the two women, Elspeth Robertson and Fiona Mathews, here at Kidlington and, for those interviews, I also want you to get the inquiry agent from Newbury here at the same time."

Both Teagle and Duggan looked surprised. Duggan asked, "What's on your mind, sir?"

"Just another thought. It was a young woman disguised in a Muslim headscarf who met the agent and commissioned him to find Charlie-boy and his gang. I thought that maybe it was Elspeth or Fiona who visited the agent in disguise; if it was, then he might just recognize her or perhaps recognize her voice; you'll remember, Teagle, he especially mentioned her voice. It's just another possibility worth checking."

"You think one of them went there acting on behalf of the aunt, sir?"

"Something like that. We know it was the aunt who got the agent's address, but we know she didn't visit him. Elspeth and Fiona were in contact with the aunt around that time."

"See what you mean, sir. Worth looking at. I'll get it all set up."

After they'd left him, the superintendent called the family solicitor in Dorchester.

"Thanks for calling back, Chief Superintendent. I wanted to tell you that I've received an expert legal opinion, and I was correct. The nondisclosure agreement can only be enforced against the aunt, who is now dead, and she, in her lifetime, did not breach it. Its obligations can't transfer to Miss Mathews, the current guardian, nor could it be enforced against Miss Sheridan."

"That's helpful, sir, because Miss Sheridan has suddenly remembered some of what happened and told Sergeant Teagle."

"So I understand; the family doctor has told me. Good news apparently; there's now hope Miss Sheridan may make a full recovery, especially as that quack medical specialist has gone. That's why I wanted to let you know. Anyway, I've always believed the wretched contract would be unenforceable if tested. Are you now going to act against those responsible?"

"I'm certainly going to do my best, sir."

CHAPTER 14

The following day Duggan reported that the pathologist had a match. The superintendent went with her into Oxford to see him at the laboratory. Doctor Watson, the police pathologist was in good humor.

"We've identified the third body for you, Superintendent. We're almost certain it matches the evidence DC Duggan obtained about Robert McClennon. So that's three out of four. Well done. Lionel and I had a bet you wouldn't do it; I'm pleased to say that my faith in you was justified. I won, and Lionel now owes me a dinner."

Professor Lionel Cornelius was there as well and added, "I must say, Superintendent, that you've surprised me. Your methods certainly work. I feel that the good doctor has duped me; he has local knowledge of you."

"My advice is to avoid taking bets with him. Is there any doubt about the identification, Professor?"

"No doubt in my mind that it's Robert McClennon. We always give ourselves a bit of wriggle room, just in case. But it's him all right. Dental records are a match, and his is the largest and tallest of the bodies which matches the other information DC Duggan obtained."

The superintendent smiled. "His nickname was 'Big Mac.'"

"Well, there you are. So you've only got one to left to find. Any progress?"

"I'm almost certain who it is but can't yet find the evidence for you. I've been looking back at your original report. You indicated that one body might have some African descent."

"That's right; I remember. Actually, it's the body still unidentified, if that's any help to you."

The superintendent grinned. "My suspect had an African grandfather. He was given a second name Yakabu in honor of him. Would that fit?"

"Interesting. Yakabu is a west African name, usually Nigerian." Cornelius looked at the pathologist and smiled. "What do you think, Doctor Watson?"

Watson was grinning and patting his ample stomach. "My dear Lionel, I think that you are about to lose another bet."

McClennon's parents, despite being separated, arrived at Kidlington together. The superintendent met them with Duggan.

McClennon's father asked, "Are you certain that it's Robert?"

"There's very little room for doubt. The forensics evidence is compelling. I need to ask you some questions please."

The parents looked sadly at each other and held hands together.

"Robert had some friends at Oxford. They were apt to behave rowdily together. Are you aware of that?"

The father looked up and spoke quietly. "We thought he was mixing with the wrong people. There was an incident which got him arrested and charged. I received a call from a lawyer in Oxford explaining that Robert had got himself into trouble, but it could be sorted out by paying off the complainant. Said it was a better option than Robert getting a criminal record, and all that stuff. I wasn't happy about it and told Robert what I thought about it; he said that it was blown out of proportion. They'd been a bit boisterous in a restaurant or bar. They'd not caused much damage, but people objected just because of who they were. They didn't like well-off undergraduates; police got heavy handed. At the time

Ginny and I had our own problems. We were in the middle of our separation, and I was busy with other things. Anyway, I paid up to get the charges dropped."

"How much?"

"I think about £15,000 from memory."

"Do you have the details of the lawyer?"

"I think I've still got something at home. As I said we had our own problems, and I did wonder if Robert was misbehaving because of that for some reason. You know what children can be like?"

"Not sure that I do, sir. I shall require details of the lawyer and what you paid. Was there any incident around the time Robert graduated?"

"Not that I remember. No, I'm sure there wasn't; this all happened before then. We didn't go to the ceremony, couldn't manage it. He came home and seemed very subdued. Left us soon afterwards, said he was off to do his own thing, and I didn't see much of him after that. We separated about the same time. Don't know if he kept in touch with you, Ginny?"

The mother looked up. "No, I didn't see much of him either. We all went our different ways, lost contact. Sounds awful, I know, but it just happened. How did Robert die?"

"He was murdered, but we don't know how. It would have happened around seven years ago. He hadn't been reported missing by you."

Their horror and shock were obvious. The mother sobbed, and the father turned to her. She pulled her hand from his grasp and sat hunched with her face held in both hands. Nothing was said until the superintendent asked, "Do you want to see his body, his remains? I'm afraid there is only a skeleton and some fragments of clothing to see, but it is Robert."

The father spoke softly. "We ought to see him, yes, please."

"Dc Duggan will arrange it and take you into Oxford. It won't be possible to hold his funeral until after an inquest."

It was the following morning when Duggan returned with the details of the lawyer; he was Vincent Roper, and his office was in Oxford. McClennon's father had paid him just over £16,000.

"His father's got plenty of money, sir. The payment didn't seem a great deal to him. He tried to explain it to me, to justify it all. Blamed Robert's behavior on mixing with the wrong people at Oxford and didn't want his future jeopardized because of that. He said the annual cost of his son's education came to much more, and so it was a small price to pay. They never saw a great deal of Robert. He was educated at a boarding school and then went to Oxford; didn't report him missing because they didn't know he was missing; they'd simply lost contact with him. Sounded weird to me. These people live in a different universe."

"I couldn't agree more, Duggan, but I don't like it."

"What do you want me to do next, sir?"

"Get me more details about Vincent Roper and discover if we know anything about him, but be careful. I don't want him, or anyone alerted yet."

She nodded and said, "The obvious place to ask is at Oxford Central."

"True, but steer clear of Oxford Central until I've checked something. Can you also contact Robin Scot-Wadham's parents and inquire if anything similar happened with him?"

After Duggan had left, the superintendent sat thinking. He was unhappy. This had a sniff of police corruption at Oxford Central. He hoped not, but maybe James Marsden could enlighten him about Vincent Roper. He put a call through to Newcastle.

"Vincent Roper was a nuisance to us, Chief Superintendent," Marsden said. "He usually popped up after some students had got into trouble—bad behavior, drunken behavior, that sort of thing. We'd get called to out to a disturbance, take the students into custody, charge them, and then usually bail them until a court appearance. Then he'd appear and tell us the complaint had been withdrawn, and he'd insist we drop the charges. If we objected, we'd then get a call from Kidlington HQ telling us to drop it. As I told you before, it was the way things worked in those days. I imagine it's still going on."

"How do you think Roper got involved? Someone must have contacted him each time, surely?"

"We assumed he'd get contacted by a college to help smooth things over. The message we got that was that the colleges didn't want Oxford students to get a reputation for bad behavior just because of a few idiots. Roper was the fixer for the colleges. We couldn't win at Oxford Central. If we turned a blind eye to yobbish students, we got complaints from the townspeople. If we took them into custody, then we got accused of being overzealous by the colleges, who then complained to HQ."

"Do you think anyone at Oxford Central tipped off Roper?"

Marsden hesitated. "I don't think so. In fact, I doubt it very much. We all disliked him. We also disliked the way HQ behaved. Our standing orders were to treat students like anyone else, but when we did, then we'd sometimes get overruled by HQ and told to drop the charges. In my opinion, the colleges were too close to HQ, if you understand me, sir."

"I think I get the message, Chief Inspector. Did Roper get involved on the night Charles Caterham and his gang attacked Amelia Sheridan?"

"One of my officers told me that he'd shown up at Oxford Central, but I didn't see him. I think he heard how serious the attack was and went away; it was not what he usually handled. Instead, I had a visit from two senior college officials, as I told you. I refused to release the four students as they wanted me to. The chief constable was then on to me very quickly. Someone at St. John's or Keble must have spoken directly to the chief constable; that's the way I see it, sir."

"That's interesting. Tell me, who usually contacted you from HQ when Roper got involved?"

He could sense Marsden thinking about it. "I can't speak for those times I wasn't on duty, but I can only remember a chief inspector at Kidlington contacting me. I talked about him with the other inspectors at Oxford Central. It seemed we all had the same bad opinion of him, so I guess it was usually him."

"Do you remember his name?"

"Oh yes, how could I forget? Chief Inspector Eddie Wiggins. We didn't like him. He was the chief constable's leg man in those days, did his dirty work for him. Is he still around at Kidlington?"

He didn't have the heart to tell Marsden that Wiggins had received rapid promotion to chief superintendent on the strength of doing the chief constable's dirty work. "No, he retired a couple of years after you transferred to Newcastle."

"Good riddance to the old bastard. You're well rid of him, in my humble opinion. Glad I'm out of all that now. How are you getting on with your investigation, sir?"

"We're making progress. Hoping that I can tell you all about it before too long. Have you had any further contact from Paul Rigby?"

"Not a dickey-bird. I'd expected to hear from him again but haven't, I'm pleased to say."

Afterward the superintendent sat alone in his office thinking about Roper. He was almost certainly dodgy, possibly corrupt, but perhaps Oxford Central was not involved with him if what Marsden said was true. That would be good news.

Meanwhile, he had someone waiting to see him. Eddie Wiggins had decided to come to Kidlington, with his chosen solicitor. The superintendent and Teagle met them in an interview room.

After the introductions, Wiggins's solicitor had something to say.

"My client, Chief Superintendent Wiggins, has explained to me the circumstances of him being here, and clearly you have been harassing him. In addition, you've used your authority to entrap him into a motoring offence. Before we continue, can you assure me that you will arrange for the motoring charges to be dropped?"

The superintendent stared at the solicitor for a moment and then turned his gaze to Wiggins.

"If Mr. Wiggins believes that he's been harassed or entrapped, then he is perfectly at liberty to complain. There is a laid-down procedure, as you know."

"That's a pity. My client had come here to cooperate, but you leave him with no alternative but to decline this interview."

The superintendent controlled his irritation and wondered what they'd conjured up between them.

"Mr. Wiggins has the choice of being here voluntarily, or he can be put under arrest. Either way he will be interviewed."

"You don't have the authority to interview Chief Superintendent Wiggins. If you believe he has a case of misconduct to answer, you must report it to the IOPC."

So that was it. Wiggins probably thought he'd have a better chance with the IOPC. The superintendent thought it unlikely—most probably the opposite, in fact.

"Sorry to disappoint you, sir. Mr. Wiggins is retired; he is no longer a chief superintendent. This is a murder investigation, and Mr. Wiggins is a material witness. He may even be an accomplice. Therefore, I am entitled to interview him."

The solicitor looked at Wiggins, who shook his head. "No idea what you're talking about, Barnes."

"Of course, the IOPC will be very interested in what my murder inquiry throws up about the other activities of Mr. Wiggins, especially his misconduct, his corruption, his abuse of office, and so on. I shall pass all that on to the IOPC."

"Those are serious allegations, Chief Superintendent Barnes. You should be careful; otherwise, it will be you up in front of the IOPC."

Wiggins looked pleased and couldn't help himself from joining in. "You're just fishing around, Barnes. You're making it up, just as Rigby said. You've no evidence."

The superintendent smiled. "Is that what Chief Constable Rigby told you? Do you believe him? I'll bet he told you to sit tight and say nothing; probably told you not to get him involved. It's the sort of thing he would say. Of course, you've just involved him, haven't you? He'll be pleased about that."

Wiggins went quiet and looked uncomfortable.

"When we talked the other day, I told you not to expect any help or support from your old friends or colleagues. You could check if I'm correct. Why not give them a call, or have you already tried that?"

The solicitor intervened. "This is getting us nowhere. My client came here simply to avoid the embarrassment of you going to his house to arrest him. He is prepared to help you, but it is unreasonable of him to do so under your duress."

"As I've already told your client, in helping me he may just be helping himself. It's up to him. I don't want Mr. Wiggins to feel under any duress. If he changes his mind and wants to talk, then please let me know. This interview is terminated"

The solicitor looked puzzled. "Is that it? We thought you wanted to question him."

"At some point I certainly will question him. Meanwhile, I can wait."

After Wiggins and his solicitor had departed, Teagle said, "I'm surprised you let him off so lightly, sir."

"I think we'll do better to wait a bit longer. Something happened earlier which has a bearing, and I want to check it out. Duggan is getting some information for me.

"Have you made any more progress with Peter Caterham, Charlie's father?"

"Not really, sir. He owns a huge organization, a network of companies, but I can't discover much else and no apparent connection to Oxford, or St. John's so far. You mentioned a possible property connection, so I'm looking into property developments by his companies around ten years ago, hoping that might throw up something."

"Keep at it. Come and see me with Duggan in an hour please."

An hour later Duggan informed him that Robin Scot-Wadham's parents had no knowledge of Vincent Roper. They were unaware of any misdemeanors involving Robin.

She'd discovered that Vincent Roper was still operating from an office in Oxford. He called himself a "legal advisor." She was just beginning to study the records and had discovered that he'd visited Kidlington HQ the previous month. She passed the superintendent the name of the officer he'd met. The superintendent seemed unsurprised.

Teagle and Duggan were instructed to go and arrest Roper and bring him to Kidlington. He was to be charged with perverting the course of justice.

Perverting the course of justice is a serious offence that can only be tried on indictment, which means that it is only heard in the Crown Court. The maximum penalty is a life sentence. A number of celebrities, politicians, and senior officials have been convicted in recent years.

Teagle and Duggan arrived at his offices with a uniformed officer in a marked police car. Before setting off, Duggan had called to check that he was there and made an appointment posing as a potential client.

Roper's office was a small suite of rooms in a modern office block just outside the center of Oxford. He was caught unawares but offered no resistance and was quickly escorted to the police car and taken to Kidlington.

By the time the superintendent saw him in an interview room, he had overcome his initial surprise and was calm and confident. The formalities were completed.

"I'm certain that you've made a bad mistake, Chief Superintendent."

"Let's see how we get on, sir. Do you want a solicitor present, or are you happy to continue alone? There is one on stand-by here for you."

Roper hesitated before replying, "Let's hear what you've got to say first."

"Do you know Mr. Peter McClennon, father of Robert McClennon, an undergraduate at Keble ten years ago?"

Roper hesitated again before replying, "The name is not familiar."

"He was one of your clients."

"I've got a lot of clients, and ten years is a long time ago."

"He paid you more than £16,000 to get criminal charges against Robert dropped."

"It's one of the services I offer."

"How did you manage to do it?"

Roper looked less comfortable and less confident.

"I really can't remember."

"You said that it's one of your services. Just explain to me more generally how you might do it?"

Roper looked at the superintendent. He was unsure how to reply.

"Maybe it would be better if you asked some of your colleagues, Chief Superintendent."

"That's a good idea, Mr. Roper. Who shall I ask?"

Roper sat looking at the superintendent but said nothing.

"Come on, Mr. Roper, who shall I ask?"

"You misunderstand, Chief Superintendent. I am simply an intermediary between Oxford colleges and Thames Valley Police. I act to protect the colleges' interests."

"Ah, I see. So who pays for your services?"

"Well, I'm retained by some colleges. I try to avoid embarrassment or bad publicity if some undergraduates misbehave."

"Do the colleges pay you then?"

"Yes."

"All the colleges?"

"No. Only those who use my services."

"So how do you get criminal charges against undergraduates dropped?"

"I make representations to you—Thames Valley Police, that is, maybe the arresting officers—to act for the best, leave it to the college to sort out and drop the charges."

"Does it work?"

"Generally, I am successful."

"Does any money change hands?"

Roper looked uneasy. "Look Chief Superintendent, I don't think this is sensible. What I do is approved at the highest level. I really think you should ask your colleagues."

"But who do I ask? The highest level suggests the chief constable. Should I ask her if she has approved what you do, whatever it is you do?"

"This is going nowhere. I can't help you."

"You came here last month to see an officer, Chief Inspector Norman Young. What was that about?"

"I can't remember."

"What happened to the money paid to you by Mr. McClennon to have the charges against his son dropped?"

"I've nothing further to say."

"That's a pity because I have lots of specific questions to ask you. You leave me no alternative. You'll be charged with perverting the course of justice; it's a very serious offence, as I'm sure you know. We'll arrange a hearing for you to plead and grant you a conditional bail in the meantime. I shall be obtaining warrants to investigate your affairs, and it's most likely that other charges will follow. Sergeant Teagle will complete the procedures; Duggan, you come with me."

Back in his office, Duggan was instructed to fetch Chief Inspector Norman Young.

"Sit down, Chief Inspector, and tell me what has been going on. I met you the other night when you were attempting to let Eddie Wiggins off drunk-driving charges. You told me that was established practice. I've just finished talking to Vincent Roper, who indicates that you assist him in having criminal charges dropped for his clients. He says you have approval for it at the highest level. Tell me all about it."

Young sat with a startled expression, fidgeting, and stuttered a reply. "Not sure I know, sir."

"Start from the beginning. When did you first get involved? When did you first meet Vincent Roper?"

"About eight years ago. Chief Superintendent Wiggins arranged it shortly before he retired."

"Were you paid by Roper?"

"It was part of our services to the university, protecting reputations and avoiding bad publicity. It was for the general good of Oxford town as well; the chief constable approved it all. Vince Roper acted for the university or some of the colleges, which paid for these services. Eddie Wiggins was retiring, and someone was needed to take over from him. It involves extra duties, and I could be called upon any time. This was just an extra duty allowance. I've done nothing that I shouldn't."

"Let's get this clear so there's no misunderstanding. Some colleges paid Thames Valley Police to drop charges against some undergraduates to protect reputations and avoid bad publicity. Roper arranged it, and you were his contact at Kidlington who got the charges dropped. Roper made the payments of your allowance, as you put it. Is that correct?"

"More or less. I was told the colleges paid the money through Vince Roper, but it was a system agreed with the chief constable."

"Which chief constable?"

"Not sure. Eddie Wiggins had been doing it before me, so it had been going for a long time."

"Is it still going on?"

"Not so much as it used to, but yes, it still happens."

"So how does it work?"

"Well, Vince calls me; we might meet. He explains what has happened. It's usually some drunken undergrads causing a nuisance, done some property damage, that sort of thing. Oxford Central has arrested them, charged, and released pending a court appearance. Minor stuff really. I call up an inspector at Oxford Central, explain the situation, and tell him to drop the charges."

"The charges get dropped just like that?"

"Yes, but I back it up by sending down a signed confirmation. It usually says, 'Undergraduates to be subject to college discipline by agreement of Thames Valley Police. Criminal charges to be dropped.' I include names of the undergrads, charge details, and the college, etc. There's a standard form."

"Is that all? You don't seek any other authorization or report it?"

"Never have done. It was how Eddie Wiggins told me to do it."

"What action does the college take?"

"I was told they have internal disciplinary procedures."

"How do you get paid?"

"Vince pays a small retainer into my bank account each month or so. Then depending upon how much I need to do, there are additional payments."

The superintendent was surprised. He'd expected cash payments or something not so obvious. It suggested how complacent Roper and Young were, or how secure they felt.

"How much?"

Young, having become relaxed during his explanation, now looked uncomfortable.

"As I said, it varies depending on what happens. Not so much in the long summer break, and it's not been so much recently. The retainer is about six hundred a month, but I'd have to check on the other amounts."

The superintendent sat staring at him. So little for selling out and betraying his colleagues and shaming the entire force. He determined that by the time he'd finished, Young, Roper, Wiggins, and everyone else involved would suffer for their treachery.

"Are you the only one on Roper's payroll?"

"Not sure. I think so, unless the chief constable or her deputy—"

Young didn't finish the sentence. The superintendent's grim expression and barely concealed fury disconcerted him. The superintendent's words were softly spoken, but the anger they contained was obvious.

"I want a full statement, Young, details of everything you've done: who was involved and all payments, the bribes you've received—everything. You don't leave HQ until I say so. Is that understood?"

All Young could manage was a nod to signify his understanding and a sigh of resignation. The superintendent turned to Duggan. "Take the chief inspector to an interview room, then find Teagle and come back here with her."

Duggan was back with Teagle five minutes later. She'd finished processing Roper and had him bailed. The superintendent explained to Teagle what had happened with Young and instructed her and Duggan about what to do next.

He met the chief constable and brought her up to date. After he'd finished, she sat silently for a minute or two. She showed no emotion as she looked at him.

"Thank you, Graham. Keep digging away, and I imagine you'll solve the murders and find out who did it. Otherwise, I'm appalled at what you've told me. I'm angry and ashamed. How could I not know it's been going on all the time I've been chief constable? What are we going to do about it?"

"Makes me bitterly angry too, ma'am. However, I think you should be encouraged because I'm almost certain that it's confined to only a few officers, of which at least two are no longer here, and a rogue lawyer—a few rotten apples. We can quickly end it and sort out those responsible."

"Don't forget the president of St. John's and those like him."

"I've not forgotten. Leave them to me. Their turn will come later, ma'am. Meanwhile do I have your authority to cut out the rot at Thames Valley?"

She looked unhappily at him. "Get on with it. Get it done and let me know what happens. I'm relying on you, Graham."

Before he reached the door, he heard her speak again.

"Thank you for not asking, Graham."

"For not asking what, ma'am?"

"For not asking if I was on Vincent Roper's payroll."

He laughed. "Never even crossed my mind."

It was late the following afternoon when Teagle and Duggan presented what they'd obtained. Young had cooperated and given a full confession. There were details of all the payments into his bank account from Roper. But it was the warrant to examine Roper's affairs which had produced the most damning information. In addition to the payments made to Young, there were previous payments to Eddie Wiggins and some payments to Paul Rigby when he was chief constable of Thames Valley. All these payments were listed in Roper's records under the catch-all description of "Thames Valley Police—for services rendered." There was no evidence of anyone else at Thames Valley receiving payments.

Separately, Roper regularly invoiced several Oxford colleges, including St. John's and Keble. These invoices usually specified "consultancy services" or "advisory fees."

The payment from McClennon's father had shown up described as "personal legal service." There were other instances of similarly described payments received by Roper pointing to others being approached by him.

It was all very much as the superintendent had expected. Although it didn't explain what had happened on the night Amanda Sheridan was attacked, it should be enough to help things along if handled properly.

Vince Roper was instructed to return to Kidlington and arrived early in the evening; this time he was accompanied by a solicitor.

"In the light of what we've discovered, I'm expecting answers to my questions, Mr. Roper."

Neither Roper nor the solicitor replied.

"Not a promising start, but let me start by asking why you've been making payments directly to police officers."

Roper exchanged glances with his solicitor. It was the solicitor who replied, "Could you please be more specific, Superintendent?"

"How specific would you like me to be? I have a long list of bank transfers made by Mr. Roper directly into the accounts of serving police officers going back over fifteen years. We will eventually discuss them each individually, but at this point, a more general indication will suffice."

This time Roper replied, "As I explained last time, what I do has the approval of Thames Valley Police."

"I've spoken to the chief constable, and she had no knowledge of you, her deputy likewise, and I've certainly not approved of you bribing police officers."

The solicitor was quick to respond. "Superintendent, that is a serious accusation. My client emphatically denies bribing anyone."

"That's correct, sir. Bribing police officers is extremely serious. What are these payments for if they are not bribes, Mr. Roper?"

"They are for services rendered as agreed with the chief constable. Perfectly proper."

"If it could conceivably be proper, then the payments would be to Thames Valley Police Force and not to individual officers."

"You'll find that is what they are described as, 'Thames Valley Police—for services rendered.' I was requested to save bureaucratic effort and make payment to the individual officers concerned."

"Who made the request, gave you the authorization?"

"The chief constable, Paul Rigby."

"Do you have a letter of authorization from him?"

"Not sure. I don't think so, but that's what he wanted."

"You paid money directly to him as well. Why was that?"

"It was what he wanted. Why don't you ask him?"

"Don't worry, sir, we shall be doing more than that."

The superintendent sat looking at them both with a sad expression. It was a feeble attempt at a defense. He turned to Teagle. "What do you think, Sergeant?"

"Can't imagine it will be accepted by the jury, sir. Paying a police officer, a chief constable even, because that was what he wanted is not going to wash. Anyway, Mr. Roper is a legal advisor, so he'd know that it was against the law. The jury would laugh."

"If it wasn't so serious, then I'd be laughing too, Sergeant. Unfortunately for you, Mr. Roper, because of the growing evidence against you, we may have to withdraw bail. Let me ask if you about an episode ten years ago. Four undergraduates committed a very serious assault on a young woman. It happened in the boat shed at Keble college, and the four undergraduates were from St. John's and Keble; both colleges are clients of yours. What did you do to get those charges dropped?"

Roper remained silent briefly before answering, "I didn't get involved in that. I was called late at night by St. John's and went to Oxford Central to see what I could do. A police officer told me I was wasting my time. I tried to call Eddie Wiggins but couldn't reach him, so I reported to St. John's, and it decided to handle things directly."

"Were you told details of the assault?"

"Yes, the officer at Oxford Central told me; as I recall it was a serious sexual assault, rape apparently."

"Who did you speak to at St. John's?"

"Unusually, it was the president himself. Normally I'd get calls from one of his executive staff or the warden's office. It's also unusual for me to be contacted in the night; I'm generally called the day after something has happened. I got the impression this was a big issue; I remember wondering why the president was up in the middle of the night. It was after midnight."

231

"Did you discover what happened to the four undergraduates?"

"I heard that charges were dropped. I wasn't surprised, but they weren't happy about it at Oxford Central."

"One of those four undergraduates was Robert McClennon. You received a payment from his father described in your records as for 'personal legal service.' What was that for?"

"Those particular four undergraduates had got into trouble on a few occasions. Previously I'd sorted it out. Sometimes it was necessary to compensate a bar or restaurant for breakages to get the complaint dropped. It was his turn to pay—they took it in turns—but he didn't have the money, so I called his father, that's all."

The solicitor intervened, "Chief Superintendent, my client has been very frank in answering your questions. In my opinion, you really don't have a case for him to answer. I would object most strongly if you attempt to withdraw bail, as you are suggesting."

"Your client has a great deal to answer for, as you know. He is not leaving here until he has made a full statement."

It was later that night, Friday, before Roper had completed his statement. Teagle presented it to the superintendent. He read through it carefully and asked Teagle a few questions. It confirmed that only three officers, Norman Young, Eddie Wiggins, and the previous chief constable, Paul Rigby, had received payments. It was much as he'd already deduced, but the evidence was clear. It was also clear that Roper's defense would be that he was simply acting on behalf of his clients, some Oxford colleges, in an arrangement made between them and the chief constable of Thames Valley Police Force. He doubted that defense had any chance of success, especially when it came to the turn of the three police officers and the heads of the various colleges to give their side of the story. He hoped that everyone involved would be going down for a long prison spell.

"That's what I wanted, Teagle; well done. You can release Roper on his bail, then you'd better get off home. Are you still going to Dorset tomorrow?"

"No, sir. I've called Amelia and explained that I can't. She understands. I've promised to get there during next week sometime. I imagined you'd have things for me to do here."

"Excellent. We'll begin with Eddie Wiggins. Arrange for him to come here tomorrow morning with his solicitor.

"Then we'll go up to Manchester to visit Chief Constable Paul Rigby. I'll let him know to expect us; see you in the morning."

CHAPTER 15

Despite working late into night before, both the superintendent and Teagle looked bright and alert the following Saturday morning when they sat across from Wiggins and his solicitor in an interview room at Kidlington.

"There are a great many questions for you to answer, Mr. Wiggins. Since we last spoke, I've received statements from Vincent Roper and Chief Inspector Norman Young. You can imagine what they have each said. We've also obtained details of payments you've received into your bank account from Mr. Roper. He claims they're for your assistance. I'd call them bribes, but your solicitor objected to my use of the word last time. Sergeant Teagle has listed them out for you."

Wiggins looked decidedly anxious. The solicitor remained quiet. Teagle passed some papers across the table. Wiggins and his solicitor sat staring at them.

"We're very busy today, and so I'll have to postpone your full interview until another time. This morning, I'd just like to ask some specific questions about an event which happened ten years ago."

The solicitor began to object, but the superintendent raised the palm of his hand to silence him.

"Before you object again, sir, please let me finish. Last time you were disinclined to help me, and so we adjourned. That gave me time to gather more incriminating evidence against your client which has further jeopardized his position. Now I'm very interested in what happened ten years ago because it's relevant to a murder investigation. Will you try and help me, Mr. Wiggins?"

Wiggins looked at his solicitor and received a nod.

"I don't know anything about your murder, Barnes."

"Just tell me what you remember ten years ago when four male undergraduates attacked and raped a female student. It happened at night in the boat shed at Keble college? Why were they released without charge?"

"I wasn't on duty. I found out about it the next day. By then it had mostly been sorted. Paul Rigby wasn't too pleased with me being unavailable. He'd been up most of the night because of it."

"Did he tell you what had happened?"

"The way he told it, the president of St. John's had called him in the early hours. Oxford Central had lifted four undergraduates from St. John's and Keble from their college rooms and banged them up in the cells. The president demanded their release. There was an agreement with St. John's that it would handle all disciplinary matters concerning its undergraduates. Anyway, Rigby agreed he'd get them handed over, but when he called Oxford Central, the duty inspector kicked up and refused. He said it was too serious."

"So what happened?"

"Rigby ordered the inspector to release them into the hands of college officials and told the inspector to report to Kidlington later the morning. By the time I arrived, the inspector had been relieved of duty and put on leave. He later transferred out of Thames Valley."

"Then what?"

"He told me to make sure it was forgotten about at Oxford Central, and so I got the other arresting officers in to Kidlington to see Rigby; he ordered them not to discuss it again, said the matter was being dealt with confidentially, and transferred them to other parts of Thames Valley."

"What about the victim?"

"Apparently St. John's took care of her. Private medical treatment, and according to Paul Rigby, she eventually received a settlement."

"Was that the end of it?"

"More or less. All got forgotten. Rigby did admit to me that he regretted doing it. It was a very serious attack, and he'd not realized that when he agreed to free them; he took it up with the president afterwards. Don't know how that ended. Anyway, it stayed quiet, remained forgotten. I retired a couple of years later, and Paul went to Manchester. Then you started your murder inquiry, which put the cat amongst the pigeons."

"In what way?"

"I don't know what you did, but I had Rigby on the line telling me to keep away from you. He was shaken by what you were doing. Indicated the president of St. John's had been on to him. That's all I know."

"Who set up this agreement between St. John's and Thames Valley Police?"

"Rigby. He was close to the president, visited the college quite a lot. I think he'd been promised an honor by the college, but it didn't happen, as far as I know."

"Chief Inspector Young claims that you appointed him to take over from you."

"I was retiring, and he took over; that's all. I instructed him what to do. It's an arrangement to safeguard the reputation of Oxford University and the city from some stupid louts of undergraduates. It wasn't an everyday occurrence. Mostly there's not much of a problem; it's just a few students who don't know how to behave. Saves us money if the colleges handle things; that's the way I see it."

The superintendent smiled at him. "I wonder if the IOPC will see it that way. Thanks for your answers. We'll be in touch."

Twenty minutes later he was seated with Teagle in the rear of his unmarked police car on the M40 motorway heading north toward

Manchester. In the front his usual driver was at the wheel, and alongside him was another officer. Both were qualified advanced pursuit drivers.

The journey was around 165 miles on some of the most heavily used motorways in England. On a good day, a civilian driver would allow at least three hours for the journey. These drivers were using the police car's blue flashing lights and maintaining position in the fast lane throughout the journey.

The superintendent talked with Teagle as the car sped north.

"I'm hoping to get Rigby to talk about the cover-up, particularly why it was so important. He may not tell me, of course, or he may not know much. He's likely to be aggressive, confrontational, because that's his style. I'm going to try and take it gently, to treat him with respect, which he definitely doesn't deserve. I'm expecting he'll be alone, but we'll have to wait and see."

"Do you think it'll help us solve the murders, sir?"

"I don't think so, at least not directly, but he might provide some clues. Rigby enabled the cover-up and let the four culprits go free, which provoked the murders; that's still my view. If Charlie Caterham and his gang had been charged and tried in court, then they would still be alive and behind bars. In that sense you could say that Rigby caused them to be murdered. But we're still in the dark about who did it and how. All we can do is to keep digging away and hope we can get to the truth. Next week Duggan has arranged for interviews of the four witnesses; I'm hoping that'll give us something to go on."

The car reached the HQ of Greater Manchester Police after a fast drive of just over two hours. They were escorted to the chief constable's office with no delay. The superintendent introduced himself and Teagle.

Paul Rigby was a big man, tall and heavily built. He was dressed in full uniform. The superintendent knew that he was just approaching sixty years old, probably thinking of retirement. He wasn't smiling, but he was alone.

"Well, Barnes, perhaps you can get to the point. It's Saturday, and I don't have time to waste."

Teagle sat quietly, listening and watching. Not a promising start, she thought. She imagined that Rigby had canceled a golf game.

"Of course, sir. Thank you for seeing us, and sorry for the inconvenience. I'm running a murder investigation, and what I tell you is evidential, so I'd appreciate your discretion, sir. Four male undergraduates who were together at Oxford ten years ago committed a very serious assault on a female undergraduate."

Rigby sat watching the superintendent but said nothing.

"Three of those male undergraduates have been murdered. I expect that we'll soon prove that the fourth has also been murdered. Have you heard anything about this already, sir?"

Rigby stared at him. "Should I have heard anything?"

"I'm not sure, sir. The reason I asked is because all four who committed the assault ten years ago were released without charge from Oxford Central into the hands of St. John's college. The ringleader was called Charles Caterham; he was at St. John's. I'm told that you knew about it?"

"Who told you that?"

"I believe there was an agreement between some Oxford Colleges and Thames Valley Police allowing colleges to discipline misbehaving students without recourse to a police prosecution. Again, I'm told that you knew about it?"

"It is a practical arrangement for the benefit of Oxford University and Thames Valley Police. Stops the behavior of few bad students from spoiling Oxford's reputation and saves wasting police time. Works well."

"So I've heard, sir. My problem is that Charlie Caterham and his gang committed a serious crime; they raped and badly injured an innocent young woman. They ought not to have been released."

"What are you suggesting, Barnes?"

"I'm not suggesting anything, sir. Do you think it was appropriate for them to be released from police custody without charge?"

"Look, Barnes, I know about this incident. Perhaps with hindsight they should not have been released, but at the time it was thought to be a minor incident blown out of proportion. Anyway, the girl made no complaint. In the end no harm was done."

Barnes sat looking at Rigby for some long seconds before continuing.

"I'm sorry, sir, but I can't agree; dreadful harm was done to a young woman. However, I'm only interested in discovering why it was so important for St. John's college to have this particular matter kept quiet. It has a bearing on the murders; in fact it is almost certainly the motivation for the murders. What you can tell me could be key to solving them."

Rigby appeared thoughtful and hesitated before talking.

"I'd not realized they'd been murdered. I'd heard about Caterham, but his father was emphatic it was unconnected to the assault."

"Do you know Peter Caterham, Charlie's father?"

"No, not personally. The president knows him well; it was he who told me. Charlie was a bloody nuisance; he and his cronies were in trouble several times. His father refused to acknowledge it as anything other than a bit of high spirits and expected the president to sort it out."

"Do you think Peter Caterham put pressure on the president that night?"

"I know he did. The president told me when he called me in the early hours; he was agitated. Caterham's father had called the president well after midnight. He'd heard from Charlie that police officers were outside his room wanting to arrest him. His father demanded that the president sort it out. By then Charlie was in the cells at Oxford Central, and the duty inspector, Marsden, refused to release them. That's when I got a call from the president explaining that it was vital Caterham and the others were released, pronto. He told me Charlie had behaved stupidly again, and Oxford Central was being bloody minded. I promised him

I'd sort it. I couldn't get through to Wiggins, so I called Oxford Central myself and had to order Marsden to get them out of the cells and hand them to the college representatives."

"Sounds odd. The president calling you personally in the middle of the night, sir?"

"Never happened before. These things were always handled by others."

"Why do you think it was so urgent, sir? Why couldn't it wait until the next day?"

"It seems that Caterham's father held sway with the president. 'Not a man to be trifled with' according to the president. I did try and check out the father, Peter Caterham, but couldn't find out much. Owns some big companies but keeps to himself, shuns publicity. I don't know what his connection with St. John's is, apart from his son going there."

"So are you saying that the entire cover-up about what happened that night was because Peter Caterham didn't want anyone to know about it?"

"That's what the president said."

"Did you know about the settlement with the victim, Amelia Sheridan?"

"I was told a settlement, generous compensation, was paid. I don't know the details."

"Do you know who paid?"

"The president said that Peter Caterham, the father, provided the funds."

"Earlier, you said that the president had told you Charlie Caterham had been murdered. How did he know?"

"Told me you'd met Peter Caterham about it, and you were linking it to the assault. He didn't want you digging into what had happened ten years ago. He demanded that the president stop you in case it caused bad publicity, dishonored Charlie's name or something. President called me to get you stopped. I tried with your chief constable but got nowhere. The president called the Home Office. Do you really have to dig into this, Barnes?"

"Wouldn't have to dig if someone told me what it was all about."

"Well, I've told you all I know; nothing more I can tell you."

"You could tell me why the president is in Peter Caterham's pocket. You're a policeman, sir; you have a policeman's instincts. You must have wondered why he dances to Caterham's tune. He's not the only one either."

Rigby went quiet. His body stiffened, and he glared across his desk.

"What do you mean by that remark?"

The superintendent gathered his papers and stood; Teagle also stood up.

"What the hell do you mean? What are you suggesting?"

"I'm suggesting nothing, sir. I'm only interested in solving some murders. Thanks for your time."

The car sped back to Kidlington. The fast lane of the motorways cleared before them as their flashing blue lights appeared in the rearview mirrors of cars ahead.

"Did you get what you wanted, sir?"

"Confirms much of what we knew and takes us a bit closer. Rigby condemned himself by what he said. We'd each better write up notes, and then we'll call it a day."

After a while the superintendent asked her, "Why does Peter Caterham have so much influence over the president, Teagle?"

"Don't know, sir. Why does the president have so much influence over Paul Rigby?"

"That's easy: because Rigby's been bought off, bribed. I studied those payments made by Vince Roper to Rigby, and one stood out. You must have noticed it?"

"The large one of £30,000, you mean?"

"That's it, made a month after the assault. I suppose you know your Bible, Teagle? What did Judas Iscariot receive for betraying Jesus?"

"Thirty pieces of silver."

"Coincidence, do you think? I'll bet the president understood the significance of thirty. Rigby would have enjoyed being seduced by the grandeur and ceremony at St. John's, sitting at high table, mixing it with the great and the good. Schmoozed by the president and probably promised an honorary doctorate. But he was also in it for the money, and that will be what brings him down."

"See what you mean, sir. But what about the president?"

"We just need to find out why Peter Caterham pulls his strings."

"Maybe he's been bought off as well."

"It's certainly a thought."

On Monday morning the superintendent was alongside the inquiry agent from Newbury. They were watching a TV monitor and listening to Teagle talking to Elspeth Robertson in an interview room.

"It's difficult, Superintendent. Remember, it was eight years ago. There is something familiar in her voice; like I said she's a nice accent, well spoken, refined, like I remember in my office. I'm guessing she's about thirty and would have been early twenties then, which I feel fits, and she's the same sort of build. But whether it's the same woman, I can't tell, never saw her face or hair."

"That's OK. I'd like you to wait in the reception area please. When she leaves I'll walk her through there and past you. I'll make a comment to you and when you reply smile at her and say 'hello.'"

"OK, I'm with you."

The superintendent joined Teagle. "Sorry to keep you waiting, Miss Robertson, and thank you for being here. Sergeant Teagle has explained why we wanted to see you. I'd like you to take us through the events that night please."

Elspeth Robertson's description of what happened was much as they already knew. Charlie Caterham and his three cronies had made a nuisance at the party most of the evening with their loutish behavior. They were known for such behavior. She felt sorry for Amelia Sheridan, who was obviously embarrassed by what was happening. The party was ending, and Elspeth left with her three friends. They were walking by the side of the river when Amelia came running past in an obvious hurry. She disappeared into the night toward the boathouse before Charlie and his gang followed by shouting after her; they were quite clearly chasing her. Soon there was a lot of shouting coming from the direction of the boathouse, but it was dark and difficult to see much. Suddenly the lights went on, followed by a scream and more shouting. Elspeth and her friends ran toward the boathouse and arrived to see Amelia held down by McClennon and Scot-Wadham. Most of her clothes had been ripped off, and Charlie was raping her with Wagner cheering him on. Amelia was screaming and struggling, and the two men with Elspeth tried to intervene. She saw Charlie smash his fist into Amelia's face, and she went limp. Charlie got off Amelia, and the gang of four ran away shouting and laughing. Elspeth and Fiona Mathews tried to comfort Amelia, who remained unconscious. One the men called the police, and four officers arrived in a few minutes.

The rest of what she said was much as Marsden had reported. The ambulance crew came and attended to Amelia before taking her away. Elspeth and her friends knew Charlie and his gang and gave their names and colleges. As witnesses they were asked to go to Oxford Central the following morning to give statements. She understood that the police officers had gone to arrest Charlie and his gang.

The following morning Elspeth and her friends went to Oxford Central expecting to give witness statements but were told that the university authorities were dealing with the matter, and their statements would not be required.

"What was the reaction of you and your friends to that, Miss?"

"Surprised, bewildered at first. We each gave the officer our contact details presuming that the university would get in touch for our statements. But we heard nothing, and the year finished within a few days, and we went down, left Oxford. Nobody got in touch, and I felt annoyed. It did occur to me that perhaps Amelia didn't want it public knowledge, but even so it felt wrong."

"Did you speak to Professor Plowright about it?"

"I did. She was horrified and said she'd take it up. Later she contacted me and said that the college was dealing with things but wanted it kept quiet. She indicated she wasn't happy about it. She knew Charlie and didn't like him—none of us did."

"Did you hear any more about it again or discover what happened to Amelia?"

"No. Perhaps I should have tried, but I went to work in Canada for nearly two years."

"Did you keep in touch with your friends who witnessed the attack?"

"Kept in touch with Fiona Mathews from time to time. Messaged her a few times and maybe spoke by telephone, that was all."

"Did you ever discuss the events of that night with her?"

"Once or twice, I think. But life had moved on by then. Sorry if it sounds uncaring. I wasn't close to Amelia. She was someone I'd met at Oxford."

"Do you keep in contact with Professor Plowright?"

"No. As I said, I went to Canada after graduating."

"Did you try and find out what had happened to Amelia Sheridan after you returned from Canada?"

"Sorry but no. It sounds bad of me, I suppose, but, as I said, life had moved on. Anyway, I'd only known her during my last year at Oxford."

The superintendent paused and smiled at her. "Thank you, Miss Robertson. That's very helpful. I'm grateful for your time, and it may be that we need to talk again, but that's all for the moment. I'll see you out if you'd please come with me."

Elspeth walked alongside the superintendent into the reception area. Teagle followed behind. The inquiry agent was seated in the waiting area, and as they approached, the superintendent turned to him and said, "Thank you for waiting, sir. I should be with you in a few minutes."

"No worries, Chief Superintendent." As the inquiry agent replied, he stood and turned toward Elspeth, smiled, and said, "Hello, Miss."

Elspeth immediately stiffened and looked flustered but managed to reply with, "Hello."

Teagle, following behind, could sense the tension and alarm in Elspeth. Teagle watched as the superintendent continued and escorted her to the entrance and shook her hand goodbye.

As he returned the three of them went into the interview room, and the superintendent turned to the inquiry agent.

"What do you think, sir?"

"I think she recognized me, Superintendent, and although I can't be certain, she also looked familiar to me despite not having seen her face. The way she walked and held herself as well as her voice. I reckon it was her who came to my office."

"What do you think, Teagle?"

"She was alarmed, sir. Flustered and taken by surprise. The normal reaction would be to smile when saying hello."

"Interesting. OK, let's repeat the exercise with the next witness."

Fiona Mathews was already in an interview room, and as before the superintendent with the inquiry agent looked through the one-way glass and listened as Teagle talked with her.

"She doesn't ring any bells, Superintendent. Wrong build, and her voice is quite different to the first woman."

"OK. Please wait in reception and I'll walk her past you as well just to gauge her reaction."

The interview with Fiona Mathews was much along the lines of Elspeth Robertson. In the reception area, she replied with a relaxed smile and "Hello" to the inquiry agent's greeting.

Shortly afterward Teagle sat with the superintendent to discuss the interviews.

"What do you think, Teagle?"

"They both lied sir. We know that they visited Amelia's home and met her aunt, but they denied it. I was surprised you didn't press them about that."

"Yes. I wonder why they did that? Why would they try to hide those visits from us? Elspeth Robertson is now on the alert if her reaction to the inquiry agent is as we think. Let's give them a week or two and see what they concoct together. I imagine they are conferring already."

"You know why they lied, sir: you believe they're part of the murders conspiracy."

"They're hiding something, that's for sure."

"Do you think Professor Plowright is involved?"

"I think that's unlikely, Teagle. She has pointed the finger which has eventually led us to the aunt and Elspeth Robertson. The professor thinks that an injustice has gone unavenged, but we know that the four murders are retribution for it. I rather think that if the professor knew about the murders, she'd see it as justice of a kind and not want us hunting for the culprits, don't you?"

"I take your point, sir. Unless the professor now has her sights set on bigger game like the president of St. John's or the principal of St. Hilda's."

The superintendent sat thoughtfully, looking at her.

"What a devious and suspicious mind you have, Teagle. It must be a product of your Oxford education. Academics are in a different league to the usual criminal brain, as you rightly have just reminded me."

"What do you want me to do next, sir?"

"Use your devious and suspicious mind to find everything you can about Peter Caterham and his property deals. According to the Home Office, there was something peculiar happened about ten years ago which could throw up a link to St. John's."

Teagle spent time thinking about how to find a link between Peter Caterham with his property companies and St. John's. From her time at Oxford, she knew that important decisions affecting any college were made by its governing body. The president of St. John's may have influence and authority, but even so he would need the approval of a committee of more than fifty members, who were mainly academics. The St. John's governing body met twelve times a year, and its minutes were publicly available.

It still took a deal of delving and a bit of luck. The published minutes were heavily summarized and brief. The reports they referred to were not included in the minutes and not necessarily readily available. There were separate subcommittees with delegated responsibilities and whose minutes were also not easily obtained. She'd concentrated her efforts on the year before the attack and the year following. In one set of minutes was an item called "Brentford Park Development." It concerned a property redevelopment.

That was the clue she was looking for, but it then took her more than a week to uncover the connection.

During the week Teagle also found time to visit Amelia Sheridan in Dorset as promised. Amelia seemed relaxed and delighted at the visit. Teagle stayed overnight at the grand house in a bedroom overlooking the coast and enjoyed her time there with Amelia and Carol Reynolds. The events of that night at Oxford were not mentioned.

"I think you might be interested in what I've found, sir."

He looked at the thick pile of papers which Teagle had with her.

"OK, Teagle, give me the short version please."

She grinned. "Around the time of the attack, Peter Caterham, or more precisely one of his companies, was finalizing a commercial and residential property development project in West London, along the A40 between Hammersmith and Heathrow airport. It was a large, valuable deal which had taken years of effort to set up: economic assessments, architectural schemes, obtaining the necessary planning consents and permissions from the various owners of the land and property, etc. It involved the demolition and redevelopment of existing properties and met with heavy resistance from those affected. There were planning inquiries, and government inspectors were involved, but eventually the necessary consents were obtained and finalized six months after the night of the attack."

"What's so unusual about it?"

"There were rumors of bribery to get consents, but nothing came of it; and afterwards there were complaints of strong-arm tactics to gain empty possession of some existing properties. You can imagine, sir, but eventually it all happened, and the scheme was completed about six years ago."

"Property development can be a dirty game. So, what's your point, Teagle?"

"I thought the timing was a coincidence, sir, and you don't like coincidences."

He sat looking at her and could sense her amusement.

"Come on, Teagle, out with it: What do you find so funny?"

"There's another coincidence. A chunk of the property involved is owned by St. John's college. Its property endowments are not just confined to the Oxford area."

He sat for a moment looking at her. "How valuable was the deal?"

"When completed its overall value was estimated at around £900 million. I can't tell you how much it was worth to St. John's. But I've discovered that Peter Caterham's company had spent and risked well over £60 million before gaining the consents, and without the commitment of St. John's, the deal would have failed. St. John's governing body didn't give its approval until two months after the attack on Amelia Sheridan."

He sat staring at her as he analyzed the possible implications. Negotiations between Peter Caterham and the president of St. John's for a big payday still not settled, which the publicity arising from his son, Charles's, attack would have scuppered, leaving huge financial losses.

"Anything else, Teagle?"

"Professor Jane Plowright sits on the St. John's governing body. Would she have voted for the deal knowing Charles Caterham's father was behind the development?"

He thought about it before answering.

"Maybe not. Perhaps she didn't know, and still doesn't, that Peter Caterham was behind it. We know he keeps a low profile in his dealings. We'll ask her in due course. I need time to think this through, Teagle. Good work, though, and well done; it certainly provides a strong motive for the cover-up. The problem is that all we have is supposition and guesswork; we need facts. Can we find out what St. John's or its president got paid by Peter Caterham?"

"Not without warrants, sir. I've gone as far as I can."

"I'm not sure we've got grounds for those yet."

"I've been wondering, sir. We've warrants to go through Vincent Roper's affairs, and we know he's been making payments to police officers. He says that they are funded by St. John's college, and if we could demonstrate that, it should give us grounds to get a warrant to look at St. John's finances and affairs, shouldn't it?"

He sat back and smiled at her. "Smart thinking, Teagle. You'll make a detective yet. Get on to it. I need to get thinking as well. If you get more bright ideas, let me know."

Teagle was back in the superintendent's office the following day.

"I think I've found something interesting, sir."

"Tell me about it."

"It might be better if you join me to hear what Vincent Roper has to say. I've put him in an interview room."

Teagle conducted the interview, and the superintendent sat alongside her listening. Roper sat with his solicitor.

"Mr. Roper, I'd like to repeat our discussion earlier today in your office. You've previously explained that the president of St. John's telephoned you in the early hours of the night of the attack. You told us it was unusual to speak directly to him. Is that correct?"

"That's right. I usually spoke with someone from his office. It was also unusual for me to be contacted in the night. His call was well after midnight, but he said it was urgent."

"What happened?"

"The president instructed me to go to Oxford Central and arrange for the immediate release of some undergraduates who'd been arrested. When I got there, I was told to go away, that I was wasting my time; it was a serious assault case. I tried to phone Eddie Wiggins but couldn't get his phone to answer, so I called the president to explain and said that I couldn't help."

"What did the president say?"

"He was annoyed and said something like 'That's not good enough; we'll see what the chief constable has to say,' and he rang off."

"Did you receive any further calls from the president?"

"About three weeks later, he called to instruct me to make a special payment to the chief constable, Paul Rigby. It was a large payment of £30,000, and I said that I'd need funds in advance because I couldn't meet the amount myself. He replied that he'd arrange it.

"The thirty thousand arrived in my account some days later, and I made the payment into Rigby's account in the usual way, except that I recorded it as 'Thames Valley Police—special services,' and I sent an acknowledgement receipt to St. John's as 'Thames Valley Police—special services."

"You normally invoiced St. John's for advisory or consultancy services without a mention of Thames Valley Police. Why did you change it?"

"Not sure. I suppose it was out of the ordinary. The president had referred to it as a special payment."

"What happened next?"

"Got a call from the president's office to say that it had not paid the money to my account, and it returned my receipt. I checked my bank account and saw that thirty thousand had come from a different account, not from St. John's. The transaction was described simply as 'St. John's funds,' but I don't know who sent it."

"Was that the end of it?"

"Yes, it was a one-off. After that it returned to the usual pattern, although things have been much quieter in recent years. It seems that undergraduates are better behaved these days."

"Thank you, Mr. Roper." She turned to the superintendent. "Do you have any questions, sir?"

"Thank you, Sergeant. Tell me, Mr. Roper, what do think the payment of £30,000 was for?"

"I don't know. I didn't ask, Superintendent."

He smiled at Roper, "Come on, Mr. Roper. You must have thought about it, have a guess? You've been doing this service for St. John's for years, and this was an unusually large sum. Why not ask the president what it was for if you didn't know?"

The solicitor spoke instead. "Chief Superintendent, I'm advising my client not to answer that question."

The superintendent looked at them both. He could sense Roper's unease. "Probably very wise, sir, because I imagine that Mr. Roper knows exactly what the payment was for."

The solicitor started to object, but he was interrupted. "Weren't you interested in who had sent you the funds. It would have been easy for you to ask through your bank, Mr. Roper. Receiving money from an unknown source would be unprofessional, illegal even."

"At the time I thought it was from St. John's on the instruction of the president."

"But then you discovered that it wasn't from St. John's. Surely you would have checked its source, unless you already knew where it came from."

Roper looked at his solicitor, who just gently shook his head.

"Well, I didn't check. It didn't seem necessary."

"That's a pity. We'll have to try and inquire ourselves, but I imagine it'll take time as it was ten years ago. Do you have anything to verify that you acted on behalf of the president? Perhaps you received a written instruction?"

"No."

He smiled at Roper. "So you claim that the president of St. John's telephoned you and instructed you pay £30,000 to the chief constable, which you did without question with money from an unknown source. Is that correct?"

Roper managed a quiet. "Yes, that's what happened, but I didn't know it was from an unknown source at the time."

He smiled again at Roper before turning to Teagle. "What do you think, Sergeant?"

"It's difficult to believe, sir. Unless the president confirms it, there's no evidence to show he was involved at all. It looks bad for Mr. Roper, especially as he says he has no idea what the payment was for or where the money came from. Not the type of behavior you'd expect from a professional legal man, someone who knows the law. Can't imagine a jury buying his story."

"I agree, Sergeant. I certainly don't believe it. OK, Mr. Roper, is there anything else you want to say? Remember that your release on police bail was only because you cooperated with us; that can change."

Roper looked unhappy and glanced at his solicitor before saying, "It's all true, Superintendent, what I've told you. I simply acted on the president's instruction; he is my client. I didn't realize the funds hadn't come from St. John's until afterwards. Maybe I should have checked the source, but I didn't. Nor did I ask what the thirty thousand was for because I assumed it was connected to the night of the attack and getting the four undergraduates released from custody."

The superintendent looked grimly at him. "That's a serious admission, Mr. Roper. You acknowledge that you paid £30,000 to the chief constable for securing the release of four undergraduates from police custody without charge."

The solicitor intervened. "That's not what Mr. Roper said. He said he assumed the payment was in connection with their release. We don't know how the chief constable used the payment. Mr. Roper was simply following instruction from his client, the president of St. John's, who is a highly respected man."

"That's no defense, as you well know, and I doubt the highly respected president will try to come to your rescue. On the contrary, he'll deny any knowledge. By contrast, Mr. Roper was seen at Oxford Central on the night of the attack trying to gain the release of four arrested undergraduates and was turned away by the officers on duty. However, shortly afterwards, following the chief constable's intervention, the four are released without charge, and subsequently Mr. Roper pays £30,000 into the chief constable's bank account. Those are indisputable facts. It won't take a jury long to reach the obvious conclusion."

There was silence in the room. Roper and his solicitor looked shocked.

"Mr. Roper, I strongly urge you to go and think carefully; try to remember something which will corroborate and substantiate your story. This interview is terminated. Remember that you're still on police bail."

Teagle followed the superintendent into his office.

"That was interesting, Teagle. But unfortunately, the crafty president has managed to distance himself and St. John's from that particular bribe."

"There is a bit more to tell you, sir."

"Go on then."

"I managed to trace the source of the thirty grand. It was easier than I'd expected, and Roper's bank was very helpful—took them only a few hours despite it happening ten years ago. It came from the account of one of Peter Caterham's companies."

He grinned at her. "Now that is interesting, Teagle. Are you certain?"

"I need to double check—there's not been time—but it looks certain. I thought it should provide grounds for a warrant to go through Peter Caterham's affairs, and that could give us the connection to St. John's, sir." She grinned back at him.

"It should indeed, Teagle. Smart work. You seem more than a match for the Oxford academic mafia. What do you think happened?"

She paused and gathered her thoughts. "Well, sir, I think that the seriousness of the attack wasn't realized by the chief constable at the time. Charlie-boy was on his phone when Inspector Marsden and his officers went to arrest him; I think he was calling his father, Peter Caterham, for help. So father calls the president at home and wakes him up to say Charlie-boy has misbehaved again and demands he sorts it out pronto before any bad publicity messes up the property deal. President calls Roper, who is shown the door by Oxford Central and can't help; so the president calls Chief Constable Rigby and tells him to sort it. Rigby orders Marsden to release the four and in doing so is told what's happened and that a victim, Amelia Sheridan, is in the John Radcliffe Hospital. The four get released without charge, but Rigby is worried. He gets back to the president, and they sort out what to do.

"Rigby later realizes the risk he's taken and tells the president that he's gone out on a limb and negotiates the thirty grand payoff. The president sets it up with Peter Caterham but is cunning enough to distance himself from the payment. In fact, he may have deliberately made sure that Peter Caterham would be in the frame if anything went wrong. That's my take on it, sir. What do you think?"

"I couldn't have put it better myself, Teagle. I think that's exactly what happened. Well done and good detective work. However, I expect that we'll find that the president and St. John's, as well as Keble and any other college using Roper's services, will have made sure they can disclaim any knowledge of bribery of police officers. Meanwhile, check your facts and obtain that warrant to look at

Peter Caterham's companies' dealings with Roper and St. John's college. Let's see what reaction that causes."

"I'll probably need help, sir. The data we're looking for is up to ten years old or more."

"I imagine you will. It's not likely to be straightforward, and we can expect pushback and objections from Peter Caterham; he'll probably get his lawyers involved, so the warrant will need to be specific with evidence to counter that. Our fraud team ought to know what to do; enlist it to work with you. As well as that bribe to Chief Constable Rigby, we need to inquire into all dealings with St. John's and its officers and servants. Also include the settlement payments to Amelia Sheridan's aunt for the nondisclosure arrangement. Rigby told us it was funded by Caterham, and the payments to the medical specialist retained by St. John's to treat Amelia."

She grinned at him. "I expect this will cause alarm all round, sir."

"Let's hope so, Teagle. Of course, we've still got the murders to solve, but one thing at a time."

The arrival of Teagle and the fraud team at Peter Caterham's offices with the warrant did indeed cause alarm, and Caterham's lawyers swung into action to get the warrant canceled. They immediately went to court arguing that the superintendent was still on a "fishing expedition"; that he was harassing Peter Caterham; that there was no evidence to support the warrant; and so on.

The superintendent was summoned to court. He presented evidence of the payment from a Caterham company made to Roper described as "St. John's funds," which was subsequently paid into the account of a police officer as a justification. The warrant would enable the facts to be established. He explained that the warrant would also assist an ongoing police investigation involving perverting the course of justice. He made the point that if Peter Caterham or his company officials had done nothing wrong, then there was no need to fear the warrant.

The hearing had not interrupted Teagle and the fraud team examining the bank accounts of Caterham's companies despite a lack of cooperation. By the time the court had upheld the warrant and dismissed Caterham's lawyers' objection, the payment to Roper and those authorizing it had already been identified, as had the payments made to St. John's to fund Amelia Sheridan's settlement. Soon afterward details of various other payments to St. John's, mostly relating to the property development, were uncovered. There were also some payments relating to St. John's that appeared to go directly to the personal account of its president.

The superintendent spent time carefully studying the information and discussing it with Teagle and the fraud team inspector. Duggan had also been busy collecting Roper's telephone log data around the time of the attack.

The superintendent thought about where to begin. He decided to talk again to the president as the first step.

They were shown his office at St. John's. The president was not alone and introduced his lawyer.

"I assumed this was a formal interview, Chief Superintendent, and I thought it best to have legal representation."

"Probably very wise, sir. Although I just want to clarify some facts to help my investigation. I assume you're happy with that."

The lawyer interrupted. "The president is always happy to help you where he can, Superintendent."

"Excellent. Now, sir, do you know a man called Vincent Roper?"

"He acts for the college from time to time, I believe."

"So you know him then?"

The president was wary. "Not personally, of course, but I am aware of him."

"What exactly does he do for the college?"

"Assists with occasional undergraduate issues, I understand."

"Can you be more specific please, sir?"

"He interacts for us with the Thames Valley Police in connection with minor legal infringements involving undergraduates. Students sometimes behave thoughtlessly and get apprehended by the police, and he intercedes, that sort of thing. He tries to help undergraduates get out of trouble, saves the police force wasting its time. Is that specific enough for you?"

"Very succinct, sir; thank you. Is there a formal arrangement with Thames Valley Police?"

"I'm not aware of one. The college just retains Roper's services to assist undergraduates."

"Do you know Paul Rigby?"

"Naturally I do. He was chief constable of Thames Valley until he moved to Manchester. We endeavor to maintain good relations with the police. He visited St. John's socially, dined here, that sort of thing."

"Did you ever discuss with him your arrangement with Vincent Roper?"

"Don't think so, but I may have done."

"Do you know the present chief constable, sir?"

"Never met, as far as I recall."

"You surprise me, sir. She has been in post for nearly eight years."

"I suppose we may have met sometime, but she's not a visitor to St. John's. She probably wouldn't enjoy dining at high table."

"You're probably correct, sir; it'd hardly be 'my cup of tea' either. Sergeant Teagle might enjoy an invitation."

The president stared blankly at Teagle.

"Have you spoken to her, the present chief constable, over the telephone, sir?"

"Only recently."

"Why was that?"

"It was to complain about you and your unnecessary intrusion into college affairs."

The superintendent paused as if considering what to say next. "Have you ever spoken to Vincent Roper?"

The president hesitated and looked at the lawyer, who then spoke. "Look, Superintendent, can you please tell us the purpose of the question?"

"It's a simple question. I'm trying to clarify if the president knows Mr. Roper."

"The president has told you that he knows of him, but that is all."

"That's right, he has. That creates a problem for me." He looked to Teagle, who then passed him some documents. "Please look at these telephone logs, which are marked up for you. Note the date and times and tell me about them please."

The president and his lawyer studied the logs with two calls highlighted.

"These date back ten years, Superintendent. You can hardly expect the president to remember them."

"Let me help refresh his memory. It's the night four undergraduates attacked and seriously injured a young woman; it's a night the president does remember. This first call is from the president's private telephone at 1:09 a.m., middle of the night, to Vincent Roper's private telephone. The second call is from Vincent Roper's mobile telephone at 2:25 a.m. back to the president's private number. I'm interested: Why did the president telephone Mr. Roper, someone he claims not to know personally, in the middle of the night?"

"Superintendent, you can't expect the president to remember something like that ten years ago. Anyway, do you have a warrant to examine the president's telephone calls?"

"The president remembers it very well. This data comes from an examination of Vincent Roper's phone logs."

"I'm advising the president to say nothing further. You must terminate the meeting."

"That's a pity; I've much more to ask. We'll be in touch to arrange for him to come to Kidlington for questioning."

"Unless you can demonstrate sufficient grounds, he won't be coming. Two phone logs from ten years ago is hardly that. It doesn't prove the president was on the line. Someone else could have used his telephone."

The superintendent smiled. "Someone impersonating the president you mean? Interesting thought. Anyway, as I said, I've much more to ask. The president was very busy that night and its aftermath. Come on, Sergeant, we'll see ourselves out"

"A bit of a disappointment, sir. Didn't seem to get us far."

They were in the car returning to Kidlington.

"Oh, I don't agree. We were hardly likely to get a confession. That was a warning shot; you could see the president was not his usual pompous, overopinionated self. He was cautious today. He's realized that we're on to him; I expect Peter Caterham has been in touch. We've got more work to do before we next interview him. Good news for our chief constable, though."

"What do you mean, sir?"

"He doesn't know her, and she's kept away from the corrupt bastard. I imagine she's not been invited into the president's fold because she's a woman. 'Don't imagine she would enjoy high table,' he said. What do you think?"

She pulled a face. "I agree he's a corrupt bastard who doesn't rate women."

"We'll give Paul Rigby a call when we get back to Kidlington. That should push things along. After that I'd like you get a warrant to examine the president's phone."

The call got quickly through to Paul Rigby. Teagle was listening in on an extension.

"Graham Barnes from Thames Valley here, sir. Something odd has come up which I need to check with you."

"Go ahead, Barnes; I'm listening."

"We've had Vincent Roper in for questioning, and he's given me an explanation about a payment of £30,000 he made into your personal bank account. It was ten years ago. I'm hoping you can tell me why the payment was made, sir."

The line went quiet.

"Hello, sir; are you there?"

"Yes, I'm here. I'm trying to remember. What does Roper say?"

"Can't tell you that, sir; he's under investigation. I can say that his explanation is very worrying. The payment has been confirmed by his bank. It went into your account, and the amount is hardly something that would go unnoticed by you."

The line went quiet again. The superintendent waited on the line.

"Look, Barnes, I need to check my records. I'll have to get back to you."

"Please do that as a matter of urgency, sir. As I said, Roper's explanation is very worrying."

He rang off and turned to Teagle with a smile. "When you examine the phone logs of the president, focus on the time around the attack and the weeks afterwards. Also look at these recent few weeks. I want the traffic between Caterham, the president, Rigby, and Roper. I expect you to find that Rigby is on the phone to St. John's president at this moment."

Duggan had, with the help of the Swiss authorities, eventually tracked down Jacob Wagner's parents and obtained his dental records and physical description. She delivered the good news.

"Dr. Watson confirms that the fourth body's remains belong to Jacob Wagner, sir."

"Thank you, Duggan. It's as we expected. You'd better inform the Swiss authorities so that they can break the news to his parents."

"Already done that, sir."

"Good; well done. When can you complete that dossier for me?"

"A few days, sir, now that we have Wagner's confirmation. I'm nearly there. There is one more thing. Professor Cornelius sends his congratulations, although unfortunately it means he owes Doctor Watson yet another dinner."

The superintendent smiled. "He should resist wagers with our devious police pathologist. I expect Doctor Watson will enjoy many more dinners as he dines out on the story."

"He certainly gave that impression. Anyway, the professor has a request: he says the whole process of our identification of the remains has intrigued him, and he'd like to use it as a case study and would like me to help him with the details. I'm happy to do it if you agree, sir?"

He looked at her as he thought about it. Duggan had done well and would probably enjoy helping the professor. Likewise, the professor had given his time freely and been instrumental in providing the clues they needed; it would be a goodwill gesture.

"That's fine, Duggan. We appreciate his assistance. Usual anonymity of course. The case is still ongoing, so he can't use it until it's solved or closed, if we don't manage to solve it."

"He knows that, sir, although he has absolute confidence that you'll identify the murderers."

"Does he indeed? I hope he's not bet again with Doctor Watson?"

She laughed. "The good doctor offered, but he was politely declined."

Peter Caterham sat alongside his lawyer in the interview room at Kidlington.

Teagle completed the formalities.

"Mr. Caterham, I'm investigating the murder of your son, Charles, and the events leading up to it. You already know this. Would you like to tell me what happened ten years ago on the night Charles was arrested and taken into custody in Oxford?"

"Nothing happened. He was quickly released without charge."

"How did that come about?"

"I don't know. I can only assume that the police realized its mistake."

"Did you receive a phone call from Charles, a plea for help for you to arrange his release?"

"I can't remember receiving such a call."

"Did you call the president of St. John's college to ask him to intervene?"

"I can't remember doing so."

"Do you know a man called Vincent Roper?"

"I'm not sure that I do."

"Can you tell me why your company, about three weeks later, made a transfer of £30,000 to an account of Vincent Roper in Oxford?"

"My companies make thousands of payments. How can I be expected to remember one from ten years ago?"

"I'm sure you can remember. That payment was to bribe a police officer."

It went quiet. Caterham looked to his lawyer, who intervened.

"That's quite an accusation, Superintendent. I hope that you have evidence to support it."

He smiled grimly at the lawyer. "You can rest assured that I do, sir."

"Are you intending to charge my client?"

The superintendent looked gloomily at them both. "I certainly am. There will be several charges in due course. In the meantime, let's talk about events of the night Charles Caterham and his gang were arrested.

"Charles, or Charlie-boy as he was known, viciously assaulted and raped a young woman, whom he left unconscious in a boat shed. He ran off laughing about it—"

"How dare you! My son is murdered, and you try to destroy his good reputation for your own ends. You simply can't leave this alone. No charges were made; it never happened. You're just stirring things up because you can't find his murderers. You're a disgrace; I shall have you removed." Peter Caterham's outburst suddenly ceased, and he sat staring angrily at the superintendent. His lawyer looked serious as he spoke.

"Superintendent, that was surely uncalled for. Another extraordinary accusation without any evidence no doubt intended to provoke my client in his grief over his murdered son. It is despicable of you, and we shall be complaining about your conduct."

He smiled at the lawyer. "You shouldn't be taken in by your client's feigned outrage, sir. On that night, he was only concerned about bad publicity arising from his son Charlie-boy's activities upsetting a valuable deal he had going with St. John's college and its president."

Caterham was stony faced; he said nothing. His lawyer looked uncertain.

"To begin with I thought it was the president of St. John's driving the cover-up. It's now clear that he was just doing Mr. Caterham's bidding. Whatever, it was a knee-jerk reaction, ill-thought out—instant decisions in the middle of the night to clear up Charlie-boy's mess and keep things quiet; anything so long as the deal wasn't jeopardized.

"Unfortunately, Charley-boy's mess was bigger and more costly to paper over than was realized at the time. Even so, two months later they got the deal over the line. St. John's governing body voted in favor, which enabled your client to clean up on his development. The payoffs, bribes, corruption, and disregard for the victim were insignificant when compared to the value of the deal."

It went quiet as they absorbed his words until the lawyer spoke. "That's an extraordinary list of assertions and accusations, Superintendent. I can't imagine any of it being substantiated; I can't see it ever getting to court or having the slightest chance of being believed by a jury."

The superintendent gave a weary smile as he replied. "Did you ever meet Amelia Sheridan's aunt, sir?"

He hesitated before replying, "Should I have? I don't understand the relevance."

"I always try to do my homework, sir; it sometimes helps me. In your case I know that you have been Mr. Caterham's personal lawyer for more than fifteen years. You are familiar with all that has gone on, the relevance of what I've said. The reason you think it can't be substantiated is because you've taken care, where you can, to insulate him or protect him from, shall we say, things which might cause him embarrassment.

"However, on that night when your client received the phone call for a 'get-out-of-jail card' from Charlie-boy, you weren't involved. A lot went on during that night, but it was only afterwards that you pitched in, rather belatedly, to try and pick up the bits. But you do know of Amelia Sheridan and her aunt even if you never met because you were involved in that disgraceful nondisclosure agreement forced on the aunt by St. John's and paid for by your client. You knew of the savagery of the attack on Miss Sheridan because of the size of that settlement. You are as guilty as your client in perverting the course of justice."

Lawyer and superintendent sat looking at each other until eventually the lawyer gave a faint smile. "Well, the best of luck proving that, Chief Superintendent. What do you intend to do next?"

"I'm going to let you both go whilst I tie up some loose ends, after which I intend to arrest and charge your client. Meanwhile that'll give you time to complain again about my conduct and appeal to your client's powerful, influential friends and associates to have me removed and my investigation stopped."

They stood up, and Teagle was escorting them out when the superintendent caused them to stop and turn.

"Why am I not surprised you haven't asked?"

"Asked what?" the lawyer said, looking puzzled.

"Asked how the murder investigation is progressing. Your grief-stricken client, as you called him, doesn't seem interested, must have more important issues on his mind."

Caterham looked uncomfortable. "What progress have you made?"

"We've made a great deal of progress. I'm limited about what I can say, but I can tell you that we've identified the remains of four bodies, all murdered and then dumped together. They are your son, Charles, and the three other undergraduates in his gang. Something for you to think about."

Teagle asked him later, "Were you deliberately trying to goad Caterham and his lawyer, sir?"

"What on earth makes you think that, Teagle?"

She laughed. "OK, it's as if you're encouraging them to complain."

"I certainly hope they will. I want them to realize that they no longer have friends in high places."

"You're too smart for me, sir. How did you know the lawyer wasn't involved that night?"

"Couldn't be sure, but everything was done in a panic. Peter Caterham, the president, Chief Constable Rigby, and the principal of St. Hilda's—all involved in the middle of the night, desperate to get it covered up before dawn. I can't see the lawyer letting Peter Caterham get himself exposed like that. His role is to make sure that Caterham doesn't get tarnished by his shady dealings."

"So what happens next?"

"I want this wrapped up. We know what happened. There's plenty of hard evidence, and you've got warrants to search for anything else connected; you know what to look for. Gather it all up, and we'll put the case together. Let's then get those involved arrested and charged. While we're doing it, I'm hoping there'll be another summons to the Home Office."

"Why do you want that to happen?"

"Because I intend to make sure that all those involved are disowned by their friends in high places and pay for what they've done."

"So that's why you want them to get together and complain about you?"

"We'll make a detective of you yet, Teagle."

It was a week before he was summoned to the Home Office. During that time Teagle and Duggan had made good progress, and the corroborating evidence was stacking up.

The chief constable called him in. "As you wanted, Graham, the permanent secretary requests your presence. I suggest you take Teagle with you."

"Won't you be coming, ma'am?"

"You don't need me, and I'm not expected. It's your show, and I expect you'll do well. Tell me about it afterwards. Good luck."

He left her office rather puzzled, slightly worried.

The permanent secretary had alongside him a younger man.

"Hello again, Chief Superintendent. Meet my personal assistant, Robert Fellowes."

"Good to meet you, sir. Let me introduce Sergeant Teagle."

Fellowes and Teagle smiled at each other.

"Nice to see you again after all this time, Alice."

She grinned. "You too, Robert; a pleasant surprise."

The permanent secretary looked at them. "You two already know each other. How?"

"We met at Oxford, not seen each other since."

"Interesting. Anyway, enough reminiscing. You have been busy stirring the pot, Superintendent, involving yourself where you shouldn't apparently—likely to cause us acute and unnecessary embarrassment according to your detractors. Is it true?"

He hesitated. "Depends on your point of view sir."

"Please give me your point of view."

"I first need to give you some background. I'll try to be brief. It goes back fifteen years. Two unconnected things happened which created the circumstances.

"The president of St. John's befriended the Thames Valley chief constable, Paul Rigby, and introduced him to the splendor of Oxford academic power and ceremony. To safeguard St. John's reputation being sullied by a few undergraduate yobs, the president exploited Rigby. Don't prosecute my yobs, waste of police time; we can discipline them ourselves, and I'll arrange some financial recompense, plus seats at high table, hobnobbing with the great and the good, and maybe an honorary doctorate along the way.

"Two years later Peter Caterham courted the president of St. John's with an offer of riches for St. John's and his 'finger in the pie.' Caterham had invested heavily to bring about a huge property development west of London. A parcel of the land which he needs is owned by St. John's, and he lures the president into his corrupt scheming. Unfortunately, Caterham includes, as part of the arrangement, his son, Charles, as an undergraduate who subsequently creates a problem. I think you already know about the property development, sir?"

The permanent secretary nodded. "It failed the 'sniff test,' Superintendent, but please continue. Your narrative is fascinating."

The superintendent hesitated and looked at him; "fascinating" was an odd word to choose.

"Thank you, sir. Caterham and the president are both extremely devious, cunning manipulators. Caterham is more basic. His motivation is the quiet accumulation of vast wealth, and he corrupts others to achieve it. The president is more complicated. He is turned on by his status and influence and his supremacy in Oxford academic society but is not above lining his own pocket."

"Ten years ago, things were at a delicate stage; inclusion of the St. John's land in the development had to be voted through by the governing body—around fifty members, some perhaps less than enthusiastic. The president had extolled the benefits, appointed subcommittees and generally cajoled members. The meeting to approve it was imminent.

"Then son, Charles, and his three friends go on a night rampage in Oxford. They viciously assault and rape a woman undergraduate. Just before he's arrested, Charles calls his father for help, to get him off the hook, as he'd done on previous occasions. Realizing that unwelcome publicity might derail his plans, father immediately calls the president of St. John's, who in turn calls Chief Constable Rigby. This is a much-abridged version of what went on during that night, but the result is that Charles and his friends are immediately released without charge. In the process Rigby discovers the victim is in hospital seriously hurt; she is a St. Hilda's undergrad. The president contacts Dame Mary Knight, principal of St. Hilda's, and she consents to assist in having the victim quickly removed to a private clinic and out of sight.

"In the cold light of the following morning, the seriousness of what's happened becomes abundantly clear. But Peter Caterham and the president are only concerned with keeping it quiet; publicity would almost certainly scupper their plans. So they embark on an audacious cover-up involving Rigby, who is later paid off for his compliance.

"Two months later, during the summer, when many of the governing body members are distracted elsewhere, the vote is carried, opening the door to a huge payday for Peter Caterham and a hand in the trough for the president."

It went quiet as the superintendent paused and waited. It was the permanent secretary who spoke first.

"You're certainly not pulling your punches, Superintendent. This colorful presentation is not your usual style. No wonder the participants want you restrained. Can you prove it?"

The superintendent stared at him. The culprits had already had their say, that was clear. He wondered how much they'd influenced the permanent secretary.

"Please hear me out, sir. There is more to tell.

"The unfortunate victim, Miss Amelia Sheridan, was traumatized, unable to remember the attack. The president and Caterham contrived to keep her that way. She is sent to live in isolation at the home of her elderly aunt, who is also her adoptive parent. Medical supervision involving drugs is arranged by the president to keep her from remembering her attack. The aunt accepts that Amelia was involved in some drunken horseplay which simply went wrong, just an unfortunate accident of some sort.

"The aunt is advised that Miss Sheridan is unlikely to recover and needs to be confined and cared for at home. A large settlement is offered by St. John's to fund this lifetime care in return for a nondisclosure agreement—paid off to say nothing. The aunt reluctantly agrees. The settlement is funded by Caterham through St. John's. Things go quiet. Miss Sheridan and the events of that night are forgotten.

The superintendent paused again and looked directly at the permanent secretary. It was Robert Fellowes who broke the silence and spoke to Teagle.

"Alice, the name Amelia Sheridan, it's familiar. Don't we know her?"

"We do. I didn't remember until I met her. It's Bunny."

"Of course. She was at St. Hilda's. Dropped out after two years."

"That was the story. Now you know the truth."

The permanent secretary interrupted, "This is all very dramatic, Superintendent. Do I need to know the details? Can you prove any of it?"

The superintendent sighed. "I've spared you the details; this an outline. It's much more complicated, and there is a huge amount of detailed evidence of conspiracy. I can prove it to my satisfaction, sir. I believe I could prove it to yours also. Whether I could get convictions in court is not so certain, but it rarely is in this type of case."

"So, what will happen? What can you do?"

"There's a bit more to tell, but I'm nearly finished. Recently the remains of four bodies were discovered together in a pond on a farm. Those remains belong to Charles Caterham and his gang, Miss Sheridan's attackers.

"That investigation is ongoing, so I can't say much, but I can tell you that there is clear evidence they were each tracked down some years after the night of the attack. I have no doubt that they were murdered by others in retribution for what they did to Amelia Sheridan.

"You asked what will happen, sir? Without doubt Chief Constable Rigby and two other Thames Valley ex-officers will go to prison for accepting bribes. The evidence is conclusive. The president's fixer who paid the bribes will also go to prison. Caterham and the president will be slippery. Caterham with his smart lawyer will be difficult to convict, as will the president, although he is more vulnerable, but Rigby and the president's fixer will not go quietly, so who knows what might come out? The doctor who treated Miss Sheridan with drugs will be struck off at the least and should go to prison, and he'll implicate the president. I do have some cards yet to play."

Robert Fellowes asked, "What about the St. Hilda's principal, Superintendent? Surely, she is also guilty? She betrayed Amanda."

"I'd not forgotten, sir. Professor Knight has not yet indicated why she played her part. She's still in denial, but I shall find out."

It went quiet again until the permanent secretary finally spoke. "I'm sorry if I sounded doubtful earlier, Superintendent. What do you want me to do?"

"I'd like you to support me, sir, or at least not to interfere with the process. Tell those who petitioned you that you do not intend to intervene on their behalf. There will be embarrassment when the various cases go to court, not least for my chief constable, but that is unavoidable. I suspect that none of those petitioners has expressed to you any concern for the unfortunate Miss Sheridan, who has been denied justice by their actions."

It went silent again for a moment. The permanent secretary looked at Fellowes and then Teagle; it was obvious what they thought.

"Thank you, Superintendent. How much embarrassment will it cause your chief constable?"

So that was it. He'd not invited her; he was considering what to do about her. The president had got his poison in, probably Rigby too.

"It should cause her none, in my opinion. This all predates her

271

appointment. However, she abhors police corruption and feels acute personal embarrassment simply because Thames Valley is her force. She is the best chief constable I've ever served, and probably the best in the entire Police Service. She deserves your full support, sir."

"Do you believe she will resign?"

He weighed his words before replying, "In due course, I believe she'll feel she must, sir."

They sat together in the rear of the car. There was no conversation; the superintendent was lost in his thoughts. Teagle wanted to talk but was constrained because of the driver overhearing. It would have to wait until they got to Kidlington.

He stood in front of her desk looking serious.

"Sit down, Graham. From your expression I imagine it didn't go well. Tell me please."

"Not quite what I'd hoped for, ma'am. I'm unsure that I have the permanent secretary's full support."

He looked at her. She gave a wry smile. "I expect he now rather wishes he'd reined you in when he had the chance. You've now caused a political problem, and his masters won't be happy. Did he try to call you off?"

"No, but nor did he encourage me to press on. He seemed preoccupied with the consequences, the fall out, any embarrassment, that sort of thing."

"I'd call that a success. Anyway, he realizes you've gone too far to stop; there's too much evidence. He's now thinking ahead to the possible consequences for the Home Office."

"What do you want me to do, ma'am?"

"Do your job. You're a good policeman. Let others worry about the consequences."

"Can I talk to you please, sir."

It was late that evening, and Teagle stood at his door. He gestured her in; she closed the door and sat in front of him.

"I'm concerned about the meeting at the Home Office. What's going to happen?"

He grinned at her. "We're going to finish what we started and enforce the law. What did you expect?"

"That's good to hear, sir. But what about the chief constable? Will she really resign?"

He paused. She noticed he looked weary.

"This is between the two of us, never to be discussed elsewhere. Yes, I believe she probably will, although I sincerely hope not. What has been allowed to happen due to Rigby has deeply distressed her."

"Thank you, sir. I think I understand. Our chief constable is a remarkable person and deserves better from the Home Office. I hope she doesn't become its convenient scapegoat. Rigby operated as he did under the Home Office's nose, which later promoted him to head Greater Manchester."

"Well said. But we have a job to do; let's do it."

He watched Teagle leave. He wondered if she thought his words to the permanent secretary had condemned his chief constable to become the scapegoat. It pleased him Teagle had seen through the Home Office's charade. She was an excellent and clever detective; her promotion was well overdue, and it was time he got that sorted out.

CHAPTER 16

Two days later Teagle took a call from Robert Fellowes.

"It was good to see you again, Alice. Look, I've been thinking about what's happened to Bunny—Amelia. Do you know how she is?"

"She's made an improvement recently. She was being wrongly treated by a specialist who tried to keep her sedated under St. John's instructions, but that's stopped. I've spent some time with her, and the doctor is now hopeful she'll make a recovery. It was a dreadful assault."

"I'd like to talk more about her; maybe we can meet soon. Meanwhile I've been thinking about Professor Dame Mary Knight, St. Hilda's principal, and her role. I vaguely remembered her attempts to get male undergraduates accepted into the college; maybe you can remember it?"

"Sort of, but I didn't pay much attention."

"Well, I've done a bit of research. Professor Mary—by the way, she wasn't a dame then; that came later, as you'll see. Anyway, she was in the middle of trying to get the fellows of St. Hilda's to vote to admit men. Always thought it amusing that fellows of St. Hilda's were women."

"Sort of thing that male undergrads would find amusing, Robert."

"Yeah, OK, point taken. What I thought was that publicity of

275

the attack on Bunny by a gang of four male undergraduates could undo things, cause the vote to fail. It was a close-run thing at the time. It could be a compelling reason to keep the attack on Bunny under wraps. What do you think?"

She pondered on it. "It sort of makes sense, but it's an awful thing to do."

"I agree, but the superintendent said that the true extent of the assault, what really happened, wasn't realized until the next day. Maybe she didn't realize at the time, but by then she'd thrown in her lot, and it was too late to backtrack. Just my thoughts."

"I'll let the superintendent know. I'm sure he'll be interested."

"There's a bit more. Professor Mary was made a dame in the next honors list on the back of getting St. Hilda's to admit men. So she had a personal interest."

"She can't have known that would happen at the time."

"I wouldn't be too sure, Alice; you'd be surprised what goes on."

She liked Robert but for some reason found his comment annoying.

"After the meeting at the Home Office, I suppose I shouldn't be surprised at what goes on."

"What do you mean, Alice?"

She couldn't help herself, and the words came out.

"I thought that the superintendent deserved your full support. Instead he had to justify himself. You gave credence to a bunch of influential, well-connected crooks and were more interested in avoiding embarrassment to the Home Office instead of finding justice for Amelia. I expect you'll make our chief constable the scapegoat for your own failings."

The line went quiet for a minute.

"It's not as simple as that, Alice. You don't understand the full implications. The permanent secretary needed to be sure the superintendent knew what he was doing. He has to consider all the consequences and prepare for any repercussions."

"Ha. You ought to listen to yourself, Robert. Tell me about the full implications, and I'll try to understand. Maybe you can express it in simple terms? I suggest you check out the superintendent when you've time and then tell me why you felt the need to doubt him."

"I'm sorry, Alice, I didn't mean to offend you; only trying to help. Thought you'd be pleased."

"In that case thanks for your help. I'll follow it up and let you know how we get on."

She put the phone down. Her hand was shaking. Why hadn't she stopped herself? Why did she feel so angry? She disliked the attitude of the Home Office but that was hardly an excuse.

She sat alongside her solicitor in an interview room at Kidlington HQ, looking angrily at the superintendent and Teagle. Professor Dame Mary Knight initially refused to attend until faced with the alternative of being arrested and brought in.

"Professor, I'm hoping for your cooperation this time. Remember this is a formal interview; you are under caution."

The solicitor replied for her. "Chief Superintendent, Professor Knight is happy to try and cooperate, but as she's already told you, she has nothing to add to your previous attempts at questioning her. Threatening to arrest her if she refused to come here amounts to harassment."

He smiled at the solicitor. "Did she mention that she attempted to have me ejected from St. Hilda's, sir?"

"She told me you behaved abominably and tried to pull a cheap trick."

"Is that what she told you, sir? Let's see how we get on this time. Professor, do you remember Amelia Sheridan, a St. Hilda's undergraduate?"

"She got involved in an incident years ago."

"Rather more than an incident, Professor. She was brutally assaulted and raped and beaten senseless."

"I have no knowledge of that. I understood she was involved in drunken horseplay which got a bit out of hand."

"But you did know that she ended up in the John Radcliffe Hospital?"

"I can't remember that."

He grimaced at her. "I find that impossible to believe."

"I don't really care what you find impossible to believe."

He paused, considering what best to do before continuing.

"Professor Knight, I am about to charge you with perverting the course of justice. There is ample evidence to support the charge. It is a very serious offence. Do you understand?"

She gasped, and the solicitor spluttered, "You can't do that, Chief Superintendent. This is outrageous. Dame Mary is a distinguished person with high position. It will be a scandal. You have no grounds for this. You are exceeding your authority."

She recovered from her shock. "There, you see: another attempt at harassment. I'm leaving; I've had enough of this."

Teagle moved quickly and placed herself by the door as the superintendent spoke. "Sit down, Professor, and just listen to what I tell you."

She looked at her solicitor, who nodded, and she reluctantly sat and glared at the superintendent.

"On the night Amelia Sheridan was attacked, at around three in the morning you received a phone call from the president of St. John's. You then instructed a St. Hilda's official to proceed to the John Radcliffe Hospital to have Miss Sheridan released into his care, officially into the care of St. Hilda's. An ambulance had been arranged to transport her to a private clinic. You had another telephone exchange with the president."

She sat staring at him but said nothing.

"Later that day you had further telephone exchanges with the president. Did you visit Miss Sheridan to see how she was?"

She spoke quietly. "No, it wasn't necessary. She was being well looked after."

"How do you know that?"

"The president told me there was no need to worry."

"Did any of St. Hilda's officers visit her?"

"I don't think so."

"Did you notify her aunt, her next of kin, that she'd been seriously hurt?"

"No, the president of St. John's took care of that for me. He felt a responsibility. Anyway, I wasn't aware she was seriously hurt. She never made any complaint as far as I know."

He looked at her with unconcealed disdain.

"I'm going to show you, once again, a photo of the crime scene. You threw it back at me when I showed you in your office. I'm sure you remember. You accused me of making it up, trying a cheap trick."

He placed the photograph in front of her. She flinched, and the solicitor looked shocked.

"You can see how badly Miss Sheridan was attacked. It's not a cheap trick but a police photograph of the scene they were called to. There are also witnesses to the attack. You, Professor Knight, by your deliberate actions, had Miss Sheridan removed from sight, so enabling her attackers to go free. You perverted the course of justice."

"But I knew nothing of this; it was a minor incident. I only did what I did to protect the college."

"Which college were you trying to protect?"

She hesitated. "St. John's. The president was concerned about the publicity; it would have been embarrassing."

"Embarrassing? Why?"

"Bad publicity is always a problem. Stupid students misbehaving is always blown out of proportion, and the good get tainted by the bad."

"Would public knowledge of the attack on Miss Sheridan by four male undergraduates have been embarrassing to St. Hilda's?"

"Of course, it would."

"Is that why you joined in the cover-up?"

"It seemed a minor thing at the time. I'd no idea."

"But you knew this wasn't a minor thing."

"No, I didn't."

"But Miss Sheridan did not return for her final year."

"That could have been simply because she was embarrassed by what she'd done. Anyway, students regularly drop out. It means nothing."

"But you knew the real reason. You had an exchange of correspondence with Miss Sheridan's aunt, who was herself a St. Hilda's graduate. She wrote to you complaining, told you that Miss Sheridan was too unwell to return, but you fobbed her off with your replies."

She looked surprised. "How do you know?"

"I've seen your correspondence. In fact, in your final letter, you indicated that St. John's would make contact about it. I'm trying to understand why you didn't try and put things right."

"We did put things right. We arranged her graduation in her absence. She still obtained a good degree. The president made a settlement with her aunt."

"You participated in a cover-up and enabled her attackers to go free."

She glared at the superintendent. He realized that she still believed she's done no wrong.

"You've no idea about the difficulties of running a college, Superintendent. Oxford colleges depend upon endowments, donations of money, to create the facilities to attract the best academics and students. Knowledge of this would have crippled my plans for St. Hilda's."

"Did your plans include admitting men to St. Hilda's?"

"Of course. That was essential to my plans to develop the college and bring it into the twenty-first century. Knowledge of this attack would have played into the hands of my opponents."

It went quiet.

"Sergeant Teagle will take a statement from you, and then you'll be charged."

He turned to her solicitor. "I suggest you advise your client to cooperate fully so that we can release her on police bail pending a hearing."

As he reached the interview room door to leave, she said, "That is vindictive, Superintendent, and simply another attempt to embarrass me. You know the case will never get to court. We couldn't have undone what was done, even if we'd wanted to, nor would it have served any purpose."

He turned to look at her and spoke to Teagle. "Include all that in the statement, Sergeant."

Later Teagle sat with the superintendent; he'd read through Professor Knight's statement.

"Well done, Teagle. It's a confession, although the professor doesn't see it like that. We'd better get on and charge all the others. Set things up; you know what to do. Thank Robert Fellowes for his help in getting Professor Knight charged and ask him to let the permanent secretary know what we're about to do."

"But you already knew about the professor's motive without Fellowes's input."

He smiled at her. "But it'll help us if we let him believe he was instrumental in getting her charged."

"How?"

"The Home Office can hardly complain about it now thanks to Fellowes's intervention, although I doubt the permanent secretary will be so pleased."

She grinned. "I learn from you every day, sir."

"There's a bit more to say. Are you still visiting Amelia Sheridan?

"Due to see her this weekend."

"That's OK, but please be cautious about getting too close and about what you say. Bear in mind that her solicitor will eventually mount a claim for damages on her behalf against Thames Valley Police; he can't do otherwise. He'll also go for St. John's, St. Hilda's, and Peter Caterham, and maybe others."

"Is that what the Home Office is concerned about?"

"Amongst other things."

"Is that also worrying our chief constable?"

"One of the things. I expect Thames Valley will come to a settlement; it has no defense. As these cases come to court, it will cause a media feeding frenzy with Thames Valley Police center stage. I doubt Miss Sheridan wants her plight publicized, so we must try to ensure her privacy."

She thought about. "Thank you, sir; I should have realized. The implications are so wide reaching. Chief Constable Rigby has a lot to answer for."

"Makes you wonder what he's got up to in Greater Manchester. I suspect that's worrying the permanent secretary."

"Hello, Robert. Alice Teagle here. The chief superintendent sends his thanks. You were right about Professor Knight's motives."

"Good to hear from you, Alice. Happy to help. Look I'm sorry about our last conversation."

"I'm sorry too. Let's forget it."

"How's the investigation going?"

"Lots to do, but thanks to you, we've charged Professor Knight with perverting the course of justice."

"Oh, really. That's a serious charge, Alice."

"It is. She's on police bail. The superintendent wanted the permanent secretary to be aware. Also, we're now ready to charge the others involved, including the president of St. John's and Peter Caterham, and we'll be referring Paul Rigby and two other officers to the IOPC. There's a mass of evidence."

"I'll pass it on. How's Amelia?"

"Ok, I think. I'm off to see her this weekend."

"Will you please mention me, pass her my best wishes if she remembers me?"

She smiled as she put the phone down. She wondered if Amelia would remember him.

The chief constable was alone when Teagle was shown into the office. She'd been apprehensive about being summoned but was greeted with a smile.

"Come in, Sergeant; take a seat."

"Thank you, ma'am."

"This is one of my pleasant duties. The chief superintendent sends his apologies he couldn't be here, but I'd wanted to see you alone anyway. Congratulations on your promotion to detective inspector. It's very well deserved."

Teagle smiled and sighed. "Thank you, ma'am."

"It means you'll be able to get out from under the superintendent's feet."

"That's a downside. He's good to work with. I respect him and learn a lot, and I'm still learning. I shall miss that. He's the best, ma'am."

She studied Teagle. "I think that too. He's probably the best detective in the police service, and he's a good man. However, you need to move on. You have a bright future."

She felt uncertain. "When you say move on, you don't mean leave Thames Valley?"

"Bad choice of words. I hope not. Thames Valley needs you handling your own cases. You don't seem happy about it."

"Oh, it's just this investigation of the four bodies. It's taken several strange twists and turns, become very complicated and in many respects dissatisfying, upsetting. It's got to me, as they say."

"Certainly not turned out as expected, not going to be a happy outcome for anyone, but that's sometimes the way things go."

"I'd like to stay on it with the superintendent until we've finished with it, ma'am."

"I'm going to talk to the superintendent about releasing you. It's not an investigation which will bring any joy to Thames Valley Police. I don't want your career tarnished with it. You need to think to the future."

They sat looking at each other. Teagle was unsure what to say.

"I'm sorry, but it would be wrong, disloyal of me to desert the case, ma'am. I'd rather be tarnished than do that. Anyway, I believe we're doing our job properly. I'm proud of what you and the superintendent are trying to do."

The chief constable gave her a slight smile and a nod of encouragement.

"Thank you, Inspector you've cheered me up. You'll do very well."

Fiona Mathews felt uncomfortable, nervous as she faced them.

"Last time we spoke, Miss Mathews, you told me that you not seen Amelia Sheridan since the night of her attack. That wasn't true, was it?"

A duty solicitor sat alongside her; the superintendent had insisted. She'd been cautioned.

"It was true. Perhaps I should have tried but never got around to it."

"But you visited her home in Dorset several times after the attack."

She felt flustered, unsure what to say.

"You went there with Elspeth Robertson, didn't you? Why are you trying to hide it?"

"Elspeth invited me to join her. Amelia's aunt was upset about what happened. Elspeth thought I ought to go, help explain things, that's all."

"Why deny it last time?"

"Elspeth didn't think it would serve any purpose. Anyway, we didn't talk to Amelia. We saw her briefly, but she didn't recognize us. She was still traumatized and sedated."

"How did you feel about that? Your visits were two years after her attack, and she'd not made a recovery."

"I felt angry. We all felt it was wrong. The police—you—had done nothing."

"Did you feel angry enough to try and do something about it?"

"What could we do?"

"Do you know what happened to Charles Caterham and his gang?"

"I know they weren't charged. They got away with it."

"You visited the aunt several times over two years or so then stopped going. Why?"

"There seemed no point. We couldn't do anything. The aunt died."

"Did you know of an inquiry agent in Newbury?"

It was clear that she was startled by the question, but she managed an unconvincing, "No, I don't."

"Think carefully, Miss Mathews. Remember, you're under oath. I didn't ask if you'd visited one, just if you knew about one. Perhaps it was discussed with the aunt."

"I can't remember."

"I'd like you to wait here and think about it. I'll come back later."

He went with Teagle to another interview room where Elspeth Robertson was waiting. She also had a duty solicitor alongside and had been cautioned.

"Sorry to keep you waiting, Miss Robertson. Last time you lied to me. You said you'd not been to see Amelia Sheridan after you returned from Canada. Why did you lie?"

"I'm not sure. It didn't seem important."

"It was important enough to lie to me about; you clearly didn't want me to know. Instead, you made up some nonsense about feeling guilty about not visiting Miss Sheridan. That makes me suspicious that you've something to hide."

"Look, I was a witness to the attack on Amelia. I offered to give a statement but instead the police didn't want one and let the attackers go free. Now you're treating me as if I'm a criminal; that's what is nonsense."

"Do you know an inquiry agent in Newbury?"

She sat silent for several seconds. "Why do you ask?"

"Because I believe you do. You recognized him last time you were here. Did the aunt put you in contact?"

"Why would she do that?"

"Because she wanted to track down the whereabouts of Charles Caterham and the others. You told her their names."

"I'm sorry, I can't remember anything like that."

"I'd like you to wait here whilst I check something. I'll be back soon."

Teagle followed him into the room where Fiona Mathews was waiting.

"Have you remembered, Miss Mathews? The aunt knew of an inquiry agent but needed someone to approach him for her. Does that help jog your memory."

"No, sorry, I can't recall anything like that."

He let them both go. He then told Teagle what to do.

It was almost a week before Teagle had gathered the information he wanted.

"You were right, sir. The aunt transferred money into Elspeth Robertson's bank account on several occasions. Elspeth withdrew it as cash. The inquiry agent confirms the amounts tally with the cash he received."

"That was careless of them. It's circumstantial, but it gives us something to follow up. I'm certain that Robertson and probably Mathews are involved in the murders, or at the least know what happened. We need something more substantial; we've no idea how those four were killed, and it still leaves the riddle of how the bodies came to be dumped together in that farm pond. There must be a connection to the farm. Let's put it aside for the time being. I need to think about it, and we've got other crimes to solve."

"A bit of good news sir."

He looked up. "We can always do with some of that."

"Not what you'd imagine. I've been invited to a wedding; bet you can't guess who it is."

"Get on with it, Teagle. I'm busy."

"Rosie Symonds is marrying Freddie Hawthorn."

"Ah, I remember you were their matchmaker."

"Hardly, sir. Anyway, I've learned the lesson."

"Glad to hear it. What are you going to do?"

"Turn it down, of course. Can't afford to be seen taking sides, might give Arthur Symonds grounds for appeal."

He smiled at her. "That's best. A policeman's lot is not a happy one, as the song goes; it can make for a lonely social life."

"Not really, sir. It just makes you careful. However, I'd like to call by and see how Rosie and Aggie are getting on, if that's OK?"

"That's OK. Use the visit to refresh your memory about that pond. There's a clue there somewhere."

When she drove into the farmyard, she was immediately struck by how tidy and organized it had become.

Rosie and her mother, Aggie, appeared happy and relaxed. Rosie herself looked younger and confident.

Ravenna Curlew had arranged for Ben Gladwell's will to be enacted so that the farm would become Rosie's on her thirty-first birthday in a few weeks, shortly before the wedding. Rosie explained that Freddie was already helping to run the farm. They had big plans for it.

They both stood together in the field looking at the pond. Teagle had asked to go there, hoping it might provide inspiration, offer up a clue about the murders.

"Thank you, Alice. Without you it would never have happened, Freddie and me."

"You'd have found a way, Rosie; I'm glad you're happy. This has been an odd case, keeps turning up the unexpected."

"It's turned out well for me and mum, and Freddie. Have you found out who put those bodies here?"

"We've made progress, and we'll get there eventually. Are many folks attending your wedding?"

"Lots: many old friends and families from the old days plus all those from Freddie's side; my grandad Ben would be pleased. We're having an enormous marquee on the lawn in front of the farmhouse. There'll be over three hundred guests."

Teagle stood looking at the pond, remembering how the superintendent had initially thought Arthur Symonds had murdered some of Rosie's boyfriends. That theory collapsed after Teagle found that all boyfriends and male visitors to the farm could be accounted for.

A thought occurred to her.

"Rosie, do you remember, I was driving you home from Kidlington after your first interview, you mentioned a friend—a girl from Oxford, I think you said."

"I do. She worked on the farm one summer. She was a student. She was nice; we were good friends. Dad didn't like it, said we were too friendly, so we used to meet here, by the pond, out of his sight. Then she didn't come any more. I'm sure that Dad sent her away; that's how he was."

"What was her name?"

Rosie looked puzzled. "You know, I can't remember. Anyway, we stopped using her name. She had a nickname, a funny one, Elephant. She didn't look anything like an elephant. She was tall and slim; that's why it was funny. When I found out, that's what I called her."

"Why Elephant?"

"Apparently, she thumped her feet running up the stairs, sounded like an elephant. I only found out because she brought a friend here one day who called her Elephant."

"You'd need a gate key to get here?"

"Plenty of keys. We each had one, although Dad never knew."

"But you can't remember her real name?"

"No, sorry. It was over ten years ago. Never seen or heard from her since. Why are you asking?"

"I'm not sure. Just a thought."

Teagle needed some photos, but there weren't any on file. She wondered what to do. In the end she got them from the Passport Office; they each had passports. Maybe there was another possibility. She hoped she was wrong but needed to be sure. Neither the Passport Office nor the DVLA, Drivers and Vehicles Licensing Authority, could help. Then she realized how to get the photo she wanted.

She was anxious when she placed the three photos in front of Rosie.

Rosie smiled as she remembered. "This is Elephant, and this is her friend. I don't know that one."

Teagle sighed in relief. She couldn't wait to tell the superintendent.

"Well done, Teagle. That's what we've been waiting for; at last we have the connection."

"Thank you, sir. It was your idea to visit the pond for inspiration. I really ought to have thought of it earlier. I reckon that Elephant had a gate key when Arthur Symonds kicked her off the farm, and she kept it. You asked Arthur Symonds if any keys had gone missing. He indicated it was always possible. When they hatched the plan with the aunt, they needed a quiet place to dump the bodies, somewhere they'd not be found. It must have seemed a brainwave at the time, with the added attraction that the gang would be together, rotting in hell for what they'd done to Amelia."

"The aunt was a formidable adversary. It's a pity she didn't feel she could come to us when she found out what had really happened to Amelia."

"She'd already been let down by Rigby and Thames Valley Police, sir, likewise Amelia; why should she think we'd be different? In a way, what they did is understandable."

He sat staring at her. She felt uncomfortable.

"Think carefully, Inspector. We can't bend the law; we're police officers. We ignore our sympathies."

"I would never bend the law, sir. But many people would have sympathy and think they were justified in the circumstances."

"Do you think they were justified?"

"It doesn't matter what I think. Our job is to solve crime. But I might hope that a judge and jury could take a sympathetic view over sentencing. I'm sorry if you doubt me, sir."

"I never doubted you, Teagle. It's been a wretched investigation, but we're getting there, thanks to you. What made you include Amelia Sheridan's photo?"

"It occurred to me that she also fitted the bill. I was so relieved when Rosie didn't know her and identified Elephant as Elspeth Robertson and Fiona Mathews as the friend."

"I'll bet you were."

"What are we going to do next?"

"This potentially complicates things for us. At least two of the witnesses to Amelia's attack are now in the frame for murdering her attackers. Let me think it through whilst we wrap up everything else. Meanwhile, if you have further inspiration, let me know."

ONE YEAR LATER

"You must be satisfied, Graham?"

He shrugged. "Not much to be satisfied about, ma'am."

She smiled. "I think that after all the years we've worked together, it's time you called me Helen."

"Mmm…brought up on formality, I'm afraid, but I'll give it a try when nobody's in earshot."

"It's a good set of results. You ought to be satisfied."

"Originally, I thought four unidentified old bodily remains might be an interesting exercise; that's why I decided to handle it myself. Turned out to be the most miserable of cases."

"Come on, Graham, it's not all been bad news. You got back a young woman's inheritance from her thieving father and had him and his accomplice put inside."

"Thanks…Helen. That was a side show as it happened, but you're right. It was a good result—satisfying, I suppose. But everything else in this case is tainted with police corruption."

"Graham, don't go soft. You've handled police corruption before, worse than this."

"But it wasn't in our force; that's the difference."

"Yes, that does make a big difference."

"Do you think we got the proper results, Helen?"

"Absolutely."

"I think our prosecution service was smart putting Peter Caterham, St. John's president, Paul Rigby, and St. Hilda's principal in the dock together. It showed them all to the jury for what they are. The jury was shocked by the graphic details of the attack, the evidence of the witnesses and James Marsden and the officers who attended. But it was the indifferent attitude of the defendants to the cover-up that night which ultimately brought them down."

"Maybe, but it was you, Graham, who provided the ammunition, found the evidence and put together the case, against a concerted opposition."

"I don't like anyone thinking they're above the law, especially the so called 'high and mighty' of the establishment."

She laughed at him. "You make that very clear, Graham."

"Actually, Professor Dame Mary Knight—principal of St. Hilda's, as she insisted on being called—did us a favor. She believed she'd done nothing wrong, probably still does. Her attitude and demeanor, trying to put herself above it all and claiming she'd just acted in the best interests of the college did not go down well with the jury. Her evidence helped incriminate them all."

"Pity she only got a suspended prison sentence."

"Oh I think that did the trick, Helen. She's lost her reputation and been forced to resign; that's a far worst punishment for her. I'd anticipated that Peter Caterham would avoid prison, but the jury didn't buy his defense, nor that of St. John's president. As for Paul Rigby, well, he simply had no defense in the face of all the evidence. I'm surprised he even tried to plead not guilty."

"How the mighty are fallen, as they say. I guess you've heard, Thames Valley Police has settled damages with Amelia Sheridan."

"I believe that's wise of you, Helen. It draws a line. Apparently, St. John's and St. Hilda's has also settled, but Peter Caterham's company is contesting the claim on the grounds that it previously settled with the aunt for Charlie-boy's behavior."

"And the murders?"

"Ah, the murders. As you know, I put investigating them to

one side during the court hearings; it just might have complicated things. But now, we'll continue digging away, Sergeant Duggan and I. Elspeth Robertson and Fiona Mathews are guilty of involvement at the very least. They may even have done the deed."

"You never disappoint, Graham. You're like a dog with a bone."

"Ha, ha. It was a dog with a bone which caused this entire investigation."

They sat quietly until he asked. "What about you Helen, what will you do? Will you resign?"

She gave a wistful smile and gazed away for a few seconds. "No, I'm not resigning, but I am going to retire soon. It's time to go. Not how I wanted to end my career or be remembered, but we can't always choose what we want. Events have a habit of interfering."

"I'm sorry. I'd wished you might reconsider. You're the best chief constable in the service and you'll be sorely missed."

"That's very kind of you, Graham. Anyway, it'll take a while to appoint my successor, so I expect to be here for six months or more."

He smiled at her. "Enough time for something to happen to change your mind. Let's hope so."

More by **Ian Ellis** about the casebooks of Chief Superintendent Graham Barnes. Available on Amazon Kindle.

An Unfair Justice
A case of mistaken identity exposes murder and greed involving the political establishment. Against all the odds, Barnes must resort to unorthodox methods.

Follow the Trail
The trail runs to the isolated rugged north of Scotland and to the glamour of the French Riviera. Entertaining and pacey and with surprises at every turn.

Not Worth the Cost
A complicated fraud has unexpected and fatal consequences when it involves international politics. An engaging story with dark undercurrents.

Printed in Great Britain
by Amazon

43617473R00169